THE HIDDEN QUEEN

JESSICA STURTEVANT

BRUSHES & BLADES

CONTENTS

THE HIDDEN QUEEN

JESSICA STURTEVANT

CHAPTER I

A PATH CARVED
IN STONE

I timed my visit to the Seer so that I would avoid passersby and rehearsed what I wanted to say. I hadn't had any success in the library despite spending months poring over nearly every book and scroll that the Keep's library held. I had confided my concerns to the Keep's record keeper, Maester Crowsbeak, and after much deliberation, research, and scrying, the elderly man had confessed his defeat to me.

"I wish I had the answers you seek, my Queen. I believe the Seer to be the only one who possesses the wisdom to aid you."

As I crossed the threshold of the Seer's domain, I shuddered as a wave of icy air blew past me.

"Welcome, Valérikka, Daughter of Anise," a young girl's voice called sweetly. "What do you seek this day?"

The Seer of Sitica rounded the corner, clad in shades of blue, silver, and white. She always maintained the form of a young girl, and even when the stars descended to reclaim her, she was always returned to the Seer's

Sanctuary within the same moon cycle—always with the birthmark of a crescent moon on her neck.

I had only gone to see Alva Seidrkona twice in the time I had been Queen. Both times, her responses had been true.

"Good evening, Alva," I greeted, dipping my head to her.

Despite her childlike appearance, she was hundreds of years old and had the ability to See in ways mortals could never imagine. As I debated how to begin the request, she motioned for me to sit beside her at the hearth.

"You wish to know about your dream, yes?"

I froze, wide-eyed, and gave a small nod. "How did you know?"

"Maester Crowsbeak has sought wisdom, too," she said, her voice high and clear. "What exactly do you wish to know about it?"

"Everything," I stammered, taking a breath and steadying my nerves. "What does it mean? Why am I having this dream, night after night, always the same? Is...is it prophecy? Am I destined to kill my husband?"

Alva sighed and took a small velvet bag from her pocket. Pouring its contents into her hand, she picked out a few tiny bone fragments and gemstones, then clenched the remaining sandy dirt in her fist. She closed her eyes and whispered in ancient Nordmaarian, and when she opened them, I shivered. Her eyes had glazed over with a foggy white film as she murmured incantations over the fistful of dirt. She threw it into the fire and the flames exploded, turning a blinding white so bright my eyes hurt.

"Your hand, please," she murmured, setting the gems

and bone pieces in a small bowl on her lap and holding my outstretched wrist in a vice-like grip.

Slicing through the flesh of my palm faster than I anticipated with a blade I hadn't even seen, she caught my blood in the bowl until the bone and gems were saturated. She set the bowl between us on the flagstone, inhaled deeply, and whispered a strange word. The blood, gems, and bones rose from the bowl, and with a flick of her finger, they shot into the flames. Scarlet red quickly overtook the white and Alva scrutinized the dancing flames with her foggy eyes. She sighed softly and the flames died immediately.

"What? What does that mean? What did you see?" I asked, failing to keep the panic from my voice. "Please, tell me what you saw!"

"I saw nothing," she said quietly. "The gods have closed my eyes to this path, Your Grace. I believe that you are to journey blindly. I'm very sorry. I have no answers to give you, but...if I may, I would encourage you to search and seek out answers for yourself. Prove to the old gods that you are not bound by fear and hopelessness. I know of what terrors you dream. I see the fear drip from your blood...but I also see you, Valérikka Varggson. You are stronger than you realize. I know that despite my inability to give you answers, the information remains. Hunt it down and make the stars tell you what you want to know."

"I'm the Queen of Tachá," I replied. "How am I supposed to leave my people? My duties...and my husband? He would never allow me to remove my crown, anyway."

"Does he know of your torment?"

"No."

"If he did?"

I scoffed. "Ragnar would laugh. He would not fear a dream and there's no way to convince him that it may be more."

"What makes you so certain of that?"

I paused as I collected my thoughts. "It's *so* vivid. Much more than what a normal dream should be. It's always the same, too. Not similar...but *exactly* the same. That's not normal, and it's certainly not normal to dream about pouring out your husband's lifeblood!"

Alva smiled sympathetically and took my hand in hers, my adult hand dwarfing her tiny fingers. Turning my hand over and peering at the lines of my palm, she traced some of them and cocked her head curiously.

"I can tell you one thing, irrevocably true," she said. "Your love will save him or your love will end him. The choice is yours and yours alone. The path ahead of you has been carved in stone, and though I don't know how you will alter it, I know you will. You must. You must leave your husband to save him. If you do not, he will surely die by your hand."

CHAPTER 2

LOVE'S LIE

I thought he might simply deny me when I asked for a furlough, even if it wasn't the whole truth. I imagined him saying "no," with that growl of authority I'd heard rumble at those we governed. Though it pained me to admit, even to myself, I'd had the fleeting worry that he might laugh at the idea and dismiss it completely. His silent answer stole the breath from my lungs as the very air between us grew thick. In one fluid motion, faster than any normal man could move, he crossed the room and swept me into his arms, holding me tightly enough that I couldn't squirm free.

"Why does my Queen want to leave me?" he whispered, his soft, gravelly tone bringing its familiar goosebumps from my head to my toes. "Have I brought shame on her? Have I been unworthy as her husband? Have I lost her love?"

How could I even begin to explain this turmoil that churned inside my mind and heart? If I told him of my dream, he would only dismiss it, never believing such an outcome could be even remotely possible. I couldn't let him carry the weight of it, either. The worry, the doubt, the pain, the heartbreak: those were mine to bear. This was not his war to fight, and not a battle he could ever win.

"My love, you know I have no greater honor than standing at your side, than ruling our homeland as your Queen. I am a Northern-born daughter of our land...you know I am not any more content locked behind the stone walls of our keep than you are. I was a Huntress trained by the best of the Northern Hunter's Guild, I *still* am. You know their laws and my oaths and fealty to them. I want to see, to walk, to conquer the lands again, and-"

"*Min Kona*," he said quietly, brushing his fingers along my jawline, "you are free to walk upon every part of our land. I'll send a party to accompany you for a day or so. The steel of my soldiers will keep you safe-"

"I don't want to be safe!" I cried out, balling my hands in frustration. "I want to be free!"

"Are you not?"

"No, and you know this!" I said. "I want to explore parts of our land I haven't walked before."

"The Wall? You wish to go to the Wall of Valthor?"

"South of the Wall and beyond."

He chuckled, igniting a flame of anger inside me.

"Why do you laugh at me?" I snarled.

"It's not my intention to laugh at you, *Min Kona*," he said gently. "You make your own path, one that I cannot control, and while that fills my heart with pride, it also gives me fear. I cannot protect you if you're not at my side."

"I don't need to be protected, Ragnar," I said, my

anger simmering. "I am not a caged bird. I was raised and taught by the best hunters in the north, I have fought many battles against both man and beast, and I have lived."

His jaw tightened in silence as his hands came to rest on my waist, nearly encircling me as his fingers tightened their grip. He pulled me flush against him, and as I looked up into his eyes, my back arched instinctively, drawn by a natural power he radiated that I could not deny.

"Valérikka, my wife," he whispered, gazing so deeply into my eyes that I could feel him searching my very soul. "You could ask me for anything in this world and I would grant it. I would give you the world. But how could I willingly allow you to step into danger? I would rather die than see you injured from my negligence."

My heart broke, torn between the pain that radiated from him and the warning my mind was still screaming. How could I leave him? Especially knowing it would destroy him. He would search the lands for me, tearing through the countryside until he found me. How could I make him understand? Would my efforts be in vain? Alva was clear: if I stayed, I would be ensuring his death.

How could he understand? I dropped my gaze and relaxed my shoulders, leaning into the safety that was my husband's embrace.

"I could be content with exploring our homeland. Thank you for sharing your heart about this, my love," I murmured, hating myself for my dishonesty toward him, especially after his vulnerability.

I couldn't bring myself to meet his eyes, not with the taste of dishonesty and betrayal still bitter on my tongue. I yawned, feigning exhaustion, and Ragnar swept me into his arms. In a few long strides, he carried me to the great four-post bed and drew heavy fur blankets over me. When he slipped beneath the furs beside me, the chill of the room gave way to the warmth of his body against mine. Soon, the furs were cast to the cold flagstones below, joined swiftly by his leather and my linen.

THE FIRE CRACKLED QUIETLY in the hearth, its golden glow casting dancing shadows along the cold stone walls of our bedchamber. The heavy scent of cedarwood and musk lingered in the air, mingling with the faint remnants of sweat and passion. The thick bearskin blanket lay draped over our naked bodies, cocooning us in heat and silence.

I turned ever so slightly—just enough to see my husband relaxed, without a single worry on his mind. It was a rare state I had never found in him while he was awake. The heavy burden of his kingly duties, his ever-watchful eyes over his warriors, the endless political tirades—none of that touched him here. His arm was slung lazily over my hips, his fingers tracing idle patterns around my navel, daring to drift lower until my breath caught. I glanced at him, eyes closed as the corner of his mouth turned upward, and realized I had never seen him so at peace. He let out a deep sigh of contentment and I smiled.

"I could stay like this forever," he murmured, his voice thick with peace, want, and sated need. "Here with you... naked beneath the fur, sticky with sweat and-"

"Ragnar, you beast!" I laughed, cutting him off as he pulled me over his hips, holding me firmly in his steady hands.

Straddling him, I rested my hands on either side of his face and bent to kiss him, slow and unhurried. I savored the taste of his lips and wished we had all the lifetimes in the world. I pulled back and sat upright, smiling as his tired eyes met mine. He reached for the long tendrils of my hair that had swept in front of me and gently wrapped it around his fingers.

"The gods are too cruel to let this last," he said softly. "A soldier never knows peace until he meets his honorable end."

His eyes, sometimes colder than the ice that crowned the mountains of our homeland, studied the rafters as if the answers to his unspoken questions were carved in the timbers themselves. When his gaze found mine again, that icy hue had softened to the blue of a cloudless sky.

"But your presence makes me want to believe they might," he whispered, brushing his thumb along my cheek.

Words failed me. My lips remained still. Though my mind could not yet understand, my heart already knew. This moment was fleeting. Ragnar stretched out his arms, his muscles flexing like ropes beneath his skin. I leaned forward again, pressing gentle kisses to his temples, his cheeks, and finally, his lips. He sighed as sleep claimed him. I began to loosen his hands from around my hips, ready to roll to his side, when the bed shifted strangely beneath me. Slowly, deliberately, a dark shadow slithered beneath the blankets. Against my thigh, cold scales slithered slowly upward, and a small serpent, as black as onyx, emerged from the blanket, its forked tongue flicking against my skin. I froze as every hair on my body rose. My hands trembled, but the snake didn't recoil or strike, it slithered into my grasp, instead.

Something was wrong.

The serpent stiffened and its scales hardened into iron. Its coiled body straightened, its tail tapering to a sharp point. Cold, unyielding metal pressed against my palm. Without question, I gripped it tighter as steel replaced snakeflesh. The dagger's hilt molded to my hand as if it had been forged for me alone. I raised it, catching the firelight, and though I didn't recognize the blade, I knew it was mine.

My gaze fell upon the man beneath me, the greatest soldier in all of Tachá's history, perhaps all of Fareland. Completely unguarded. Entirely mine, as I was his. I could still taste him on my lips, still feel the lingering sensation of his fingers as they trailed down my spine. I knew that he loved me. I rested my free hand on his chest, rolling my hips forward as the soft sound of pleasure escaped his throat. The steady beat of his heart lay just beneath my palm, and the slow rhythm of his breaths, full of trust. He had given me everything. His kingdom, his loyalty, his love.

In one swift motion, I plunged the icy blade into my husband's throat.

His eyes flew open, not filled with rage or battle-hardened instinct, but with shock, disbelief, and heartbreak. He clutched my wrist, his strength fading with every pulse of blood that spilled between us. He blinked, truly seeing me at last, and where I expected fury, I found only betrayal. Gurgling through his blood, he choked out three words, "Min Kona...why?" The light left his eyes and his hand slipped from my wrist, falling limp at his side. He lay half-covered by the bear fur, surrounded by a pool of dark, sticky blood. His trust, his love, and pride, all spilled out from the cold iron I betrayed him with. My hands trembled as my head swam, and a gasping sob burst out from my throat as I woke.

～

I CLAPPED my hand over my mouth, muffling a scream as I lay entangled in Ragnar's arms, his warm breath heating the back of my neck as he sighed, burying his face into the crook of my neck. *Alive! He's alive!*

I knew without a doubt that the dream was a warning of exactly what was to come if I didn't leave my husband's side. I would rather die than allow this nightmare to come into reality.

CHAPTER 3
THE VOWS

13 Years Ago

~

The Bridegroom, Ragnar

"You're really doing this?" Floki asked as he drained another mug of ale. "I remember you swearing up and down the coast that you'd never-"

"I know what I said," I interrupted, "but that was a long time ago. A lot has changed. I've changed."

"You've certainly gotten fatter," Floki said with a chuckle, dodging my blow. "Slower, too!"

"C'mere and I'll show you slow," I said, not bothering to hide my laugh. "I've made my decision, and even you have nothing rude, crass, or negative to say about this wedding, or her. Floki, she's the one I want. I've waited long enough."

Floki quieted and nodded after a moment.

"She certainly does bring out the nicer side of you. You haven't shed blood in the Great Hall since she arrived two months ago! It was quite a deal you worked out with that Winchester of the Hunter's Guild, too, very under-handed and political of you, making him see the benefits of having the Queen of Tachá as an Officer of the Hunter's Guild...very clever."

"I didn't do it for the sake of politics, Floki. You know me better than that. I did it to have her at my side and not have to share her with that damned Guild."

"Regardless of why you did it, it was a wise move, Ragnar. How does she feel about her new title? And all those new responsibilities?" Floki asked, unusually focused after his eighth mug of ale.

"She wants to be Queen about as much as I want to be King. But I love her, and I think she loves me. I think Tachá needs someone like her to rule."

Floki raised a brow, the one that was jagged and dotted with scars, and paused before he spoke. I shot him a glare and he stayed silent for only a moment before speaking.

"I'm just thinking it might be wise to make sure she's going to be there tomorrow morning. It's gonna look bad on you if she's not."

"She'll be there," I said with a stern glare, standing suddenly as my chair scraped the flagstone floor.

"Maybe it'd be wise to wait until the morning," Floki said. "You'll be sober...well, mostly, and she'll not be expecting it!"

"Damn you, Floki," I grumbled, unwilling to admit he was right.

"G'night, my liege!" he called out, laughing loudly as he lifted his mug to his lips.

~

The Bride, Valérikka

I HAD BATHED last night in scalding hot water, the steam had filled the air around me as my handmaidens scrubbed the layers of dirt from my pale skin. Bodil and Meridya had brushed out my long blonde hair, picking out twigs and pine needles that had burrowed into my braids. With my hair braided simply for the night, I had crawled into bed and shivered, the linens icy against my gooseprickled flesh. I fell asleep to the fire crackling in the hearth, and my nerves gnawed at me. Realization that I would be sharing a bed with Ragnar brought both anxiety and flushed excitement, and I tossed and turned for what felt like hours.

~

THE NEXT MORNING, the ladies woke me with beaming smiles and joyful songs as they rushed me into a warm overdress. Pulling tightly and securing snugly, the women wove my hair into beautiful, intricate braids that were befitting of a royal bride. A headache formed as the tight braids pulled at my scalp and I grit my teeth.

"Like golden silk, My Lady," Meridya cooed. "Your hair is just beautiful."

"Thank you, Meridya," I said. "It's a bit tight, don't you think?"

"Oh, no, my Lady, it must stay this way to last the entire ceremony, it would shame us all if your braids loosened in the midst of your vows!"

As I remained seated, Meridya brought a pair of silver

silk slippers, the heel high enough to raise my height as if I were standing on my toes. They fit well, but gave my toes no room to wiggle, and the straps were tied snugly.

"We can't risk you losing your footing and taking a tumble, my Lady," Meridya apologized as she tied the laced straps. "Stay seated until the dress fitting, please."

I nodded in understanding and Bodil attended to my face, applying a dark kohl to my eyes and, with intricate strokes, scrawling ancient runes from the nape of my neck down to the middle of my back whispering the translations of happiness, abundance, fertility, and protection as she applied them carefully.

"Time for the dress, my Lady," Bodil whispered excitedly, tears forming in her eyes. "You look so regal and beautiful already, and you've already received your first wedding gift!"

"What? From who?" I asked as a young woman with long, pointed ears brought in a long, thin box.

"A fellow royal, the Elf-King, Rofellos," Meridya muttered, clucking her tongue. "He's no' exactly a friend of us Northerners, but a gift is a gift, and…oh my…"

Her voice faltered and trailed off as she held up a white gown, so bright it seemed to glow in the woman's hands. Made of silk and lace that seemed delicate enough to shatter if I sneezed toward it, Bodil gasped and wiped her hands on her gown before she touched it. The women fawned over it, carefully touching the smooth silk, and I was stunned. I had never seen anything so fine, let alone been gifted, and as Meridya removed my outer dress and my linen shift, Bodil unlaced the corset strings and I stepped into the gown. Strangely warm, it clung to me like a second skin, and the women fussed and tightened the corset strings, tighter than a new set of leather armor.

My spine stiffened as the boning forced me upright, a regal posture, and the sleeves, long, flowing, and snug kept my arms from moving too wildly. As my hand-maidens drew back, they wiped tears and smiled.

"My Lady, my Queen," Bodil whispered, her voice cracking with emotion, "you look radiant!"

"Like a real Elvish Queen," Meridya added. "You're just glowing!"

I turned to the mirror and froze. A stranger looked back at me, our faces matching only in confusion and astonishment.

"Thank you, thank you both," I said, struggling to walk in the dress as the fabric pooled at my feet.

I bent to pick up the dress's train and stopped short, the restrictions of the dress preventing me from bending. A bead of sweat grew on my brow and I tried to fill my lungs with air, struggling as I carefully tugged at the lace-adorned neckline.

"Where is my dagger going to go?" I asked as the women balked.

"My Lady," Bodil said, chiding in a motherly way. "You cannot wear a weapon to your own wedding! The chapel forbids weapons! Besides, you have nowhere to stow it!"

My heart began to beat heavier and my breath came in bursts. As Bodil drew close, patting my brow with a clean cloth, I noticed a neatly folded parchment on the floor. I motioned to it, unable to even fully extend my arm from the dress, and Meridya picked it up, her eyes wide as she passed it to me. The sigil of a stag sealed it shut, and I broke it without a second thought. Written in elegant calligraphy and in the traditional elvish language, I mumbled the words as I mentally translated them.

. . .

To the newly crowned Queen of Tachá,

I have seen fit to send this gown as acknowledgment of your recent elevation, despite the unlikeliness. Named Lúnë-vael by its makers, it was woven beneath a full moon by the hands of the finest artisans, spun of silk no loom beyond Thyuland could hope to rival, and imbued with grace and power your lands have never known. Such craftsmanship is not gifted lightly. It is an honor rarely bestowed and never upon one unworthy of being improved by it. Wear it well. It is far more than Tachá could ever give you.

You may find the gown allows for limited freedom of movement. This is intentional. True refinement is never unre-strained and it is best learned early that grace is not found in excess motion, nor in displays of strength unsuited to one's station. Consider it a kindness, structure imposed where instinct might otherwise prevail.

King Rofellos -High Sovereign of Thyuland

"WHAT AN ABSOLUTE ASS," I muttered, tossing the note on the dressing table. "That Rofellos is probably the most smug son of a-"

The door to my chamber burst open suddenly, the women shrieked and I was on my feet instantly, pushing them both behind me as I grabbed the knife hidden underneath the tabletop. Ragnar stood in the doorway, confused as he paused before entering. Bodil and Meridya bowed deeply and as I tossed the knife back to the table, I tried and failed to cross my arms.

"You can't just come in here, Ragnar!" I cried, louder than I'd intended. "What if I'd been...indecent?"

The corners of his lips turned up as he considered it and he addressed the handmaidens.

"Leave us," he said, catching my eye and adding, "please."

They bowed and scurried away without delay and closed the door as they vanished. Ragnar approached and took a breath, pausing as I put my hands on my hips, barely able to make contact with my hands.

"You look…" he stammered, trailing off as he frowned. "Y'look awful. What are you wearing? Where did you get that? Why didn't you wear the one I gave you?"

"Ragnar, do not test me," I growled. "I *cannot* move, everything has been pulled and poked and bound and I can't even breathe properly!"

"Well, I can imagine why!" he cried with a chuckle. "You look like a peacock!"

Fury bubbled, not simply because Ragnar had laughed, but his humor at my expense was my breaking point. I swung a fierce left hook but failed to connect, the restrictions of the dress too confining. In my failure, overwhelmed by the inability to move, to protect myself, to protect others, an angry sob escaped my throat. My vision blurry with hot, furious tears, I glared at Ragnar and I shook my head in defeat.

"Is this the sort of Queen you want?" I asked plainly, close to defeat. "A damned silken beauty who stays still and quiet? That's not me, Ragnar, and I thought you knew that. I can't be this…this *thing* you want. I can't do this. I can't be your Queen if my life will look and feel like this."

"Who ever said I wanted any of this?" he said, resting his hands on my slimmed waist. "I want you to be exactly who you are. I *know* who you are, Valérikka. That's why I love you. Besides, I had a dress sent that was...more suited for you."

"Tell me the truth. Is this marriage a political move to get in bed with the Tacháan Hunter's Guild?" I asked sharply. "I've heard people talking. They say it was a brilliant scheme to get the feral woman in your bed to have the Guild in your pocket, and-"

"No."

"What do you mean, *no*?" I said with a snarl. "Ragnar, I *hear* what they call me! The wild Huntress, that savage woman...what other dress are you talking about?"

"I mean, the people don't know you, not yet. Where the hell did this dress come from, anyway? Loric!"

We waited for Ragnar's loyal steward to appear and I continued.

"Rofellos sent it as a wedding gift," I said with a groan as the corset boning poked my ribs. "He can have this thing back and-"

"What did you say?" his tone cleared the air and I stilled. "Who sent that dress?"

"Rofellos. The note is there on the table," I said, pointing awkwardly. "I hate this thing, and the shoes, and my hair."

"That bastard gave you this? Take it off," Ragnar said, a sudden suspicion and animosity in his tone as he turned his head toward the still-closed door. "Loric!"

"I *can't* take it off," I replied curtly. "It took both Meridya *and* Bodil to get me into it, let alone my hair pinned up like this and these shoes on my feet. Ragnar, I can't take it off myself. It wouldn't surprise me if they stitched me into it."

Entering quietly with a bow, Loric appeared.

"Where is the dress I had made for her? What is this Elvish thing? Fetch me her real dress, Loric."

He nodded and vanished silently and Ragnar sighed.

"Valérikka, this dress is *not* what I want for my Queen, my *wife*. I never wanted you to be...like *this*," he said, gesturing to my hair as he shook his head. "The woman that put me on my ass for underestimating her, I want *her* as my wife."

A soft knock sounded and Loric appeared, I saw Bodil and Meridya's eyes locked on me. I gave them a subtle nod and they relaxed. Ragnar's ferocity had a long-standing history, I was glad to have two strong women to keep at my side. Loric laid the linen garment bag down on the bed and bowed as he took a step back.

"Would my King like the Lady's handmaidens to tend to the matter?" he asked.

"I'm not done here yet," Ragnar replied, his eyes returning to me. "I'll send for them when we're ready."

Loric bowed and left, as the door opened, he whispered to Bodil and Meridya, who nodded in understanding. I took a step toward the linen bag that lay on the bed where Loric left it and realized I wasn't even capable of taking a full stride, reduced to much smaller steps. I wondered what sense of fashion the Elvish designers had as I grunted, straining against the surprisingly strong material. Ragnar opened the bag and the gown poured out. He held it up and I gasped in awe.

"I found a seamstress and a tailor to create this for you. The cloak is fur from a Tacháan snow deer, and the beading details are bone, glass, and gemstones, all of Tachá's provision. I had custom insets and hidden folds for your daggers, as well."

I met his eyes and saw how proud he was of this

craftsmanship, and my heart melted. He set the dress down and closed the distance between us.

"It's breathtaking, Ragnar, truly," I whispered. "I would love to marry you in that gown instead of this instrument of torture. I don't know how to take it off. It's not as fragile as it looks."

Ragnar stepped even closer and wrapped his hands around my waist, trailing his fingers up my spine as I shivered. As his fingers swept downward, he tugged at the lacing of the corset, finding it unmoving. He pulled harder, but still it remained tied fast. He swore under his breath and grabbed the small dagger that I had tossed onto the tabletop, slicing through the silken cords with ease as he tossed the blade aside. Despite the loosened ties, the dress remained snug. Ragnar gripped it, ripping the fabric with a loud tearing sound as breath filled my lungs again. I held the corset to my chest as he ripped the snug sleeves off one by one, as strips of the dress pooled at my feet. He bent, tore the straps off the shoes and tossed them aside. He met my eyes and took hold of the corset, holding what remained of the silk gown in his grasp. Ragnar dropped the corset and it pooled to the floor between us. Slowly, as I stood completely exposed in front of the man I was to marry in mere hours, I held his gaze and raised my hands, slowly pulling the pins from my hair as he watched. One by one, the braids loosened and began to unravel. With my long hair covering my upper half, Ragnar struggled to hold my gaze as I stepped forward, pressing against him, and began to methodically unfasten each button of his tunic, agonizingly slowly, if only to tease him.

"The hell with this," he growled, the want thick in his

voice as he pulled the tunic off with one arm, the other pulling me flush against him as my feet left the floor.

In a tangle of linens and limbs we were one, my hair loose and wild as his hands grasped a handful of it. I arched my back into him and he swore as he exhaled sharply.

"I've waited too long for you," he moaned. "I won't wait any longer."

In a whirlwind of need, love, and sweat, a moment that I wished would never end, our union was written in history, and as I regained my senses, dizzy, breathless, and sated, I looked at the man next to me, breathing heavily and just as sated, a grin on his face as he met my eyes.

"Shall we get married now?" he laughed between breaths.

"Yes, I suppose so, now that I have a suitable gown," I said with a laugh. "People have been waiting for this moment, we should at least show up. I just wish it wasn't in front of the whole damn country."

"I wish the same..." he said, trailing off as his brows furrowed for a moment. "What would you say to a change of plans? Only slightly."

"What do you have in mind?"

"Venue change. Meet me under the Willow Tree in the southern grove in an hour."

I agreed, and he kissed me before dressing quickly, carrying his boots in his hand. As I pulled a linen shift over myself, he reached the door and paused.

"Will you have your braids like...yours?" he asked, a small smile brightening his face as I nodded. "I'll send in your handmaidens. One hour."

Bodil and Meridya gasped as they saw the shredded

gown on the floor, but as they spied the Tacháan gown nearby, they smiled. I stepped into the gown and it fit beautifully, providing the flexibility and movement I hadn't had in the Elven gown. Meridya held out my daggers carefully and I placed them in each of the three braces Ragnar had had fitted, one at my thigh, one hidden in the folds of my gown, and the other behind my back, concealed beneath the thick white cloak. Bodil sighed and touched my hair, combing her fingers through it.

"Will you braid my normal style, please?" I asked Bodil. "I'm a Tacháan woman. The braids before were so beautiful, but they weren't me."

"Of course, my Lady, I would be honored," she beamed.

MY LADIES ACCOMPANIED me to the southern grove as the snow fell in fat flakes, and the immense willow tree that rooted deeply in the earth stood, radiating not only a warmth, but old magic in its appearance. The Fire Willow stood apart from the rest of the forest, surrounded by a wide ring of snow that stopped where its deep orange and red leaves brushed the ground. With bark as white as the freshly fallen snow, ancient runes had been deeply etched into the trunk, but by whose hands no one knew. Drawing close to the thick wall of warm leaves, we walked through the curtain of the Fire Willow, where green grass grew freely, untouched by snow or cold. The leaves swayed as if in greeting, and at the base of the tree stood Ragnar with his back to me as he spoke to some-one. No banners flew, no horns sounded. It was quiet, private, sacred, and intimate, a comfort I didn't know I needed. My gaze fell upon Ragnar as I stepped closer, and the world fell away as he turned to me. He stood tall and strong, wearing a dark fur cloak, a deep cream tunic, and a sword lashed to his belt. His gaze locked to mine, unwavering as I neared his side. Floki, to my surprise, inclined his head to me, and I blinked, but Ragnar's gaze never left me. Bodil and Meridya took their place near Loric, who stood a short distance away, and already they tenderly dabbed at their eyes.

Ragnar held out his hand and I took it without hesitation.

"See now? Floki said to Ragnar with a wink sent my way, "I told you she'd come."

"What's going on?" I asked as Ragnar turned to me, a soft, hopeful smile on his face.

"I thought perhaps a more intimate ceremony would be better suited for us," Ragnar said quietly. "Floki has offered to marry us."

I raised a brow. Floki had never taken anything seriously, except for war, and doubt crawled up my back. To my surprise, Floki faced me and saluted, the gesture a solemn and respectful motion I hadn't expected.

"It would be an honor, my Lady," he said, the wry grin and sarcasm void from his tone. "My Queen. We will begin now. Join hands."

I slipped my right hand into Ragnar's and glanced at Floki. He pulled a triple-braided cord from an inside pocket of his coat, one of the cords dyed blue from the native frostberries, another black from the ash of a hearth, and the last cord a long strip of softened leather. He raised it above his head with a reverence I'd never seen and lowered it as he spoke. He wove it around our hands with slow, purposeful movements, never hesitating in his actions.

"We stand strong under an ancient magic, where even winter dare not rest," he said, his tone steady and focused. "The Fire Willow stands as a reminder of the sacred power of Tachá, as old and strong as time itself. The blue wool cord represents the royal standing, a vow to rule together in unity for the welfare of your people. The black is death, the inevitable end of all things, and the leather throng is your love. Softened and well handled, it will protect you both as long as you maintain and care for it."

As if in response to Floki's words, the branches swayed and the leaves whispered around us, sending a current of warm air around us. Floki chuckled under his breath and nodded to himself. He turned to Ragnar and his demeanor grew gravely serious.

"Ragnar," he spoke in Nordmaarian, an unquestioned authority in his voice. "King of Tachá. Leader. Warrior. Wolf. You kneel not to the unseen gods of old and you swear your oaths by what your eyes see, by what your hands can touch. You swear your oaths to protect those you care for, and for those who will stand beside you at world's end. Do you swear to take Valérikka, daughter of Tachá, to be your chosen kin, your shield, and your home?"

Without hesitation, Ragnar affirmed in our language. "*Ek vil*," as he gazed into my eyes, and Floki gently pulled the cords taut around our fingers.

"Valérikka, you have sworn your oaths to something else, your fealty to the Hunter's Guild paramount. You have been offered the leniency in binding yourself to Ragnar, however still belonging to the Guild. This is understood and your allegiance to the Guild is not in question. But for the man that stands before you, do you swear to bind yourself to him in mind, body, and soul, to take him as your sword, your hearth, and your strength?"

"*Ek vil*," I murmured with a nod, the Nordmaarian language rolling off my tongue with eagerness.

Floki smiled widely, his eyes shining brightly.

"For as long as this realm shines with the light of the sun and moon and holds the favor of the old gods, may this union flourish and be blessed. You are bound," he said, "bound in flesh, bound in spirit, and bound in will."

We released our hands and the cords remained together, the knot that had been made forming a lump in my throat. I was married now, to a man that I loved wholly, and who I knew, without a doubt, loved me in return. Floki drank deeply from his flask and sighed as he grinned wickedly.

"I'll witness that consummation, eh?" he chortled, the juvenile quip stopped by another swig of ale.

Ragnar shook his head as he clapped Floki on the back, and Bodil and Meridya wept tears of joy, bowing deeply to us in reverence. Loric, approaching with a bow, asked for Ragnar's ear, and my husband bent, laughing a moment later.

"Return to the keep, to the chapel, or wherever everyone else has gathered, tell them they missed the ceremony, but to have their fill of ale and wine at the reception. We'll follow shortly," he said, eyeing me carefully as he sent a subtle wink. "I must have a private meeting with my wife first."

CHAPTER 4
THE STOLEN HUNT

My handmaidens, Meridya and Bodil, strong, steadfast women who had served many years as trusted friends, had been diligent in their preparations. Ensuring both saddlebags were secured to my waiting mare, they stood quietly as I approached. Dappled gray against a thick white coat and bred for the arctic tundra, Astrid had been a gift from Ragnar, something he had long saved for the right woman. The thought made the sting of my betrayal cut deeper. I loved her dearly and I knew she trusted me. Waiting in the stable, she stamped her hoof impatiently, sensing my unrest almost too well for a horse. My handmaidens stood beside her in silence, one gripping the leather reins as I approached quietly through the dark.

"Are you sure you need to do this, my Lady?" she whispered fearfully. "My Lord the King will be furious with us when he finds out we assisted your departure."

"He will not harm you, Meridya. He won't retaliate against either of you," I said, grasping her hands in mine.

"His anger will lie with me, not you. I know him well enough to promise you that."

She pulled me into a tight embrace and whispered a blessing of safety into my ear before releasing me into Bodil's grasp, another blessing of protection and love bestowed. I hauled myself into the saddle and glanced around for Kona. As always, my white wolf was never far from my side, appearing like a ghost from the shadows.

"Where will you go?" Bodil asked as my horse took a few steps forward.

"I don't know yet," I said with a deep breath, filling my lungs with the sharp northern air. "But I'll return, I swear it."

"Be safe, my Queen," she said, bringing her fist to her chest and bowing her head to me as Meridya followed suit.

I returned the Tacháan gesture of respect and Astrid trotted toward the outer gates of Wolfstone Fortress. The great city of Sitica had been my home since marrying Ragnar almost fifteen years ago, but the frozen forests of Ravenscourge and the Hunter's Guild hidden within had raised me since childhood. When the wind screamed through the trees, I heard my name in its voice, calling me back to the timber.

My duties as Queen of Tachá should have taken precedence, but the Vow of the Hunter's Guild held greater sway, a truth known and understood by Ragnar. He had been proud to have a Queen who could hold her own in battle...at least, he had been, until I left. That training would be my only line of defense beyond the thick walls of the stone castle.

Shaking away my intrusive thoughts, I pressed my heels into Astrid's sides. Followed closely by Kona, Astrid never slowed pace as she trotted through the gates. The eyes that watched us held no knowledge that their Queen, with her face and identity hidden, was riding out of the fortress. I had left a note, hastily scribbled, offering no reassurance. There was no time to craft an explanation, there were no words that could have borne the weight of the heartbreak, fear, and desperation I carried.

Forgive me.
I love you.

It was an awful way to leave, and if he banished me, divorced me, or stripped me of everything I had, I would understand entirely. I knew that abandoning my king and my country was dangerous and may have crossed into the realm of treason, but I hoped that Alva and Maester Crowsbeak would have space to explain on my behalf. I prayed that my husband would be merciful and control his rage. Ragnar was a formidable foe both on and off the battlefield, unmatched in strategy, power, and wisdom, with a sharply keen mind. His strength paired equally with his devotion to his country and his kin. However, Ragnar's love for me was measured with an intensity that left everything else in the dust. I could only hope that he would still love me after all of this was over with.

I STAYED on the main road, keeping my hood pulled forward to conceal my face. My fair skin, bright blue eyes, and yellow-blonde hair easily identified me as a native of Tachá, and though I was fairly confident no one outside the city walls would so easily recognize my face, I couldn't take any chances. I'd wrapped my brooches, clasps, hair pins, and jewelry in a soft fur, and tucked them safely in a chest in our bedchamber. The one piece I could not and would not part with was the thin, hand-crafted ring of iron on my left hand. Ragnar had commissioned the best ironworker in all of Tachá to craft the wedding band with a sapphire that he said was reminiscent of my eyes. I kept it as a reminder of the very reason I fled. I loved him enough to leave him. As I swayed along with Astrid's loping walk, my eyes grew heavy as the sun sank behind the mountains of the western land. I knew I'd come across an inn to stay the night in and a stable to house Kona and Astrid, and after two more hours of Astrid's leisurely walk, lights in the distance pierced the darkness.

I paid a few pieces of silver for a stall, hay, and water, and triple that for my own lodging. As the woman behind the bar paused to stare, her inquisitive eyes fixed on me, I offered her a silver coin and subtly put a finger to my lips. She gave me a discreet curtsy and pocketed the coin as she returned to the kitchen with an armful of plates to wash. I was determined to leave before first light, aware of the risks of being identified in my own homeland, though I hadn't fully considered the implications. The Queen of Tachá traveling alone, without a guard, especially toward the Wall, was bound to give rise to rumor and suspicion. Past the Great Wall of Valthor, however, no one knew my face or my skill with steel, so a quick attack to defend myself would be easy enough.

Before the sun rose, I was shouldering my pack and quietly descending the wooden planks from the upper level. The woman was waiting at the counter and as I neared, she brought out a small bundle of wrapped rations and set the coin I'd offered last night on top.

"Be safe, my Queen," she whispered, placing the bundle into my hands. "Not a soul will know that your presence has passed by. It has been an honor to serve you."

"My husband will be looking for me," I warned quietly. "If he questions you-"

"Has he brought you pain or shame, my lady? Is this why you flee him? I had always thought him a hard man. Fair but firm. Am I mistaken?"

"No, he has a gentle heart and kind hands, he's an honorable man without question. I flee for *his* safety, not my own," I stammered, unsure of why my words spilled from my lips. "I fear he may be in danger and I *have* to save him from it."

"Then may the old gods watch over your journey, give your mare sure footing, and provide the answers and satisfaction you seek."

She reached out and cupped my cheek in her hand, a bold move to touch the Queen as such, but I sensed the motherly affection in her action. I didn't see another soul as I saddled Astrid and we left the city under the cover of the quiet, pre-dawn slumber. By the time the birds began to sing, I couldn't see the smoke from the inn's chimney anymore. The sun rose and perched above my head, and the only sounds that filled my ears were the steady impacts of Astrid's hooves against the packed earth, slow and rhythmic. Kona's paws left soft imprints in the snow, but aside from a whine every now and then, she was her usual silent self. I pulled Astrid to a stop and she nickered, throwing her head nervously. Kona growled, the deep rumble radiating outward as her head lowered toward the thick forests westward.

That's when I realized that there were no birds singing or soaring...no rabbits digging out sweet grass from under the snow...no deer loping lazily...nothing. A chill ran up my spine and I watched Astrid's eyes widen with fear and Kona snarled as she lunged behind me. I didn't even have time to draw my sword before a massive white arm, matted with blood, snow, and twigs, launched me backward off of Astrid's back. I hit the ground eight feet away, flat on my back, and the air emptied out of my lungs. Astrid bolted to safety and I rolled to my feet, drawing both of the blades that hung on my hips as Kona returned to my side. Bellowing with a roar that brought a shudder of fear and icy cold to my bones, a lone yeti rushed toward me.

Black claws slashed the air in front of me as I dodged another frenzied attack and we locked eyes, my blood running cold. Snarling, its claws tore through the air again, this time catching my arm and slicing through the thick furs and wool I wore. Warm and sticky with blood, my left arm weakened as I struggled to maintain a grip on my sword. The yeti roared, the scent of my blood rich in its nose, and Kona darted forward, sinking her teeth into the yeti's thigh as she tried to shake it off balance. The yeti was starving, and the scent of my blood drove it into a frenzy as I gripped the hilts of my swords and readied for the attack. The claws came, and as I dipped away, my steel blades sang as they cut through fur, flesh, and bone. The yelping warped into a furious scream as I severed the yeti's arm at the elbow, the weak, jointed connection of the arm bones giving me the only upper hand I would get. It turned and fled, the snow crunching under its feet as I dropped my blades and drew the bow strapped to my back.

"Kona, stay at my side," I commanded her, ignoring her whining pleas to chase the wounded beast.

Nocking a raven-feathered arrow, I drew back and hit the yeti in the shoulder, the arrow sinking deep into the muscle. It continued and seemed to disappear in the snow-covered terrain, the camouflaged predator injured and furious. Astrid nickered and trotted to my side, and as the adrenaline slowed, the pain in my arm increased to dizzying levels. Wrapping the injury with a clean cloth, I gingerly mounted my horse and continued after the wounded creature.

Even without Kona's keen senses, the blood trail was easy to follow, the bright crimson spots staining the snow in a crooked line toward the woods. I stowed my bow and drew a sword, keeping a firm grip on Astrid's reins in case she spooked and bolted again. The blood led to a hollowed-out formation in the forest floor: a cavern that sank its tunneled entry deep into the earth. Dismounting Astrid, I stopped to look, listen, and feel, Kona's ears swiveled, listening for any sound. Stepping into the mouth of the cave, the air was cool and damp, the only sound in the quickly-enveloping blackness was my nearly-silent footsteps and Kona's single sneeze. The hairs on the back of my neck stood up and I whirled around, slashing my blade through the creature's midsection and slicing through its jugular with my second sword. Kona sprang behind it and leapt, her teeth embedded in its wounded shoulder as she used the momentum to knock it off balance. Gurgling and spraying blood, it staggered backward, swiped at Kona weakly with a limp claw, and fell, the sickening crack of its skull echoing throughout the cave.

"Well, that was fun," I murmured to the white wolf, pausing as a threatening growl came from her throat.

Following her gaze, I saw three men at the mouth of the cave, relaxed and standing at ease with the sight of the downed yeti between us.

"I think you'll be coming with us," a man said, flanked by two companions, all heavily armored and wielding swords and bows *much* larger than mine.

He sheathed his sword and gestured at me, and seemed surprised when I scoffed and shook my head.

"I'll be on my way, actually. Come, Kona," I replied. "Move aside, please."

The skinny man, wearing a long, mud-colored jacket, reached in his pocket, pulling out a pinch of sand. He grinned widely as he threw it toward me and Kona and muttered under his breath. Despite the distance, the sand hit us in the face, echoed with the man's words. I coughed and wiped my face clean as Kona fell, her paws folded underneath her as she slept soundly.

"She don't look like no elf!" the man exclaimed as the other two approached warily. "She should be sleepin' too!"

I drew my swords, but I was no match for three men, one of whom began chuckling under his breath. Looking at me, he held his hand up and whispered, *'lights out,'* as my vision slowly began to fade. I stayed conscious and my grip on my swords tightened. Blinded and furious, I listened as their footsteps shuffled closer and paused. I could smell their fear.

"Listen, little lady," a voice came from ahead, "we don't want to hurt you, it's just that you took our kill, that's all, and we kinda needed that. We don't think a woman of your...*delicate stature* should be out here all by yourself, see, so we're gonna...accompany you back to our hold."

"I'm not going anywhere with you," I snarled, slashing at the air with my steel.

They whispered, too quiet for me to hear, and one of them sighed heavily. Footsteps approached from both sides, and a surprise blow to my head knocked me out.

CHAPTER 5

A KING WITHOUT A QUEEN

Ragnar

The sun had just crept over the mountains when I stirred. Suppressing a groan as my bones ached in the chilly morning air, I rolled to my side and reached out to pull Valérikka and her radiating body heat to my side. My hand brushed over cold linens, and reaching farther resulted in the same. No warmth, no wife, just an empty bedchamber and an eerily quiet dawn. I sat upright and blinked away the foggy haze of eye slumber, and stared at the vacant part of the bed that she had warmed for so long. She wouldn't have left this early, not without waking me, and as dread mixed with frustration, I caught sight of a folded scrap of paper with my name written in her hand. I leaned over her side, the cold sheets chilling my skin, and I snatched the note. My eyes followed the soft, hurried script, and the world stilled.

Forgive me.
I love you.

My heart slammed hard as if trying to burst free from my body. Once more it beat, and again.

Then the rage came. Without my wife to quell the waves of fury, I was anger unbridled.

My feet were tangled in the bearskin blanket, frustration reigned as I flung the thick pelt off the bed. It landed in a crumpled heap with an audible thud and as I set my bare feet on the stone floor, the cold shocked my senses. Unbothered and without care, I stormed from the chamber stark naked as anger coursed fiery hot through my veins. The morning bustling was brought to a sharp halt as gasping ladies scurried away and wise men cleared the area, knowing my temper flared and things had a tendency to fly across the room.

"WHERE IS SHE?!" I bellowed, my roar echoing through the vaulted hall.

No one moved, not a soul spoke, and as I took hold of a heavy wooden chair, I threw it over my head and it shattered against the stone walls.

"WHERE IS MY WIFE?!" I shouted, the rage blurring my senses.

"My Lord, the Queen-" one of them began, "she… is she not in her chambers, my King?"

"If she was, do you think I'd be demanding to know where she was?" I replied with a snarl, the man cowering before me.

I stomped over to the floor, my feet melting the frosty chill that covered the flagstones, and I seized the massive oak table that lay in the center of the room. With a furious roar, I flipped it over, two of the carved wooden legs snapping off from the tabletop with a deafening crack as the goblets, plates, and utensils that lay on the table scattered in cacophony. It would take a handful of my strongest men to pick up that table, eight men were needed to bring it into the hall originally, but I didn't care. I didn't care about anything or anyone. I wanted answers. As the last plate stopped rattling on the floor, silence grew. No one dared to speak, and the great doors suddenly burst open as men stormed inside, looking for the cause of the pre-breakfast clamor.

"My King, please," my steward Loric stammered, holding out a long tunic to me as he bowed, averting his gaze.

I slapped it away and repeated my question, perhaps yelling loud enough that even my men looked shaken. One of my men stepped forward. I knew his face, Bernodon, a brave man, fearless in battle. His eyes held fear as I loomed over him. He swallowed and opened his mouth.

"She was seen leaving the grounds before dawn. A hooded figure on a dappled gray Tacháan mare...with a white wolf at her side."

That was her, *that* was my wife. She had left of her own volition, *willingly*.

"No one stopped her?" I snarled. "Your Queen is *gone!* And you let it happen!"

"She gave no orders, Your Grace," Bernodon spoke, his tone clear and unwavering.

"She didn't *HAVE TO!*" I roared, slamming my fist into a stone pillar, the impact cracking the stone as dust fell from the ceiling.

A small figure stepped forward from the safety of the crowd. A woman. I recognized her face. She was trembling head to toe, white as snow, and her eyes stayed on the flagstone. She gave a curtsy and her name floated to the forefront of my mind as she waited to be addressed.

"Speak, Meridya. Where is she?"

"She asked for my help, my King," she said, her shaking voice barely a whisper. "I-I gave it."

Silence thickened in the room and I grit my teeth in fury as I looked around the room for anyone else that had shown as much bravery as this woman. Not one. The eyes of fellow handmaidens had welled with tears and I realized that every servant in the room expected her to be struck down. I stepped toward her slowly, my steps the only sounds in the room. She kept her eyes down, I didn't know if it was in modest protest to my nakedness or in anticipation of the judgment I was about to pass. I placed my hand on her shoulder, gently, and she flinched. I knelt in front of her and Loric approached again. I allowed the tunic to be pulled over my shoulders, and he retreated to the crowd, leaving Meridya alone.

"You are not to blame," I said softly, the rage gone from my voice as it cracked. "My wrath lies not upon you, but myself. I let her slip away, I...I did this."

Her eyes met mine, welled with tears...for me.

"I'm sorry, my King. She said she would return, but did not tell us where she was going. Please, I believe you will see her again, Your Grace."

As if she had realized the situation, she gave a hasty curtsy and retreated to the safety of her companions. I stood and scanned the crowd. Every eye remained full of fear and with a growl and a wave of my arm, I dismissed them. They scattered, fleeing like mice, and I was left alone. The hearth was roaring and my feet were numb with cold. As I approached, another wave of anger washed over me.

"Loric!" I shouted as the man approached. "Where is Lady? I'll send Lady to bring my wife back whether she wants to come back or not!"

From the hearth across the room, the white direwolf raised her head, clearly annoyed as she resumed basking in front of the warm flames. A chuckle, high-pitched and giggly, sounded from the corner. I groaned at the sound and waited for Floki to join me.

"I'm pleased to see your manhood well covered," Floki said with a grin, knife in hand as he tossed me a slice of the apple he was eating. "Makes keeping my breakfast down a little easier."

I swatted it away and the tall, lanky limbed man stood beside me.

"Your plan is to send your *former* wife to fetch your *current* wife?"

"Oh, shut up, Floki," I spat, annoyed at his words. "That myth has gotten out of hand as it is. What would you have me do instead? She's *out* there in Tachá, doing gods know what, in...in danger I'm sure of it."

I hung my head, overwhelmed by grief and fear. Floki clapped me on the back and sighed.

"Fear does not become you, friend," he said quietly, a rare sincerity in his voice.

I didn't answer, struggling to put into words what exactly brought that unwanted tightness in my chest.

"I need her, Floki," I muttered, swallowing the thick emotion I wouldn't allow myself to feel. "I need her here."

"Why?" he asked, urging me to keep talking.

"She...she keeps me sane. She keeps that part of me that just wants the world to burn...she keeps it under her foot. She keeps me from ripping off the heads of... everyone."

"She makes it look so effortless, too."

"Seriously, Floki. I don't know how to explain it. She helps me do better. She makes me a better man. I'm afraid of what I'll become while she's gone, and I'm afraid that if she comes back...she won't come back to me."

"So without her you're a piece of shit, and with her you're a slightly more tolerable, muzzled piece of shit," Floki said simply. "I remember who you used to be, too. I don't think you're that man anymore, but I think you shouldn't dwell on him too long. Ghosts can come back, even our own. She told her ladies she was coming back, so she'll come back. Keep the kingdom in running order for her until she gets back."

"What if she-"

"Have you forgotten *who* you chose as your wife and Queen?" Floki said, cutting me off. "Did you think all of her knowledge, her skills, and her capabilities just *flitted out the window* when she accepted your hand? Ragnar, she's *fine*. Probably."

"How can you be sure?"

Floki gave a shrug. "Either that or she's dead and you'll need another queen."

He ducked as I swung my hand at his head, giggling as he rose again.

"Have a little faith in the woman, Ragnar," he said. "If anyone could handle our motherland, it's her. Like I said, if she can put *you* on your ass, she can survive Tachá with ease."

I grinned, recalling the first time I had ever set eyes on who I knew in an instant would be my wife. The ferocity in her eyes as I landed on the bar floor, coupled with a stinging punch square in my mouth, revealed more about her than traditional courting ever could.

"Feel better now?"

"Piss off, Floki," I said, exhaling as my feet finished thawing. "I know she'll be okay, as long as she stays within Tachá's borders."

Floki's sarcastic retort was cut short as my steward approached.

"Yes, Loric?" I said, waving him forward.

"My King, a letter from Ibria," he said, placing the sealed note bearing the sigil of the desert country in my hands.

Floki spat. "What does the Pharaoh of Cowardice want?"

I opened it and recognized a different signet seal at the base.

"It's not from him, it's from his son, the Prince."

To His Majesty, King Ragnar of Tachá,

From the Hand of Prince Azran Ra'zír of Ibria,

May this letter find you in strength, wisdom, and the enduring favor of the gods.

I write to you privately, not merely as a prince nor as a suitor soon to be wed, but as a man burdened by the truth and driven by purpose. The union between myself and Princess Valeria Vael'Quinalis is not just one of love and alliance, it is the beginning of a reckoning long overdue.

My father, Pharaoh Tekhmet, was once a noble ruler. He has in recent years become ensnared by fear and manipulation. After much investigation, I have discovered that, under the subtle chains of King Rofellos and the shadowed dealings of the Trifecta, my father has allowed Ibria to become a silent partner in their conquest. Our mines now bleed gold into their coffers and our deserts—vast, empty, and cruel—are littered with hidden camps, where prisoners and dissidents labor under the sun until they are dust. My father, whether by fear or folly, has become a steward of their dominion.

But I am <u>not</u> my father.

Upon my ascension as Pharaoh, I intend to sever these poisonous ties immediately. The Trifecta shall no longer drink from Ibria's wealth, nor exploit its lands as a crucible of torment. I will free my people, expose the crimes buried in the sand, and raise Ibria into a realm that stands with justice, not beneath tyranny.

However, I cannot accomplish such a mighty feat alone. I know of your strength. I have heard of Tachá's resilience, its unbending spine in the face of the Trifecta's reach. You are a king unbowed, a ruler of mercy and justice. I seek your alliance—not in ceremony, but in cause. When the time comes and the Trifecta realizes they've lost their grip on Ibria, they will turn their gaze to me with fury. I will need an ally who will not look away.

Let us forge a bond greater than blood or banner. Let us bring the dawn to an empire of shadows.

In faith, fire, and freedom for our people,
Prince Azran Ra'zír
Heir to the Twin Bloodlines of Ibria

"Good ol' Rolly's been playing in the sandbox," Floki said, a dangerous glint in his eyes. "Perhaps we should bury him in that sand. I knew he was working with the Trifecta, those bastard thugs."

"At ease," I murmured. "I need to think."

"No time to think!" Floki shouted. "I'll raise the

banners and rouse the men! Finally, a time to bathe in the blood of our enemies!"

"Ah, yes, Floki," I said through gritted teeth. "Now, where *is* the Queen to proclaim such a war declaration?"

Floki's arms dropped and he shouted, a mixture of frustration and rage as he beat his chest. He turned to the white direwolf, who was actively ignoring us as she dozed.

"Ah! Where's Lady? Lady! Go fetch the Queen, bring her back so we can go to war!" he said, the urgency in his voice dampened by defeat. "We can't go to war without the Queen's permission...why do we have that law? It's a stupid law, Ragnar."

"We have it so bloodthirsty savages like yourself aren't off creating wars. Women have level heads. Most of the time," I replied coolly.

"Damn that law," he muttered. "I need to beat something. I'm going to the Pit."

I agreed with him, though I'd never admit it. Nothing could have truly quenched the raw pain I felt, but beating a handful of men to bloody pulps could have definitely helped distract me. It would do Floki some good, going a few rounds in the Pit, a sunken, underground ring where Tacháan men and women fought to earn respect and clout. I hadn't been in a very long time, my wife had been able to talk sense into me whenever I got that itch. Thinking of how she would distract me from bloodying my fists, I glanced at the letter from the Prince and sighed. Val would have a few things to say about this letter, one of them would be to attend the upcoming nuptials, out of a polite manner, and also use the occasion to speak with the Prince to solidify alliances. I wasn't sending a damned gift. That was Val's job to arrange a gift for the newlyweds, I was absolutely not doing that.

"Loric!" I called, waiting only a moment before he arrived. "I need to head south. Alert Bjorn, tell my son I need to see him before dinner tonight. Tell him to pack a bag, too."

"Sir?" he asked, slightly braver now that I wasn't screaming anymore. "Is everything alright? Are you..."

"Don't worry, Loric," I said, patting the man's arm, the unintentional force sending him reeling. "Sorry, er, I'll explain after I speak with Bjorn."

He nodded, bowed, and left, leaving me in the empty room with nothing but my thoughts.

CHAPTER 6
THE WARDEN
OF THE NORTH

Before I opened my eyes, I listened to my surroundings, the training of my hunting years springing to the forefront of my mind.

The earthy scent of the air around me tickled the back of my mind, memories from long ago calling out. From all around me, the dry snapping sticks and crackle of logs sounded, and the accompanying warm air gave evidence for multiple hearths. The shuffling of boots, from thick iron boots that scraped to soft leather soles that brushed the floor, passed by and as I opened my eyes, the face of a woman filled my view. Stern and mildly amused, she stood with her arms crossed, as if waiting for me to wake up. I sat up and winced as pain flashed across the back of my skull, sharp and biting. Gingerly touching for a wound, I found nothing but a goose egg, and the woman let out a chortle.

"Don't ya worry about that," she said dismissively as I stood, brushing my hands on my pants. "What I *would* worry about is coming up with a good excuse as to why the Queen of Tachá is traipsing 'round the tundra, cutting down yetis and frolicking about in the snow. Care to answer that?"

She raised an inquisitive red brow, a similar shade to her braided fiery locks, pinned back with long bone shards polished smooth and sleek.

"You're a sight for sore eyes, Ylsa," I said with a grin, catching the twinkling eyes of my old mentor. "You've gotten old."

She smiled widely and swore at me in our native tongue as I stood up, blinking hard as the swaying room began to still.

"And you've gotten slow, Valérikka," she said, my name rolling off her tongue easily. "Rollan, Aerin, and Vyggo say they got the drop on you. What do *you* say?"

"*I say* I may have stolen their hunt," I said, adding, "unintentionally, of course. When I refused to go with them, they blinded me and knocked me out. Rude of them. Where's my wolf and my horse?"

"They're safe under my protection, eating their fill in the stables. I may have told those boys that you were a *very* experienced, highly respected huntress, with a keen sense of revenge...and a deep love for your companions. They begged for mercy, and before all was said and done, your wolf bit two and your horse kicked the other," she said with a laugh. "They're definitely smart creatures. Come with me, dear."

I followed her down a tunnel-like hall as memories of my youth flooded the forefront of my mind. The sharp sound of steel kissing steel made my hand itch for the sparring practices that formed my muscle memory. I smiled to myself at the pained yelp that came as we passed a wide doorway; three pairs of young men, barely out of their teens, practiced their swordplay, footwork, and close combat skills in a large, well-lit room. As we passed, they all stopped, touching their right fist to their chest in salute to Ylsa. She nodded her head at their gesture of respect and briefly returned it. I hadn't realized I'd done it in return until Ylsa chortled under her breath.

"Old habits die hard, eh?"

I raised a shoulder and continued alongside her, fully understanding that here, under the unrivaled, unquestionable leadership of the Warden of the Northern Hunters' Guild, I wasn't the Queen. I was Valérikka, a huntress who had once risen through the ranks and had fought tooth and nail for the respect that I had earned and held in the Guild. I'd apparently been absent from the halls long enough for the newer pups to not recognize my face, and right now I was thankful for it. I didn't need whispers and rumors getting back to my husband that his wife was reverting to her wild days of being a Huntress of Tachá. As we continued down the hallway, I realized where we were heading, and I absently began stretching my arms, rotating the joints and sockets that were about to get a workout.

"Y'know, it was sheer dumb luck that the damned yeti didn't spill your guts out in front of you," Ylsa said, opening the thick wooden door to the magically immersive practice room. "When's the last time you held a sword for more than a painted portrait?"

"It's been a while," I admitted, slowly realizing that she may be more right than I'd care to admit.

"Gear up, we'll catch ourselves an uglabjorn," she said, tossing a quiver full of arrows to me.

The dimly lit room shifted, the magical enchantments creating a thickly wooded evergreen forest around us, seemingly with us right in the middle. Snow fell in fat flakes and melted on my bare skin, and my breath billowed like dragon's breath as the temperature dropped. I knew it was all an illusion, but it was still an incredible thing to behold, and best of all, it *felt* real. After strapping two swords to my hips, I chose a maple wood shortbow, the curve of the red bow catching the sunlight through the trees. We were supposed to be finding an uglabjorn...and I knew that if we were searching for *it*, it was searching for *us*, too.

I recalled the mistakes that I had made during my first hunt for an uglabjorn; I hadn't anticipated such a large bear-beast being so silent, but despite its size, the thick white fur that covered its massive paws provided an insulated warmth as well as soundproofed steps, perfect for stalking prey. Dappled grey, white, and pale brown, depending on the season, the camouflage of the uglabjorn was legendary, inspiring similar patterns that many of the past and present hunters of Tachá adopted. Sharing mannerisms and appearances similar to the great tundra bears of our frozen land, many hunters had been shocked during the hunt to discover the vicious, feathered head of a giant bird. With keen eyes and a sharp beak, it was able to strike faster than anticipated. The roar of an adult uglabjorn had rattled almost every new recruit: the few that could overcome the fear from those blood-chilling bellows had risen quickly through the ranks, myself included. My memories were interrupted as a stick snapped in the distance, and I nocked an arrow with a careful silence. Adjusting my footing in case I needed to dart aside, I rested my fingertips on the arrow, just grazing the crow-feather fletching as I readied to shoot.

"Hope you're not too rusty, Highness," Ylsa said with

a wide grin, stamping a foot as another branch cracked, much closer this time.

"Suppose we'll find out," I managed to say before firing an arrow into the beast that had burst from the trees, an explosion of snow, white feathers, and white dappled fur. I somersaulted out of its path and traded my bow for the two swords at my sides, drawing them simultaneously and locking eyes with the massive beast. The squawking roar made my ears ring and it rushed me. Like hitting a solid wall of stone, the soft feathers of the uglabjorn did nothing to soften the blow of the impact as my back hit a tree that was definitely going to leave a bruise.

"My compliments to your magic-weaver," I groaned as I rolled to my feet. "The forest's realism is all too accurate."

Ylsa barked out a laugh as the rage-filled uglabjorn swiped at her. Dodging with the fluidity of a cat, she drew back and threw her fist into the creature's face, the immense power behind the blow cracking its sharp beak. It squealed and fled from the woman, turning its attack to me as it stood tall on its hind legs, towering over me. Dodging the first claw attack, I severed the incoming second paw, tipped with black, razor-sharp claws, and it fell with a wet, heavy thud on the forest floor. Readying my swords for another defense, I sighed as the bloodied uglabjorn dissolved into dust, floating away as the forest that surrounded us vanished, revealing a large, dimly-lit room. Walls of stone lined with small sconces revealed a hard-packed dirt floor, cold to the touch.

"The training room seems smaller," I murmured, toeing the dirt.

"No, you just hold your ground much better," she

said, adding with a laugh, "the beast didn't throw you that far, either. You're not as scrawny as you once were."

We continued walking through the Guild's fort, a mostly-underground lair of twisting tunnels, secret entrances, and hidden doors. Ylsa stopped at a door that appeared at her approach, her hand paused mid-air, and she turned to me, her eyes searching for answers.

"We will only speak truth beyond this door," she warned. "Deceit is ill-advised."

The door was a thick mahogany, intricately covered with wrought iron runes woven into the design, the runic shapes a more delicate version of the patterns on Ylsa's boots. I knew this was her private quarters, though I had never been through this door. No one I knew had, except for Ylsa herself. I didn't hesitate to follow her across the threshold. As if I'd walked under a waterfall, a cold, fluid sensation ran over me, from my head to the very soles of my feet.

"It washes away any masquerades that someone may have," she explained briefly.

"Ylsa, I wouldn't-"

"It removes things that were not bestowed on you with your consent. It's a cleanser."

I nodded once, still mildly confused why she would find it necessary, and as if I'd said it out loud, Ylsa responded.

"We've had hunters with bounties in the past," she explained. "Some of those bounties were earned... viciously. The whole guild is enchanted with a very subtle protection ring. It's only this strong because this room holds the coveted items that others have tried to pilfer in the past."

"Who enchanted this so well? Is it the same person who upgraded the training room's enchantments?"

She grinned with a nod and beckoned me to sit at the ornate table, the wood matching the deep red coloring of the door behind us. She sat and exhaled, her shoulders relaxing as they dropped.

"Tell me what's happened, Valérikka," she said, a mixture of quiet authority and gentle sincerity.

I told her everything and left out no detail. By the end of it, her eyes were steely and her jaw was set. I knew questions were rolling in her mind, but she offered me the greatest respect by keeping them to herself.

"Tell me what you need and it's yours," she spoke quietly. "What resources I have are now yours, but tell me why. Why are *you* the deadliest threat to the greatest soldier this land has had in over a century?"

I hung my head. "It took me a while to understand. It's because he loves me and I love him in return. He is unguarded with me. What greater trust should a man have than with his wife? What greater betrayal could come than from his wife? I don't know why this is happening, but I intend to find out why, who, and how, and then I will kill them."

As I began to describe the dream that had plagued me for months on end, she nodded.

"I hate to say it, but I think you were wise to flee, child," Ylsa sighed. "And I have a feeling that this goes far beyond a wife killing her husband, or even a Queen murdering her king. I have no answers for you, but my colleague may. It won't be an easy trip, but I have faith in you."

"Who? Wherever he is, I'll go-"

"Gracious, child," Ylsa said, holding her hand up to

silence me gently. "Answers to the questions you seek will take *patience*. My colleague, Mr. Winchester, resides in Enguard. He is the Warden of the Ironclad Hunters' Guild of Thyuland. I believe he spends almost all of his time at his shop, however, to gain access to the Guild, you'll have to show...or prove, your status in our Guild. Now, I can't guarantee that he'll have answers directly, but he may know someone else that can help. I fear that if Winchester cannot give you some sort of answers, no one will."

"Thank you, Ylsa," I said, pouring my gratitude into the words.

"Let's get you packed up, your horse and wolf are in the stables. They've been well looked after by the pups."

"You're *still* calling the new recruits pups?" I laughed.

"Well, they *are* pups," she said with a chortle. "Babies, pups, greenlings...I think it's a pleasant term of my affection. They have to earn their place in our guild, just like the wolf packs that roam our lands. You remember those days, don't you? They weren't all *that* long ago, Valérikka. You would be training those pups yourself if you and your stubbornness hadn't tossed our king on his ass in a tavern and then fallen in love with him."

"It didn't exactly happen like *that*," I said, my heart swelling with the memory.

"Well, the stories told would say it happened *a lot* like that," Ylsa said with a hearty laugh. "But sometimes a bit of exaggeration and embellishment is good."

A small part of me hoped that my dreams tonight would hold memories of my first encounter with Ragnar. The bliss of slumber would be magical in itself, but dreams of my husband would be a sweet thing to remember.

CHAPTER 7

FROSTHOLM

14 Years Ago

~

We were losing. Badly. The six recruits I had been assigned to were terrified of the pack of massive frost spiders, and I couldn't blame them. We were outnumbered, the blizzard we had been racing was nipping our heels, and the village we were supposed to protect and defend was calling us inside as they prepared for the storm. Ghvain had been bitten in the shoulder and was bleeding profusely as he cut down a spider the size of a hound mid-leap.

"We have to run," a young recruit cried out in panic. "We can't be trapped out when the blizzard hits! We'll freeze to death if the spiders don't get us first!"

"We're not running!" I shouted, cutting off the hairy limb of a spider that crept too close. "We stand our ground and we fight until they flee or they're dead!"

As I slashed at another fast-approaching beast, I heard a blood-chilling scream from behind me. A frost spider had sunk its fangs into Rhyse's leg and was attempting to drag him away. Rhyse screamed my name but I was already at his side, the spider dead on its back. I tied a length of cord with a stick around his upper thigh and tightened the tourniquet until the young man screamed and paled, and then I rotated it another turn. Ghvain killed a spider that had crept up behind me while my attention was on Rhyse.

"Well done, Ghvain," I said with a nod. "Let's get him up."

I turned around to assign a couple recruits to helping Rhyse and saw their backs, sprinting toward the small village nearby. Fury burned within me as their abandonment and I slashed viciously at a spider skittering toward me. Covered with jagged pieces of ice and web, its armor-like exoskeleton split in half from the blow. We were surrounded on every side, and I was absolutely sure that we weren't going to be able to cut down every spider, and I was not about to let my recruits be killed by a cluster of frost spiders. I focused and summoned thorny, grasping vines from the snowy ground, tightly ensnaring the spiders as Ghvain and I grabbed Rhyse under his arms.

"Head to the forest!" I ordered.

"But the village is closer!" Ghvain panted, pointing with his injured arm.

"The village has already been under the spider's attack, there would be no safety there," I answered, leading the men toward the dense woods. "The beasts will have to work harder to move through the trees."

The edge of the woods was within my sight; the forest called to me and I picked up the pace as the spiders broke free from my entanglement, skittering fast. They were headed straight for us and I knew that if they caught the scent of the blood-soaked bandages around my recruits we'd be finished. I spied a jagged rock outcropping, perfect for hiding behind, and as I pointed toward it, the hairs on the back of my neck stood tall. The spiders scattered wildly as a massive creature burst from the ground, all-too-close to the outcropping I had been headed for. Frozen ground and snow exploded into the air as a monstrous, armored centipede burst from the earth, a frost spider wriggling in its pincher-jaws. The spiders swarmed around it and I knew that we had to move quickly and sure-footed. Any disturbance on the ground would grab its attention, and I knew we couldn't outrun the Burrower, especially with two injured. Despite its carapace being so thick and bulky, it could burrow under frozen earth quickly, moving at unheard of speeds to ambush its prey from below. I needed to use the overwhelming tremors from the spiders to cover our own footsteps.

As we back-tracked away from the Burrower I redirected our steps, hyper-aware that just a few miles away, a larger city lay, protected by guarded sentries with both magical and steel defenses. I just had to make it there...and survive the incoming blizzard, too. I knew this land, and while many had perished in the frozen countryside, I had studied it since I could remember, and finding my way anywhere had become an instinctual, gut-feeling. I trekked carefully, but directly, and headed toward the city of Frostholm.

"Tie yourself to us, and do not cut the rope under any circumstances, understand?" I said clearly, knotting the rope around my waist and Rhyse's before passing it to Ghvain. "If the blizzard is as bad as expected, if we get separated, we will die."

The farther we managed to get away from the Burrower and frost spiders, the colder and windier it became, and soon, *visibility was nearly zero. Instinct directed me, Tachá herself guided my steps, and if there were torchlights nearing, we couldn't see them through the stinging snowflakes. If the city called our names, we didn't hear them over the howling wind. I didn't even know how close we were to the city until I nearly walked into the massive wall of spiked posts that surrounded the city. Following it north, I ducked my head and walked we into the wind, burying my face in my furs to keep myself from freezing. The shout of a man startled me, much closer than I realized as a hand grabbed my arm, leading us through the city gate.*

"He needs a healer, they both do!" I ordered whoever would listen.

We were led to a nearby guard's barracks, and quickly surrounded by armed men, both curious and suspicious of our arrival. Shrugging off the ice-coated cloak I wore, I stood tall and met the eyes of the man in front of me.

"My companions require a healer," I repeated patiently, "there is no time to waste."

A quick glance and a nod brought four men to help Ghvain and Rhyse down the hall. I raised a brow in question.

"They're being taken by passage around the city to the healer. It would raise too much attention if they were traipsed through the square, you agree? Now that your men are seen to, why don't you start with your name and why the hell you were out in a blizzard?"

"I am under no obligation to reveal anything to you," I said firmly, shaking the remaining ice crystals from my cloak and refastening the silver twin-wolf clasp around my neck. "Where is the nearest inn?"

"You're going back out in this?" one of the men said, astonished as another guard gave me crude directions. "It's a lucky thing you didn't freeze to death out there!"

"I'm not sleeping on a cot here, sir," I said bluntly. "I'll pay for a goose-down pillow and a hot meal. When my men are healed up, send them to the inn, please."

Without waiting for an answer I left the guard barracks, bracing for the shock of cold, and followed the 'turn right, veer right at the blacksmith's forge, dead in the middle, across from the stables,' and found the inn with no issue. A gust of cold wind ushered me inside and I fought against the blizzard's strength to shut the door, unintentionally slamming it. The inn was full, it seemed that the soldiers of Tachá had decided to take shelter in the business as well, and a group of merchants watched the armored men from the back of the tavern, intimidation keeping them tightly knit. I caught the eye of the barman behind the counter and wove through the men until I was between the polished bartop and a group of very drunk, very loud soldiers, all armored in the striking Tacháan blue.

"I need a room, please," I said, raising my voice and repeating myself as the soldiers continued laughing, rough-housing, and nearly spilling their steins of ale.

I had to lean in close to hear the innkeeper, and as he mimed that there was one room left. I nodded, returned the mime, and reached for my coin. A man took a step back, staggering back and nudging me a little.

"Excuse me," I said after the man failed to even acknowledge his accident.

He either didn't hear or was ignoring me, and as he drained his stein, throwing his head back as the ale ran down his beard, he took another step backward, standing his ground as he obliviously pressed me into the bar's counter. The man was strong, but very drunk, and I was now furious over being ignored as well as accosted.

"Get off me, you drunken oaf!" I grunted as the soldier laughed and continued with his group.

I supposed he was under the impression he was reclining against the bar itself, and not the woman squished in between. The man behind the bar froze, unsure and fearful, and I growled under my breath as he walked away. Squaring my legs against the base of the counter, I wriggled my arms in front of me and used the leverage from the counter to push as hard and fast as I could. Launching myself backward, the force knocked him off balance and he staggered before falling to his knees, dropping his empty stein.

Axes, swords, and arrows were drawn in an instant as the man stood slowly to his feet, holding a hand up to the men. Weapons were lowered and the man turned around, his expression holding a bubbling rage that quickly vanished as he burst out laughing. At me. My cheeks flushed and I brought my clenched fist right into his mouth with strength that erupted from my anger. From behind him, another soldier raised a handaxe and ran at me. The tall man's eyes shifted from mine, just enough to see the defending soldier in his peripheral view, and he stepped into him, planting his feet as he delivered a shoulder-check that propelled the axe-wielder into the bar beside me.

"At ease," the tall man growled, taking a moment to meet the eye of every man as their weapons were sheathed.

I set my feet strong, tightening my core in anticipation for a retaliatory blow. The man turned to me and smirked, his bottom lip barely swollen, but bleeding a little, split where my fist had connected.

"Can I buy you a drink?" he asked, signaling to the bartender as he took a seat and pulling out the stool next to him..

"*You may buy me two,*" *I replied, matching his smirk and quelling the unusual way my heart was hammering.*

IT WASN'T *until I had drunk four more servings of ale alongside him, playfully bantering and flirting unabashedly with one another that one of the men called him by his title and name. I swallowed the mouthful of liquid and stared at the man beside me.*

"*You're...you're Ragnar? King of Tachá?*" *I asked, astonished at the lack of royal attitude the man held.*

"*I am, and you are?*" *he answered as if he was anything but the king.*

"*Surprised, to say the least.*"

He chuckled and raised a hand to the barman, who brought two more frothing mugs.

"*I like you, very much,*" *he admitted.* "*What's your name? Where are you from?*"

I squinted at him, a little drunk, but still clinging to my senses, I wondered how Tacháan the king truly was.

"*Hví skylda ek segja þér nafn mitt? Þú ert of drukkinn til at muna þat í morgin. Hefr þú vit til at skilja mik?*" *My words translating to 'why should I tell you my name? You're too drunk to be able to recall it in the morning. Do you have the sense to even understand me?'*

His eyes, brighter than the ice that capped the mountains, glowed with a sense I couldn't quite make out.

"*Djarfr ert þú, at freista konungs þíns,*" *he growled, in the common tongue 'bold you are, to test your king.'*

A wicked grin crossed my lips and I laughed.

"*Not testing, just curious,*" *I admitted, biting my lip.* "*I thought you would be too drunk to recall the mother tongue, let alone recall my name in the morning."*

He leaned in close, I found myself closing the gap.

"If I whisper your name in your ear all night, I think I'll remember it better," he whispered as goose pimples covered my body involuntarily.

I smiled sweetly, fighting my senses for control as he grinned like a schoolboy.

"I'm not some common whore for you to bed," I said, finishing my drink. "Good night, Ragnar."

I slid off my stool and walked away without a backward glance, climbing the stairs to my rented room, removing my armor in a heap and falling into my bed, empty and cold. I stared at the ceiling for a moment and sighed as the room swayed. Why would the King of Tachá pay any notice to me?

I HAD RISEN before dawn and checked on my men, ordering them to return to the Guild when the healer had released them. Greasy eggs and fried potatoes for breakfast quelled the queasy waves in my belly, and I washed them down with strong coffee. The women bustled around the tables a little faster; whispering to each other as they glanced at me. One of them, a dark-eyed young woman with long black hair, paused and dipped her head to me. Clearly, word had gotten around that I'd assaulted the king...and then gotten drunk with him. I ate and had another cup of coffee before the thunderous sound of boots made their way downstairs. Four of the Tacháan men emerged in the tavern and sat at a table adjacent to mine, and I was very aware that their eyes were glued to mine. I hadn't donned my armor, wearing a simple brown tunic and pants, delicately embroi-

dered with runes of protection, revealing a lack of weapons as my tunic clung to my curves. My left boot concealed a small dagger and my belt held another pair, if needed, but I was fairly confident I would be left alone. As my coffee was refilled, another set of boots descended the stairs, slower than the other soldiers. I ignored the king, despite the towering man taking a seat across from me, and continued eating as if I were still alone.

"Good morning, lovely," he greeted. "I would like to share breakfast with you, and I apologize if I hurt you last night."

I raised a brow. "No apology needed, you didn't hurt me."

I purposely ignored the sharing-breakfast remark, but he held up two fingers to the woman that approached and I rolled my eyes. Clearly a man like Ragnar was used to getting his way.

"You never told me your name," he said slowly, his voice holding an apprehension and...was he nervous? "Despite how much you think I had to drink, I do recall your name lacking from our conversation last night. What does a man have to do to know your name?"

"Earn it," I challenged with a sly wink, "you wage battle on the open field without hesitation, so consider this a minor skirmish of the mind."

He concealed a grin as his ears turned red, and a platter of meats, cheese, bread, and butter was placed between us. "I find myself intimidated."

"I intimidate the mighty King of Tachá?"

"You intimidate me," he murmured, his tone taking a gravelly edge to it as it lowered to just above a whisper.

I wasn't threatened, nor was I scared, though a part of my mind warned me that perhaps I should be. There was something about him that drew me nearer, closer than I should have been. "What's the difference between the King of Tachá and the man that sits before me, Ragnar?"

"Mere words and titles that people bestow on me do not make me who I am," he clarified, the furrow between his brows growing deeper.

"Is my name all you really want to know?" I asked as he passed me a plate of sausages and freshly baked rolls. His hands were scarred, calloused, and as big as the plate he presented.

"Names are just a doorway."

"To what end?"

"Depends on where you're going, I suppose," he said with a devilish grin. *"I have to confess, my library may be full of books, but the poetry books have a thick layer of dust on them, clearly."*

I threw my head back and laughed.

"I'm glad of that," I said, meeting his eyes without fear. *"I would not be so easily moved with empty words and silliness."*

"But you are moved by me?"

I paused and my breath caught in my throat. I was moved, very much so, whether by the command that he seemed to carry without effort, or the way his men respected him so loyally, the strong stature of his body, built and born for labor and war, or perhaps it was the way he looked at me, as if I were a treasure that he was reaching for.

"I am," I confessed, failing to hide the creeping redness in my cheeks.

He smiled, the corners of his eyes crinkling as he chuckled.

"Alright, you want me to earn the right to know your name?" He said after draining his coffee and meeting the eyes of the barmaid. *"I accept. Ask me anything."*

"Oh, no," I replied, the corners of my lips turned up. *"I think you'll be asking the questions. Ask me the right questions and I'll tell you my name. Perhaps I'll lie with an answer, and if you detect my false answers, you'll win that round."*

Ragnar grinned as if he had already won. "Woman, what is your name? That is my first question."

"My name is Brigitte," I replied coolly, sipping the steaming coffee.

"That is your first lie," he said confidently.

"Correct. Next question?" I confessed with a smile that made him nearly drop his cup. "Also, questions may not be repeated."

"Where are you from?" he asked. "I mean, where do you live currently?"

"Ravenscourge," I answered truthfully.

His eyes widened for a split second before he feigned knowledge. He knew exactly who I was without knowing my name. Ravenscourge was the formal name of the thickly wooded forest that surrounded the Ironclaw Hunter's Guild.

"Never heard of it," he said slowly.

Who's lying now?" I mused.

"There are...some things that surpass the bounds of kings."

"That's a curious way to put it. What's your next question?"

"What's your weapon of choice?"

"Poison," I purred.

"Bullshit! Poison is for the weak, and you are anything but! You knocked me on my ass last night," he barked.

I laughed again and he joined me, the full sound of his laugh seeming to rattle the window with its intensity. We had earned the attention of every soldier, all of whom had emerged from their rooms to eat. As they suddenly became very interested in their food when their king burst out laughing, Ragnar centered his attention back to me.

"I prefer my twin blades," I responded. "They are usually either on my back or they sit on my hips."

"I would very much like to inspect that craftsmanship," he

growled, locking his gaze with mine in a way that took my breath away.

"I may not be armed with those right now, but I warn you I am armed."

"I would expect nothing less."

"Oh? Where are my weapons, and what are they? If you guess correctly as to the location of all three, I'll show you."

He swallowed and thought to himself for a moment before giving a scoff. He reached down, under the table, and drew a long knife from his boot, laying it down on the table.

"Mine lives in my right boot," he said with confidence. "Yours however, is tucked in your left."

"Are you sure?" I challenged with a wink.

"About that and many other things," he responded, his eyes drifting up and down my figure. "You favor your left hand as you eat and drink. Your knife is in your left boot. Show me."

I grinned, thoroughly enjoying this game. I reached down, locking my gaze on his storm-colored eyes, and presented a thin dagger from my boot, resting it on the table opposite his. The size comparison was laughable.

"That's one," I said with a wicked grin. "Where's the other two?"

His gaze dropped from my eyes to my neckline again, dropping further until it met the table, and he raised a brow.

"If you're as talented as I think you are, there's no way I could find them, even with a very, very thorough searching, but I do assume they're well within grasp."

"You would be correct."

Ragnar fell silent as he watched me, and I had to work hard not to get lost in his gaze. Soft, yet as firm as stone, his eyes held emotions that he had worked diligently at keeping under the surface. I wondered why he was allowing me to get a peek at them. He blinked hard and cocked his head, glancing at his men.

"I'm leading my men back to the capital, to Sitica," he said quietly. "Would you like to come with me?"

I paused, keenly aware that I had two wounded recruits at the healer's hut and a handful of failed recruits in the neighboring village. Why would he ask me to accompany his men to the capital? Regardless, it was on my way back to the Guild, the protection of the king's men could be beneficial, even if I chose to leave after a while.

"Why?" I couldn't help but ask.

"Because I like you, and I'd like you to see the city. With me."

I rose from the table, replacing my dagger in my left boot, and set my hands on the table.

"When do we leave?"

"Whenever I say we do, I'm the king," he retorted with a cocky grin.

I rolled my eyes playfully. "Give me an hour."

He nodded once and I turned away from the table, taking only a single step before turning back and leaning over the table. He leaned in to meet me and I didn't bother trying to hide the blushing in my face, only mere inches away from his.

"My name is Valérikka."

AFTER I'D DRESSED MYSELF, *donning my armor and weapons with years of muscle memory, I headed toward the healer's hut to check on my recruits. Gvhain and Rhyse had been mended well by the healers of Frostholm, their wounds cleaned and wrapped and the minor frostbite almost healed completely. They struggled to stand and salute me, and as I returned the*

gesture, they suddenly bowed deeply, crying out and wincing at their strained wounds. Their armor had been cleaned and hung beside their sick beds.

"What are you doing?" I asked them, as they maintained a low bow, wincing as I knew the strain on their wounds. "Stop it!"

I turned and saw Ragnar leaning against the door frame.

"What the hell are you doing here?" I asked not-too-politely.

"Captain, ma'am, we are in the presence of the King of Tachá! Ragnar Varggson is in our midst!" Gvhain whispered, his voice a thin line of panicked fear and respect.

"I don't care, quit bowing to him," I said shortly. "He's not here for you, anyway."

"Ma'am?" Rhyse asked, confused.

"You two are to report back to Ravenscourge, directly to Ylsa on my command, do you understand? Tell her she should expect a letter from me soon, tell her I am...delayed," I said, shooting an annoyed glance at Ragnar, "and report to her about the frost spiders, the Burrower, and the other recruits. They failed their task, they are not welcome back."

"Yes, Captain," Rhyse said, limping toward me and inclining his head as he whispered to me. "I've heard stories about the king, ma'am, please be wary."

"I'll kick his ass if he tries anything untoward," I said with a grin.

I saluted them both with the respect that they'd earned and turned toward the door, finding Ragnar blocking most of it.

"Captain?" he murmured as he followed me from the healer's hut. "That's very impressive for someone of your..."

"If you say it's because I'm a woman I'll put you right on the floor again," I warned.

"*I'll just have to pull you down with me,*" he whispered in my ear, making my heart hammer as I burned inside.

I ignored his remark, assuming that he was well-versed in wooing, flirting, and subsequently bedding the women he came across. After all, who wouldn't want to share a bed with the King of Tachá, even for a night?

"*I have a horse waiting for you,*" he said, pulling my thoughts away.

"*Thank you,*" I said, "*I wasn't too sure you'd make me walk.*"

"*Never,*" he said as we found his men waiting near the gates. A massive Tacháan horse, tall and strong with a thick black coat, stamped its hoof impatiently until it saw Ragnar. Standing taller than any other horse I'd ever seen, it looked perfectly sized for the unusually large man that walked next to me. The horse beside his was regularly sized, but seemed dwarfed. He waited for me to mount, offering a hand up, and grinned when I mounted the mare easily without his help. Astride the horses we moved forward, most of his men on foot while a couple officers, scattered in the ranks, rode horses of their own. As we left Frostholm, we rode in a comfortable silence for a short time before Ragnar cleared his throat.

"*Have you ever been to the city? To Sitica?*" he asked, bringing his horse close to mine.

"*No, what's it like?*"

"*Massive stone walls surround the city, the Keep itself is impenetrable, a fortress of iron, stone, and ice. How does that sound to you?*"

"*It sounds awful,*" I said with a playful, exaggerated grimace. "*Like you're stuck in a prison.*"

"*Glad we share the sentiment,*" he said with a soft laugh. "*I hate it there.*"

"*Oh? Where would you rather be?*" I asked, genuine

curiosity getting the best of me. "Don't say the battlefield, either, that's silly."

He smiled sadly, his eyes drifting to a far away place and he cleared his throat. "I think I would much rather be in a village, small and quaint, maybe a fishing village like the one I come from."

"I grew up in a village like that, my parents were linen and fur-traders, not fishermen, though," I said, the foggy faces of my parents eluding my memory.

I glanced at Ragnar and was taken aback, finding his eyes soft and careful as they watched me. Not like a wolf stalks its prey, but as if he were committing my features to memory. I found myself staring into his eyes, swimming in an endless sea of blue, and I blushed, allowing myself to experience something completely new. I didn't want this to end, but I knew it could never last. My duty belonged to the Hunter's Guild that I had sworn myself to. I had no surname, I had no lands, I had no family, only the Guild.

"Why are you looking at me like that?" I said lightly, unused to being observed like something so...coveted?

He laughed and shook his head. "You don't understand yet?"

"Apparently not," I replied, burying the emotions that were rising, desperate to change the subject off of myself. "What kind of man are you, Ragnar? Are you fair? Just? Cruel? Ruthless?"

He shrugged. "Ask my men, they'll tell you the truth."

"I think I will," I answered, pulling gently on the reins as my horse slowed to a stop.

Ragnar glanced behind and gave a wink as he rode ahead and I took a moment to clear my mind. As the men walked on, passing me by without a thought, I called to a walking officer, who stopped immediately and bowed.

"Yes, y-" he stammered for just the slightest moment, "my lady, how may I serve you?"

"Please, call me Valérikka," I said warmly, wondering what words he had tripped over. "I'd like to ask you a few questions."

"Of course, my lady," he said.

I dismounted the mare and walked alongside the officer, the reins in hand as the horse followed along easily.

"This is your horse, isn't it, sir?"

"Yes, my lady. It is my honor to have her bear you as her rider."

I smiled. "She likes you," I said, watching the man smile warmly. "You are kind to her, which is a very honorable trait. I feel that I can trust the answers to the questions I'd like to ask you. What's your name?"

"Lieutenant Trygve Erikkson, my lady, of the King's Tacháan Army," he said, the pride he held as he spoke his name and rank clear.

"Tell me about Ragnar, Lieutenant Erikkson," I asked, "what kind of a man is he?"

"My lady, our king is an-"

"You misunderstand me, sir. I ask of the man, not the king."

He stammered for a moment and laughed under his breath. "I see now why he is so very taken with you, my lady. I will tell you about the man, as you wish. He is...possessive of his things. He does not share well. His temper is...legendary."

"Am I in danger?" I asked plainly. "Tell me the truth, would Ragnar put his hands on me if I angered him?"

Trygve stopped and looked me directly in the eyes. "My lady, it is no exaggeration when I say, with absolute certainty, that you are the safest woman in the entire world while in his presence."

"I don't understand what would make Ragnar so protective over me, we just met."

"You may have just been introduced, but he has been waiting for you for over a decade, my lady."

I rolled my eyes. "I'm not some lovestruck maiden, Lieutenant. I know that this is said to every woman Ragnar finds to bring to his chambers. I'm not-"

"He has not spoken to a woman since he lost his wife over a decade ago," he interrupted sharply. "You are...different."

The argument that had been rising in my chest deflated and was swept away, overtaken by so many questions, thoughts, and as we walked, the mare following along dutifully, I sighed softly in disbelief.

"What does he want from me? Speak plainly, please, Lieutenant."

"Is it not clear to you? He is bringing you to his home, my lady. You are to be his queen."

"He hasn't even asked me yet, what makes you so sure?"

Trygve grinned. "You put the King of Tachá on his ass, in front of his men, then socked him in the mouth, and then you drank with him! You made him want to know you, you gave him hope again. My lady, you are everything he's been searching for. Surely you know the history of his rise to rule, yes?"

I shook my head. My education as a young girl had been thorough from my parents, continued by the Hunter's Guild, and while I was fluent of multiple languages, while I knew the terrain of the lands of Tachá and could decipher and track the crudest of marks, the historical account of King Ragnar had not been in my syllabus.

"The king comes from the humble beginnings of a coastal village, and he fell in love with the Jarl's daughter."

"What was her name?" I asked curiously.

"We do not speak her name, lest we call her spirit back from her place in the halls of glory," Tryvge said. "Before he became king, he was Jarl. Before that, he was a man, who loved a woman and fought for the right to call her his. He loved her very much, and when she was killed it nearly broke him."

"How did it happen?"

"Frost giants came down from the mountains and attacked while the men were away on a hunting trip, trying to get ahead for the long winter months so no one had to go without. The giants were doing the same, it seemed. They decimated the village, only a handful of people survived. Those that were cut down included Ragnar's wife and eldest son. He led the slaughter and leveled the frost giant's lair...he left no survivors."

I swallowed the lump in my throat and we continued trudging through the snow. Ragnar glanced back and I met his eyes. I offered a small smile and he returned it. I found myself watching him more, if only to see the way his eyes shined when they fell upon mine.

"See, my lady?" Trygve murmured, "I can say that he has not looked so relieved in my years of knowing him."

I chewed the inside of my lip and handed the reins to the horseman. He sputtered and remained marching. "My lady, I cannot take them from you."

"Yes, you can, and you will," I said firmly. "Mount your horse, Lieutenant."

I spoke as if the man were a recruit of my own, and he set his jaw, but to my surprise, he obeyed. Ragnar, glancing over again, stopped his horse and glared at the man atop his mount. I shot him a look and walked through the men back to his side.

"We're almost to the city," I said, pointing to the gated

wall on the approach, "I don't want him walking into the city, it seems dishonorable."

The furrow between his strong brow pinched and I smiled at his annoyance. He extended his hand out to me; he seemed surprised when I took it, but he pulled me up, and I was seated in front of him, the warmth of his fur-clad body radiating into me. I rested my head against his chest, the soft furs warm and comforting. His right hand dropped from his saddlehorn and came to rest on my leg, just above my knee. It was both an anchor and a connection, and he inclined his head to me as he spoke softly.

"Welcome to Sitica, Valérikka," he murmured as the gates swung open.

CHAPTER 8

THE STING OF MEMORY

Ylsa sent me off with hearty rations and a set of quilted leather armor that would not only keep me from being chewed on by another yeti, but also warm. The dusty blue of our Tacháan color complemented the bright gold of my hair, and seemed to make my eyes glow an electric blue. Kona trotted ahead, sniffing out rabbits and leaving pawprints to follow in her wake. Astrid's breath came in smoky billows from her nostrils, and we approached the last sizable town before the Great Wall of Valthor. My hood concealed most of my face, and this far from home, I truly doubted anyone would recognize my face. I'd still keep to the shadows, just in case. I whistled, soft and low, and Kona's sharp ears tilted back as she paused, waiting for Astrid's hooves to come alongside her. With a glance up at me, she licked her snout, cleaning the snowflakes from it.

"Stay close in town," I commanded her gently. "We're not staying long."

We entered the outskirts of town as the sun reached its highest point and exhaustion from the long ride crept up around me. Astrid's head dipped as she nickered, Kona whined in sympathy. A sizable tavern, the swinging wooden sign painted with a decorative wolf's head tiled in a dramatic howl, the Howling Wolf Tavern sat on one corner of the city block, a long sheltered barn, aptly named the Wolfsbane Stables, was positioned across from it. I bought a stall for Astrid, Kona would share it tonight, and bought enough hay and fresh water for Astrid to last her through the night.

"I have a few old fish for your dog, ma'am," a young stableboy offered, inclining his head at me.

"That's very thoughtful of you, lad," I answered, tossing him a couple silver for his troubles. "Kona would appreciate them, and she likes her ears scratched, too."

"Her name is Kona?" he said, wrinkling his nose in confusion. "That's what my Pa calls Mama."

I laughed, and nodded. "It's our native word for wife. Kona was a gift from my husband, as was my mare, Astrid."

The boy smiled, a toothy grin, and reached for the wolf's ears.

"She's a good dog," he murmured.

"She's a wolf, you know," I answered. "She was born in a snowstorm, my husband said. His hunters found her and brought her to him, and he gave her to me to raise. She's the best friend I could have ever asked for."

Kona met my eyes briefly, as if she understood and nudged my hand with her nose. The boy let out a soft gasp and touched Kona's head.

"I've never seen a real wolf," he whispered, "I'm gonna get her some more food. I think a wolf eats more than a dog. Right?"

"You're right," I replied brightly. "I'm gonna head

inside the inn for a while, I think I can trust you to keep them safe."

"Yes, my Lady!" he cried, bowing his head to me and beaming at the responsibility.

I paid for a room, dinner, and tossed in a few coins to have breakfast ready the following morning, and as I savored the hearty venison roast soaked in rich broth, I dipped a crusty bread in the juices and passed the time listening to the conversations of the strangers around me. Nothing of remote interest tickled my ears, until I heard a familiar name. I leaned in subtly, and focused hard.

"-the queen just up and abandoned him!" the man said, spilling a trickle of ale down the front of his shirt as he drank. "The king is furious, of course, and they say he's sent his wolf-wife after her. She'll bring her back, no doubt, but dead or alive is another matter."

"You *know* that's a myth, right?" the man opposite him said with a scoff. "That wolf is just a wolf. Ain't no magic can turn a lass into a wolf."

"Now, how do you know what magic can do? Are *you* a mage? Are *you* a spell-caster, Dell? No, you're a farmer. You don't know nothin' about it."

The man called Dell dropped his head and muttered dejectedly under his breath. They sat in an uncomfortable silence, their steins empty until a woman passed by with refills, her bodice pulled low and snug as it grabbed their attention.

As their eyes followed her, my mind wandered back home. Ragnar was angry, of course he was. But I was fairly confident he wasn't sending Lady after me. My husband's legendary direwolf was feared amongst the people of Tachá, and whoever had come up with the idea that Ragnar's late wife had been reborn or transformed into the white wolf had done him a favor, as the reputation provided even more intimidation, reducing the amount of threats toward him greatly. As Ragnar had said to me, explaining the myth, *'fear lives even in myth. If my enemies fear me for a child's bedtime story when they should truly fear flesh and bone, that will be their undoing.'*

Ragnar had told me this a month after we had been married, and only after I'd confronted him directly, angry at the accusations that had been whispered as I passed by. I'd marched right up to him, planted my feet, and met his eyes. "Is it true?" I had demanded, "what they say about your direwolf? Tell me the truth!" He had simply raised a brow and sighed. "Lady is a direwolf. Nothing more, nothing less. She was a *gift* from my late wife. That's why I'm so fond of her. If the people wish to believe that Lady holds the soul of my dead wife, let them. What does it matter to me? I have bigger things to worry about," he had explained. Accepting his words, I'd nodded and he'd cocked his head as a smirk grew on his face. "You have a fire within you, my Queen, to approach me so boldly. Anyone else would have asked *and* awaited my permission to approach, would have bowed to the king, and certainly *not* raised their voice to him. You may be the Queen, but *I am* your husband. You will respect me, *Min Kona.*"

As I recalled the first time he had ever called me that, my heart ached sharply for the man I loved.

～

"Come with me," he said, *"I'd like to show you something."*

"Ragnar, I'm on your horse," I said with a laugh, *"what, am I supposed to say no?"*

He laughed and led his horse opposite his men, and I peeked around the horse's head, trying to see where we were going, but I was completely unfamiliar with the area. It wasn't until I heard the whinnies and snorts of horses that I began twisting and leaning to try and see.

"You're going to fall off of Brigo," Ragnar said, catching me as I slid a little too far. "We're almost there."

He called in Nordmaarian to a man he called Bersi, who greeted Ragnar in our mother tongue in return. As Ragnar's feet landed solidly, he turned and reached for me. His grip on my hips was tight, but not uncomfortable, a secure hold that I knew wasn't going to let me fall. My boots touched the snowy earth but his hands lingered, resting on my hips longer than needed. I parted my lips to speak but words failed me, lost again in his gaze.

"I have something for you," he whispered, stepping closer to me. "A gift."

I looked up at him, a full eight inches taller than me, and knit my eyebrows.

"I didn't do anything to receive a gift," I whispered, confused.

"You came with me, you trusted me, that in itself is a gift to me."

"Sire?" Bersi called, the gnarled old man leading a Tachán horse toward us.

Dappled gray with a snowy white coat underneath that matched her white mane and tail, the mare tossed her head and gave a light nicker, her eyes and ears on me as I gasped to myself. Ragnar's hand rested on my lower back, a comforting touch as the stunning mare was brought in front of me.

"Her name is Astrid," he murmured to me as my eyes grew wide. "She is yours, a token of my affection."

"Thank you, Ragnar."

I rested my hand on his chest and Bersi approached with a bow. He looked at me and bowed deeply, respect and admiration emanating from him.

"May Astrid serve you well, carry you lightly, and journey sure-footed, always, Your Grace," he said to me, holding the braided reins out.

Astrid was much taller than the horses I was used to, her hand-crafted saddle breathtakingly carved with runes. Ragnar thanked the old man and he departed, back to the stables that he had emerged from. He chuckled as Astrid nibbled my loose braids and as I reached up to grab the saddle to hoist myself up, Ragnar picked me up, as if I weighed nothing, and set me on her back. He left me breathless and flushed, and with every touch he left me wanting more. He handed me the reins, his fingers resting on mine for a long moment, and I followed him as he mounted Brigo, trotting to his side as Astrid seemed to anticipate my commands.

"You look beautiful on her," he said as I hesitated.

"Ragnar, why did the horsemaster call me Your Grace?"

"Did he? I didn't notice, must be getting a little senile in his old age," he said, a terrible liar as he failed to hide a grin, "I have one more request, if you'll follow me."

"I suppose," I mused playfully, urging Astrid into a canter as she continued down the empty path.

Ragnar caught up, Brigo's strong legs striding forward, and the unspoken challenge was on. Leaning forward to Astrid, I spoke to her, "Fljúg sem vindr, Astrid," urging her to fly like the wind, and she let out a squeal. I tightened my grip with my hands and legs as she unleashed her speed, her gallop smoother and faster than any horse I'd ever been on. She needed no direction, seeming to understand, and my hair, braids and loose locks of gold, flew wildly behind me. Over my shoulder, I saw Brigo failing to catch up, and I laughed.

"Alright, I think they'd had enough," I said as she slowed from a simple, gentle pull on the reins.

She slowed to a walk as we entered a meadow, and she pawed the snow away, grazing the green grass that still grew under the snow. Astrid had taken her first mouthful when Ragnar caught up. His eyes held a fire that brought fear and awe to me.

"You...you're, gods help me," he panted, breathing heavily as he pulled Brigo to a stop. "I have to assume you know why you're here, Valérikka. Tell me you know, please."

"I would never assume to know your mind, Ragnar. I'm not someone to play games with your mind, or your heart," I replied, turning Astrid to give Ragnar my full attention. "Tell me what you want with me."

"I want you, all of you, as my Queen."

"Just as your Queen?" I said, walking Astrid to come alongside Brigo. "Look me in the eyes and tell me what you want, Ragnar."

"I want you as my wife," he said softly, cupping my cheek in his hand with a tenderness that brought tears to my eyes. "Will you be my wife?"

I WIPED AWAY the tear that had fallen from my eye and glanced around. No one had noticed, save for one of the serving girls. She was watching me carefully, a mixture of sympathetic sadness and curiosity in her hazel eyes. She wiped tables clean nearby and slowly made her way over to me. She paused, mid-wipe of the already clean table-top, and spoke quietly, with wisdom that far surpassed her youth.

"Are y' hurt?" she whispered softly. "Is the one that hurt you here?"

I smiled sadly and sniffled. "No, I-just...I miss my husband. I have to be away from him for a while."

Her demeanor shifted and she touched my hand.

"That's a relief," she said, quickly stammering and patting my hand in apology. "What I mean, is that it's a relief to see a woman crying over love, instead of the pain that usually haunts our eaves."

"What do you mean?"

"I mean, lock your door and sleep with a blade tonight, miss," she said quietly, glancing around the room subtly. "He comes with the dead of night and I can almost guarantee you've been noticed by him, already. You're a thing of rare beauty, and traveling alone, as well. Barricade your quarters tonight."

"I will, thank you," I replied as she moved on, collecting steins and plates left at other tables.

I was fairly sure I knew what she meant, and though I hadn't wanted to make myself a target as I traveled alone, it had been done for me. If someone was going to try to approach me tonight, he'd be met with the sharp end of a Tacháan huntress. I knew that the woman wasn't aware that I always slept with a blade under my head, that is, until I had slept with Ragnar's arms around me. Never had I felt so safe, protected, and loved, but held tightly against his chest.

CHAPTER 9
THE DÓMHRINGR

10 Years Ago

~

"My love," I asked quietly as Ragnar pored over a small, gray pelt that had been presented to him. "Why does this give you such concern?"

As we sipped hot drinks in the warmth of the quiet room off of the massive hall, he pondered the small piece of fur in his hands. He shook his head in a way that I knew he was struggling to find the words, and he groaned. I moved to sit near him, and his shoulders fell, the weight great upon them.

"My men found this in the Frostholm market square. The back-alley dealers had a few of them, my men bought one to bring as evidence. It's the pelt of a direwolf pup."

I gasped as he held out the small pelt. "A pup? Oh, how awful! Everyone in this country knows the respect we hold for the direwolf! Why would someone do this?"

"I don't know. It's an illegal and dishonorable act to kill a *direwolf of Tachá, but to kill and skin a pup is just cruelty. I want to find out who did this. I have my hunters out looking."*

I paused. Ragnar met my eyes and he sighed, annoyed immediately.

"What?" he asked, clueless. "I know they're good hunters. They can track any animal for miles!"

"Ragnar, your hunters aren't accustomed to tracking men or collecting evidence, though. What will they do if they find them? Do they have leads?"

"My Queen sounds like she wants to pick up her bow and swords and find them herself," Ragnar chuckled, taking up my hands. "Give them another day or so, then you can call them back and...tell them how to do it your way."

A flash of anger surged through me and I yanked my hands free. "It's not just my way, it's a completely different set of skills! Tracking a man, especially one that doesn't want to be found, is more than just following footprints!"

"I know," he said, hastily backpedaling. "You're right. But it's been a long while since you've been out there, I'm sure you wouldn't be any more skilled than my men out there."

The unintended blow came like a punch in the gut as I crossed my arms, more of a self-comfort than an aggressive stance.

"That wasn't necessary," I said firmly, keeping my voice quiet as the hurt bled out. "I went from one kind of life to a completely different sort. There are parts of my past that I greatly miss, as I'm sure you do, too."

Ragnar's eyes softened and he pulled me into his lap, my dress sweeping across our legs as he held me close. His beard tickled the back of my neck as he kissed the spot between my collarbone and my neck, and he sighed, burying his face in my braided locks. He pulled back and met my gaze, touching his forehead to mine tenderly.

"I'm sorry," he murmured, "I forget how strong you are sometimes. You are wild at heart while I try to keep you safe in a cage."

"I've been locked in for almost five years. I need the outdoors," I said, almost pleading. "You can even come with me if you think I'll be in danger."

"Would that make you happy?" he asked.

I pulled back a little, the barely discernible worry in his tone concerning me. His eyes held a trace of fear mixed with love.

"I am happy, Ragnar," I said, taking his face in my hands as I shifted my weight. "I'm...I'm just bored. I haven't slept with a knife under my pillow in years!"

Swinging my legs gently as they dangled to the side, I pressed my hand to his heart, maintaining his gaze as I stared into the blue abyss. I watched as a spark ignited in his eyes, the corners of his eyes crinkling as he chuckled.

"I can understand that, my love," he said quietly. "Why do you think I always want to go to war? I would much rather be lost in the frozen tundra than behind these stone walls."

I laughed brightly with my husband, kissing his cheek as an idea dawned in my mind.

"May I ask you for something?"

"You don't even have to ask, whatever you wish is already yours," he replied.

"Go for a ride with me. We'll take Brigo and Astrid. We can leave at dawn and come back when we're ready."

He paused, watching me with curiosity as he gave a slow nod.

"Alright, we leave at dawn. I'll tell Bjorn that he'll be overseeing things until we come back. If we decide to come back."

The eldest of Ragnar's children, I knew Bjorn would not be

pleased to assume the responsibilities during our absence, even for only a few days.

~

THE SUN WARMED *our backs as it rose in the sky. I filled my lungs with the frigid air as Astrid shook out her mane, eager to put some distance between freedom and confinement. The snow held a thick enough crust that our horses' hooves stomped through the ice, crunching in a soothing rhythm. We knew the treacherous land held anything but safety, underneath the furs that kept the cold at bay, we wore armor and had our weapons within reach.*

"I think we needed this," I said to my husband as he smiled, relaxed on his steed.

"I think you're right, Min Kona," he said with a deep inhale, exhaling plumes of fog from his lips. "Do you have a destination in mind? If not, I have somewhere I'd like to take you, I don't think you'll have seen anything like this before."

"Lead the way," I said, intrigued at his offer.

Ragnar veered north slightly and I knew that from this direction, the forest line was a few hours' ride away. I'd walked and ridden across so much of Tachá's snowy terrain that I was wildly curious about a place I hadn't yet discovered. The hours passed in a comfortable silence and the icy crust melted from the snow, making the ride much less jarring as we reached the treeline. The air cooled around us, unable to soak up the warmth of the sun's rays through the thick evergreens. We rode for another hour and reached a large, circular clearing, the undisturbed snow bright and sparkling as the area seemed to glow in the sunshine. Ragnar dismounted Brigo and let his reins hang loosely around his horse's neck. I shifted my legs and slid down the thick blanket on Astrid's back, my boots sinking inches in the snow.

Everything seemed to melt away as Ragnar took my gloved hand in his, leading me into the clearing. In front of us stood twelve massive stones, each standing tall in a circle. While the ground was blanketed in heavy snow, the stones remained untouched, free of any trace of snowflakes.

"A Dómhringr in Tachá?" I whispered, awe and apprehension coursing through my veins. "How could I not know of standing stones here? I've been through this forest so many times!"

"I am surprised this is new for you," Ragnar said quietly, as not to disturb the peaceful moment. "I am glad I could share this with you, Valérikka."

He pulled me close, kissing me deeply as the snow began to fall again.

"There's no one else I would want to see this with," I whispered, my heart swelling with love.

He led me closer, and as we approached the circles, a strange warmth seemed to radiate from the stones themselves, and I shivered. Stories of the ancient magic of the standing stones had spanned the world many times over, but eyewitness accounts had been lost to time.

"How did you find out about this place?" I asked breathlessly as we crossed into the interior of the stone circle.

"It's been a story for ages," he said with a shrug. "Didn't you hear the stories as a child about the magical stones? I believed that the stones were dragon bones, and that's why they were always hot. As a child, of course."

"Of course," I grinned, giving a gentle shrug. "But, I think my upbringing was a little different. My little village was quiet, we didn't get visitors too often, and I was too young to travel far."

"*My fishing town always had people from all over the world trading their wares, fish was only one of the exports for us. Spices, furs, fish, and ice came and went through our docks.*"

Reaching the center of the stones, we saw a large slab of stone laying flat, a thin ring of green grass between the stone and the snow. Crouching next to it, I pulled my glove off and placed it against the stone, the warmth as inviting and comforting as the hearth of our bedchamber at home. I smiled and turned to Ragnar, inviting him closer. He crouched and pulled his glove off with his teeth and rested it against the stone.

"*I've...I've never felt actual magic before,*" *he marveled quietly.* "*I've always imagined it cold and distant...but this feels like...like the embrace of a lover.*"

I met his eyes and smiled softly. I reclined, resting my back against the stone, and my husband joined me, hesitant and curious. Staring at the clear sky, void of birds, clouds, or snowfall, I reached for Ragnar's hand and closed my eyes, listening to the sounds of our breath and feeling his pulse as his hand covered mine. I turned my head and met his eyes as he watched me. I raised a brow in question and the corner of his mouth turned up.

"*You're what I needed, like the gods heard me, after all,*" *he murmured.* "*I love you, Valérikka.*"

"*I love you, too,*" *I replied, concerned over his unusual verbal affection.* "*Are you alright?*"

He nodded absently and furrowed his brow, the way he did when he was deeply lost in thought. I waited patiently for him to finish, and he sighed after a long moment.

"*Can I tell you something about myself?*" *he asked, an edge of apprehension in his tone.* "*It's just a story, a myth, but I want you to hear it plainly from my mouth.*"

"Of course," I said as worry gnawed at my nerves. "You can tell me anything."

"Even if it sounds absolutely ridiculous?"

I didn't mean to, but I giggled. He shot me a look and I turned to my side, resting my hand on his cheek.

"You may tell me everything and anything, and I trust that you would never lie to me or mislead me. I trust you entirely, Ragnar. Tell me your story," I said earnestly, leaning forward to kiss him.

He cleared his throat and began, his tone steady, solid, and unwavering.

"My grandmother used to tell me as a child that I was meant for more than just slinging nets in the village. The way I was born...it was...unconventional."

He glanced at me, perhaps to gauge my reaction, and chuckled.

"Well? Keep going," I urged, playfully swatting at his shoulder.

"The seer had foretold my birth under the waning moon of the fourth month. She gave my mother and father the exact hour that she had Seen...so with another full month before my mother was due, my father went into battle against a feuding clan of frost trolls, following the orders of our Jarl. My mother fought alongside him, despite his insistence that she return home for safety."

"She fought frost trolls...pregnant?" I marveled. "What a woman!"

Ragnar grinned with pride. "My grandmother said that those who tried to stop my mother were knocked out for hours afterward. A steel hammer was her weapon when she wasn't on the battlefield, a sword and shield were her companions otherwise. Most men knew better than to argue with her, including my father. He tried his best to protect her, but she *was a shield maiden of incredible talent. Though she would never admit it out of respect, she guarded his back and protected him better than he did for her."*

"She sounds...incredible," I said, the proud shine in my husband's eyes undeniable.

"She was, truly," he agreed. "A few hours into the fight, an unexpected snowstorm descended from the mountains. She was in the middle of a skirmish against a pair of frost trolls when something happened. She told my grandmother that she felt the gods press upon her. Her waters broke right there, mixing with blood and snow, and my father called for help, trying to get her back to camp where the medics could assist her. As the men and other women surrounded and defended her with shields and swords, the gods pulled me from my mother's womb. I arrived so swiftly that she didn't even have time to suffer the birthing pains. It is said that the mountains themselves trembled in awe, but I don't believe that, not any of it."

"Why not?"

He let out a laugh of disbelief. "You know how women see things during the pains of childbirth...well, my mother swore upon the gods that my eyes flashed red, for just a moment. 'Rauðeygr sveinn,' she used to call me, her red-eyed boy."

"What is so unbelievable about that?" I asked genuinely.

"It's that and the rest of the legend from my grandmother that makes it unbelievable," he said, teasing me with a patient pause as he yawned dramatically.

I waited for a few seconds before leaping on top of him playfully.

"You beastly man!" I laughed loudly, my voice echoing in the clearing. "Such cruelty in making a woman beg!"

In an instant his hands were around my waist, planting

me firmly on him as he sat upright. His eyes darkened with want and I bit my lip.

"Careful, Min Kona," he warned, his voice a deep growl as I shifted my weight in his lap. "Þú ert mín ein, ok ek held þér fast."

"I am yours, Ragnar," I whispered in his ear, offering myself to him. "Tak mik, ok ger mik þína."

The stones were hot on our bare flesh, the sky bright as our cries of ecstasy floated above the trees. Steam rose from our breathless union and I lay atop my husband, his chest rising and falling steadily.

"Þú ert minn ástvini, Min Kona," Ragnar whispered.

He had first called me 'his beloved,' on our wedding night, and had faithfully every night since. He breathed it with such assurance that I had never questioned it, nor would I ever. I loved him more than words could express, and I wished he could understand how much he meant to me.

CHAPTER 10

THE POACHERS

"For such a sacred space, do you think the gods peek in frequently?" I asked with a giggle, tying my bodice's laces securely.

"If they do, they certainly enjoyed what they just saw," Ragnar said with a hearty laugh as he buckled his belt. "Perhaps we taught them something new."

He pulled me close, flush to his chest and I rose on my tiptoes to kiss him. He froze suddenly, his hands stilling at my waist. I pulled back and saw his eyes locked on something behind me, and I turned to see a massive direwolf, shaggy brown with amber eyes, watching us carefully from the edge of the woods.

'Help me, Huntress,' she said, her voice thin with agony.

"She needs help," I translated for Ragnar, taking a step toward her and focusing on her as I spoke. "Please, we won't hurt you."

Her head dropped as she studied me and she took a hesitant step forward, whining. Limping another few steps, she crossed the snowy clearing and stopped short of the stones. I closed the distance and approached her carefully but hurried. Clamped onto her front left paw was a steel hunting trap.

"Oh no," I whispered, squinting as I peeked around the direwolf's form. "How did this happen?"

'Men hid the traps under the snow.'

The direwolf's size was massive, her back was level with my eyeline as she looked at me and she bristled, the excruciating pain undeniable in her voice as it filled my mind. Ragnar approached and she snarled, snapping her jaws as he paused. Fear coursed as the heat from her breath warmed my face, and I swallowed hard.

"I can heal your wounds," I told the direwolf as she looked down at me, "but we have to take the trap off. I need him to do that. I'm not strong enough. We will not hurt you. Please trust us."

'He is more than a Man,' she said, a trace of fear in her voice. 'If you are wise, you would fear him. He holds...danger.'

The word she spoke held a different meaning than a simple common-tongue translation. Danger, the word she spoke, emanated with an undeniable sense of chaos, darkness, and a hint of pure evil. A memory, tucked away a few years ago, surfaced, only months after Ragnar and I had been married.

WE LAY TOGETHER on a bearskin blanket that had been tossed to the stone floor in front of the hearth, catching our breath. Rising on my elbows, I rolled to my stomach and glanced at Ragnar, the stress that normally weighed on him replaced by a tired but relaxed overlay. His eyes opened a crack and I smiled. Kissing his bare shoulder he grunted softly, at the affection.

"Will you tell me a story?" I asked as the flames of the

hearth danced, casting shadows against the wall. "One of your favorites?"

He thought for a moment and smiled. "Alright, I'll tell you a story that my grandmother used to tell me over and over again when I was a boy."

I rested my chin in my hands and waited expectantly as Ragnar laced his fingers behind his head.

"It was told to me a very long time ago...so some details may be hazy," he began. "On the eve of Winter's Solstice, the blood of war froze on the ice. A child was born in the shadows of the wolves. Centuries before our ancestors walked, back when the gods trembled at the very thought of prophecy's true-ringing bell, one god in particular was chained. Deep in the Hollow Beyond, the Great Wolf of Ending lay trapped in a prison bound by god-forged links. His howling echoed through the planes."

"Fenrir?" I asked, as the corner of his mouth twitched in a grin. "Your grandmother told you stories of...Fenrir?"

"Yes, Fenrir," he confirmed. "As he lay chained for eternity, he did not sleep. He did not rest. He waited, and still waits."

Ragnar paused to give me a moment to speak, but I stayed quiet as he continued.

"One day, not quite so long ago, something stirred in him, and the world gifted a moment so rare that the realms shuddered in the timing. During the birth of that babe, Fenrir deemed that soul his. A child of winter, a son of war, a chosen vessel. Unbound by the gods, unbroken by fear, unhindered by chains. In that instant, Fenrir, who had hidden a fragment of his soul, tucked away in secret for centuries, summoned every ounce of strength he had hoarded over the eons. Using the power of the Winter Solstice, Fenrir was able to pour his soul shard through the veil between realms. His soul fragment

became one with the babe's soul. The wolf god's essence slumbers quietly within the child, coiled like a serpent as it waits."

"Fenrir...possessed this poor child?" I breathed.

"Not quite. More like two minds became one. A pact of survival; Fenrir and the boy would grow into one eventually, when the time was right. There is a prophecy that says when Fate bows her head and Fenrir shakes the chains free, the wolf god will be reborn in flesh and fury, a god-killer within mortal muscle."

"That...that's terrifying," I said with an astonished laugh. "Fenrir sounds evil."

"He's not purely evil. Fenrir once showed me mercy when no other gods would," Ragnar said quietly. "But that is a story for another night."

QUICKLY TUCKING away the sharp memory, the beast looked at me as if she knew what I had remembered. I didn't translate for my husband and I didn't respond, either. Instead, I knelt to inspect the trap closer. It was made of reinforced steel, and the sharp teeth of the trap had embedded themselves deeply into the direwolf's flesh. The chain that dragged behind her had a long spike that held ice and soil.

"You pulled out the spike yourself...how long have you been hurt?"

'Two nights.'

"I'm so sorry this happened to you, but let's get this off of you, to start with," I murmured, ushering Ragnar closer.

"What do you need me to do, Min Kona?"

"Can you open the trap? Slowly, carefully, please," I said.

As Ragnar took a knee, he reached for the trap and the direwolf snarled out of fear. Her jaws snapped mere inches from his face, and he paused, lifting his eyes to her. My heart hammered in my chest as I quelled the rising panic.

"Don't you dare bite me," Ragnar warned her.

Wagging his finger as if she were a house dog, he seemed unintimidated by the proximity of the beast's jaws. I glanced at the massive creature and the unusual waves of fear rolled through her, and I fought to subdue the memory of his story again. Perhaps I was reading too far into the situation, perhaps she had been pursued by men similar to Ragnar, possibly the Goliath-men of the mountains.

"It's going to hurt to open the trap, but please don't bite him," I nearly begged the direwolf.

Ragnar took a steady hold on the sides of the trap, and I knew that even the gentlest movement brought immense pain. A deep rumbling rolled from the beast's throat and Ragnar pried open the steel, the hinges squeaking slightly. The direwolf lifted her paw free, now bleeding profusely, and began licking it. Ragnar tossed the trap aside, the trap snapping shut with enough force that I flinched. As I turned back to the direwolf, I realized that Ragnar had his forehead pressed against the direwolf's muzzle. He patted the furry neck and smiled as he turned back to me.

"We've come to an understanding," he murmured as I approached the direwolf's injured paw.

'He is still dangerous, but in him I see goodness. You keep Danger at bay," the direwolf said, the warning still in her tone but softened.

I nodded absently, watching the blood trickle from the deep puncture wounds, and I cleared my throat.

"The bleeding needs to be stopped, may I?" I asked gently.

She sat on her haunches and raised her paw, the blood staining the snow a deep crimson. I placed my hands on the wounds, warm and wet as my hands became stained with the lifeblood of the direwolf in front of me, and closed my eyes, whispering the words my mother had taught me long ago. It took more energy than I'd recalled, and having spent so much of my energy with Ragnar...I was bordering on exhaustion.

"Min Kona, would you ask this one where she was injured?" Ragnar asked quietly, a sense of revenge bubbling under the surface. "Who did this?"

I glanced at the direwolf, who was gingerly placing her healed paw down.

"My husband would like to know where this happened to you," I asked on his behalf.

'I cannot tell you where, but I can take you as close as I dare.'

"You'll take us there?" I replied, surprised at her willingness. "Okay, let's go."

"We leave now," Ragnar said as I washed the blood off my hands in the snow.

Astrid and Brigo waited patiently, anxious with the direwolf so close, but my reassurances calmed them, if only just a little, nickering as we set off. Without hesitation, the wolf turned north, following the curve of the stones, and we followed along. The snow was softer here, and without the icy crust, we traveled surprisingly quick and quiet.

'I will go no further,' she said after a few hours of trotting. 'Beware the traps beneath the snow.'

Relaying the message to Ragnar, he hopped off of his horse and approached the direwolf fearlessly. Taking her muzzle in his hands, he kissed her as her eyes closed.

"Far í friði; gæta þín goðin," Ragnar whispered, a blessing of peace and safety he had often spoken to his soldiers.

The direwolf turned and walked away, seeming to disappear in the low-hanging evergreen boughs, and Astrid exhaled sharply, impatient to continue.

"*Do you think it's safe to take them closer?*" *I asked quietly, fearful of the steel traps.*

He furrowed his brow and grunted. "No. I won't risk our horses. We'll tie them here where it's safe, and get them when we're done."

We gave them plenty of roaming space, and we started forward, stepping carefully and praying that there wasn't a steel trap beneath our feet. After a few minutes of careful maneuvering, staying close to the bases of trees, I caught the faintest hint of smoke, and Ragnar pointed ahead. As we continued, we came across half-covered bootprints leading deeper into the woods, erratic and in anything but a straight line.

"Should be safe to follow, right?" Ragnar said, stepping into the footprints, dwarfed under his massive boots.

"I suppose, but the way that they're scattered makes me a little uneasy," I confessed.

He turned with a sly grin. "Would you like me to carry you, O delicate Queen?" He continued on and I scooped up a snowball, hitting him square in the back of the head. Stopping in his tracks, he raised a brow, bringing a giggle from my lips as he turned around.

"Try that again," he dared playfully. "See what happens."

I bent forward toward the snow, a wicked grin on my face. I scooped up another ball of snow, revealing a frozen arctic fox as I gasped and dropped the snow. At my fright, Ragnar was at my side instantly, his hand axe already in-hand. I swept away the snow and uncovered the corpse of a small, white fox, its entire torso caught in an iron trap. I examined it closely and sighed heavily.

"She suffered," I whispered. "She died slowly and painfully. There is no reason to have these traps set. That dire-

wolf could have died, and this fox did. I want answers, Ragnar."

"You'll find them, Min Kona," he said darkly, freeing the frozen body from the trap and burying it with snow. "We'll follow these tracks to the men that have done this, and we'll take care of them."

"Will you kill them?"

"Not unless they give me a reason."

We continued in mournful silence and a small cabin appeared through the trees. Smoke curled from a stone chimney and lights flickered through a small window. Ragnar's eyes focused as he moved forward, and as I followed his footsteps, there wasn't time to react as a light click sounded beneath his foot, followed immediately by a ringing, metallic snap as the teeth of a steel trap caught Ragnar's leg. His hand was over his mouth as he muffled a roar of agony and I was at his side, uncovering the trap that had been buried under the snow. The trap had caught him just above the boot, the linen and leather of his clothing doing nothing to protect his leg from the sharpened teeth. Veins bulged in his forehead and neck, as he breathed deeply through gritted teeth. He bent forward, keeping his weight on his unaffected leg, and grunted as he gripped the sides of the trap, prying them open and removing his foot carefully. With a hand on each side of the trap, he cursed heavily in Nordmaarian, words I had rarely heard him speak, and he pulled the trap apart, wielding the pieces as weapons.

"No healing, not yet," he said gruffly. "Save your energy."

In a red-sighted rage, Ragnar limped for a few steps, then exhaled sharply as he put his full weight on his injured leg, the anger radiating from him as he left blood stains in the snow. He marched straight up to the cabin door and put his boot into it as it flew inward, completely off the hinges. I drew my daggers and slipped inside after him, disappearing in the shadows as pure chaos erupted. I counted eight men inside the small cabin, bunks stacked against the wall and a cauldron of stew over the hearth, with a thick, roughly-cut table in the middle with a few stools. The men rose and drew weapons, from axes and swords to a pair of crossbows. One man near the back of the room raised a loaded crossbow while a man beside him loaded another, and Ragnar threw half of the steel trap at him before he could fire the bolt. The teeth of the trap tore into the man's flesh, the force of the blow exposing a bright white skullcap as the man's scalp flapped sickeningly. He dropped to the floor, not dead, just dazed and shocked, and the man next to him screamed and vomited.

Gripping the other half of the steel trap, Ragnar threw a few blows that tore flesh from bone, throwing the second half of the steel trap at a man toward the back.

"We need to question them!" I shouted, catching his attention as he turned. "I need them alive!"

As Ragnar threw one of the three men that had rushed him, another man, short, balding, and missing a few teeth, grabbed me around the middle, shoving me into the wall. I brought my fists against the sides of his head and delivered a headbutt that shattered his nose. Blood streamed and he coughed as he swore heavily in Elvish, spitting blood as he staggered. A shout from Ragnar stole my attention, and I watched as he flipped the table on its edge and yanked one of the legs off, splintering it halfway down. He tossed it to me and as a single motion I gripped it and swung hard across the man's face. Splinters tore through his face and he wailed, screaming as he clawed at the wood shards piercing his eyes. Ragnar grabbed two of them, smashed their heads together, and dropped them to the floor. The man in front of him dropped his small knife and raised his hands in surrender as he soiled himself.

"You will tell her everything and anything she wants to know," Ragnar seethed. "Is that understood?"

He nodded and I stood in front of my husband as he began to pace behind me, waiting to lunge.

"How many traps have you laid?" I asked the man.

He glanced at the others and began counting on his fingers. First he held up five fingers, then eight, and finally held up all ten fingers and shrugged. I scoffed.

"Not one of you kept track of the total amount," I snarled. "Did you even think to mark the placements?"

He raised his hand like a child asking permission to speak. I crossed my arms and nodded.

"We put down a scrap o' white cloth nearby," he stammered. "Jus' didn't know it snowed so much here."

I pinched the bridge of my nose and groaned.

"What exactly are you doing in Tachá? Be very, very specific," I said sternly.

"Don't you tell that she-elf nothin'!" one of the men said brashly, sneering and spitting at my feet as he stood. "You keep your mouth shut!"

Ragnar turned and grabbed the man by the collar, lifting him up until his toes scraped the floor.

"I warned you to tell her everything," Ragnar whispered, the warning clear in his tone. "Next time, you will have no tongue to speak with."

He released the man, whose legs failed him as he crumpled at Ragnar's boots. He noticed the blood marring Ragnar's leg and scrambled to his feet, pale as a ghost.

"My apologies, m'Lord," he muttered, "I'm sorry you were injured by the trap."

"*What were you hoping to trap?*" *I interrupted, taking his attention.*

"*Anything we could catch,*" *he said, his eyes shifting from me to Ragnar, and back again.* "*Southerners pay big for those white fox hides.*"

I knew he was lying, and though I couldn't prove it, I just knew it in my gut. I hoped to call his bluff, and while I still counted the potential threats: two men were close to bleeding out on the floor, and the rest were seriously injured in a surprisingly different amount of ways, the one who had been scalped by the iron trap was still moaning on the ground, his partner next to him, trying hopelessly to make the loose, bloody flap of skin fit back on his skull.

"*My love, this man is lying to me,*" *I said calmly.* "*Maim him severely, please. I need him to be able to speak, though, so leave his tongue.*"

My husband read my intentions and had grabbed the man around the neck before he could react. His entire hand fit around the man's throat and he squeezed just hard enough to bring the man's face from a flushed red to a grayish-blue. Ragnar watched for my notice to release the man and when the blood vessels burst from the pressure in the man's eyes, turning them a splotchy red, I raised a finger. Ragnar released his grip and the man fell bodily to the ground.

"*Try again,*" *I said quietly as I knelt at the man's side.* "*Let's start with three questions. What is your name, what are you trapping, and who is purchasing?*"

"*Br-Bryndon. My name is Bryndon,*" *he gasped, coughing and sucking in air that rattled in his throat.* "*Please, I don't wanna die, I'm sorry! We was paid to get them wolves, but anything else we got was for our pockets. We...we didn't know they was so damn big! Gods, they's as big as m'horse! Ne'er seen anythin' so big!*"

"You were paid to trap...direwolves?" I breathed. "To kill them or keep them?"

"K-k-k-keep, if we could," he said, stuttering over his words.

"Where are they?" I asked darkly.

"Some of 'em are bein' held in the barn," he said, his face darkening with fear as he continued, "and the rest of 'em are in the shed."

His words sat heavy on my chest and I glanced at Ragnar. He met my eyes, and from my peripheral vision I saw the man reach to his boot and pull a knife. He stabbed wildly and Ragnar stepped backward faster than the man anticipated. In one motion, he reached behind him, grabbing the bubbling cauldron of stew off of the hook, growling as it burned his hand, and delivered a back-handed blow to the man's head, the cauldron making a dull thud as it connected with his head. He fell back as Ragnar poured the simmering contents over him, I looked away as the man screamed and writhed, his boots hammering against the floorboards.

"Go, I'll keep them all here," he said. "No one will die by my hand...unless they wish for it."

As I nodded and turned for the doorway, stepping over the door as it lay flat on the floor, one of the men stood in my way, blocking the doorway completely.

"You ain't takin' our pelts," he snarled. "We earned 'em fair!"

Filled with righteous anger over the death of Tacháan creatures, I kicked the man square in the chest as hard as I could. He staggered backward into the wall as he gasped for air, the dirty print of my boot's sole dark against his dirty linen shirt. As he doubled over, I gave him a hard push with my boot and sent him reeling into his companions.

"Valérikka, tend to the direwolves," Ragnar ordered. "I'll make sure you're not interrupted."

I gave a nod and dashed out the doorway, turning toward the shed first. A shrouded hut hastily built on a hill, it had open windows for ventilation and a trench dug beneath it. Ice had glazed over the liquid that had trailed down the trench and the stench took my breath away as the wind shifted. I knew immediately that the hut was the preparation center. Entering the hut, I kept my distance from the large vat in the corner, the stench reeked of lime, and I was glad it wasn't a mixture of urine, as it was sometimes done. Finished pelts hung in rows, organized surprisingly neatly by size; from smaller white fox furs to larger wolf pelts. On one wall, separated from the others, five small pelts lay, matching the one that Ragnar's men had brought him. We had found the men that had killed and skinned direwolf pups for profit, and my husband was holding them hostage. Rage coursed through me like a wildfire and part of me wanted the men to suffer in the same way those innocent pups had. I left the hut and headed straight for the barn, praying that I would find signs of life. I threw open the sliding door and the scent of straw, raw meat, and feces hit me hard enough to make me stagger back a step. Twelve iron cages lined the walls of a dilapidated horse barn, converted to fit the cages. I stepped inside, bracing against the smell, and calmed my mind. Direwolves, mostly juvenile or younger, filled every cage. I spied a cage toward the back that held four pups and I crouched near it. They looked safe, unharmed, and relief settled on my shoulders. I stood in the middle of the barn and every eye fell upon me.

"I'm here to help you all," I said quietly, a desperate pleading in my tone. "I know you can understand me, so hear my words. The woods surrounding this place are filled with iron traps. You can't just run out of here. Be wise, you

Direwolves of Tachá, and do not get caught. My husband and I are dealing with the men who caught you. They will never hunt again. Help the young pups to safety, and be free. Warn others of the perils of this place and don't return."

I neared the first cage and met the eyes of the direwolf. He seemed to still be young, but between his long legs and stature, he still stood eye-level to me. The cage was padlocked, and there was no key in sight.

"Where are the keys?" I asked absently as I scanned the walls and surrounding cages.

Finally, I saw an iron ring hanging near the table of roughly chopped frozen meat, I supposed food for the wolves. Grabbing the ring, I approached the cage and inserted one of the many keys in the hole and fire crawled up my arm, licking at my armor as I swiped it away. With my hair singed at the tip, I glared at the keys.

"Great, they're enchanted? I don't have time for this," I muttered angrily.

Taking a step back, I noticed the direwolf turn around and lay down in a corner.

"I'm not giving up, I'm finding another way," I clarified, watching his ears swivel to hear me as he turned toward the wall.

The hinges of the cage doors were soldered well enough that even with the best tools, it would take me a very long time to knock the pins out to remove the cage doors. The iron bars were crafted thickly, built by someone who knew what they were doing, especially with the strength of the direwolf. Brute strength was not an option to free them. Lockpicking was looking like my only option, but I had exactly five picks in my gear. Five picks to twelve locks didn't add up. I needed brute strength to beat the locks off, and the brute strength I needed was in the cabin. I turned away and the direwolf sighed, a heart-wrenching sound of defeat.

"I need help," I said, "I can't break this and I can't pick it open. I need a hammer, or an iron bar, or something!"

I searched around the cages, finding nothing but wet straw, and reached the table that had frozen chunks of raw deer meat. A rusted, dull cleaver had been used to slice the meat, and a heavy hammer had been used to beat against the cleaver to break through the frozen venison. Grabbing up the hammer and cleaver, I rushed to the lock, positioned the blade, and beat it with all my might, and by the third swing, the lock broke and fell to the floor, smoking from the lock's enchantment. I opened the heavy door and it creaked in protest, but stayed open. The direwolf took a hesitant step forward to freedom, his ears flattened against his head, until he was fully free from the cage. I had moved on to the next one, the lock bursting into flame as it clattered to the floor. It took me what felt like an hour to break the locks off of the cages, but at last, I opened the final door, freeing the pups.

"Please remember to be careful," I told them, pleading with urgency. "The iron traps are everywhere, and I don't know how many there are, let alone where they are."

"We have the scent of the men that laid the traps. We are able to smell them now," one of the direwolves said, stepping forward. "We are thankful to you for your assistance."

I nodded and watched as each one of them trotted out of the barn, disappearing around the corner of the building and vanishing into the safety of the woods, their sharp noses to the snow to scent out the traps. My heart swelled with pride as I made sure the barn was empty, and I turned back to a cage, pulling out my flint and a dagger. Sparking my steel against the flint, I smiled as the spark grew, licking at the straw as it spread. By the time I had walked back to the cabin, the barn was fully engulfed in flames and crumbling in upon itself. Reaching the front of the cabin, I saw Ragnar knelt outside, his hands buried in the snow.

"Ragnar?" I called, worrying that he had been injured.

As I drew closer, I realized that the brown shades of his leather had turned dark and wet, and he stood, turning slowly to me. His entire body had turned red, as if splashed with blood and gore. My hands flew to my mouth and I summoned my energy to heal whatever had happened. He held his hands out, clean from the cleansing in the snowbank.

"Min Kona, it's not my blood," he said quietly, turning to wash his face clean in the snow.

I paused, realizing that he was uninjured.

"What happened?" I murmured softly, walking past him toward the splintered threshold.

He grabbed my arm at the same time I caught sight through the doorway. A massacre had taken place, painting every surface within my sight with a horrific visage. Ragnar had ripped the men apart, one by one, limb by limb. I shut my eyes as he tried to pull me close but I pushed him away, unwilling to be covered in someone else's lifeblood. There was so much blood...

"What happened?" I demanded, holding him away and staring into his eyes.

"They threatened you with a fate worse than death. In great detail," he said with an animalistic snarl. "They thought I wouldn't disobey your orders. They were wrong. You are mine, and mine alone."

For a split second, faster than my mind processed, I could have sworn his eyes flashed red, and a warning pressed into my mind, the dire wolf's voice, calling my husband Danger.

CHAPTER II

THE SERPENT'S FANG

I retreated quietly to my lodgings for the night, armed myself with a dagger, positioned the lumpy pillows under the blankets, forming a petite sleeping figure, and went to the open window. A soft, high whistle pitched from my lips, and a short moment later, I saw Kona, almost invisible in the darkness, trot toward the tavern door. Only a few minutes passed before a light scratching sounded toward the bottom of the door, and I crept over, opened the door enough for her to slip in, and shut it again. Her silent paws padded toward me and Kona nudged her muzzle into the crook of my elbow and we sat quietly, invisible in the dark room, and waited for what I knew would come.

The moon rose quietly, and just as quietly, I placed my hand on Kona's back as the door to my room opened. Slowly and with patience, someone opened the door in complete silence, and Kona tensed. I knew she wouldn't make a movement or a sound without my command, and as long as I stayed motionless, she would, too. The moonlight caught the steel of the blade the man wielded as he crept to the side of the bed he supposed I slept in, and he paused. I knew, without a doubt, that this was far from the first time he'd done this, and I knew just as well that this man was a beast in human form.

Three things happened simultaneously: the intruder yanked back the covers and stood stunned as a goose-down pillow lay exposed. I threw my dagger, embedding it deep in the muscle of his thigh, and Kona lunged. She held him by the throat as he squealed and cried, and she squeezed a little harder as a deep growl rumbled from her throat. I struck a match and lit the oil lamp beside the bed and was mildly surprised to see the man that had been speaking to the man named Dell earlier that night. As he met my eyes, faint recognition dawned and he emptied his bladder onto himself and the floor.

"So you're the disgusting pig that's been assailing women almost every night?" I asked, standing over him with my hands planted on my hips. "Should I even give you the air to breathe your explanation?"

He stammered between sobs and I held up a hand to silence him. Bending, I grasped the hilt of my dagger and yanked it from his leg. He blubbered and bawled and I knelt by his face.

"Why should I show you mercy?" I whispered. "You showed those women none. Why shouldn't I let my wolf tear you apart? Tell me why my face shouldn't be the last you should ever see?"

Kona tightened her grip as the man begged for mercy, and it enraged me. His body trembled and his boots thudded against the wooden plank floor. A squeak came from the doorframe as the young woman who had warned me about this man stuck her head in, she gasped and pushed the door open.

"Papa, he's in here!" she shouted, rushing to my side and recoiling at the sight of blood coating the man's trousers, or perhaps it was the stench of his urine-soaked self.

A tall man who I vaguely recalled as serving drinks behind the bar stepped into the room and shook his head darkly.

"This is your fate, Fundus, to die at the hands of a woman," he growled darkly. "I'd have it no other way."

"He'll meet his fate at the hands of justice," I replied, wiping the man's blood on his shirt and replacing the cleaned steel in my belt. "Bind him tightly and then call the guards. They will make sure that Northern steel separates his head from his shoulders."

I stood and Kona released her grip, the spots of blood on his neck displaying the distinctive pattern of wolf fangs. The tavern owner sent his daughter to grab a length of rope and the man's face paled as his eyes grew crazed. He stammered unintelligibly and I waved my hand.

"You've dug your own grave," I said quietly. "Now lie in it."

I headed for the doorway with Kona as the girl returned with a length of cord, and as the man approached to bind Fundus, he paused.

"You have our thanks," he said, inclining his head. "As well as the gratitude of many others."

He brought his fist to his chest and I returned the respectful gesture. I recognized the crazed gleam in Fundus' eyes a moment too late as he reached for the short knife on the tavern owner's belt. His fingers grasped the hilt and he pulled it free from the leather belt as the girl screamed. My dagger sailed through the air with the flick of my wrist and lodged itself deep in Fundus' throat. He gurgled and sank to his knees, dropping the knife to grab at his throat. He pulled the razor-sharp blade from his throat and bright crimson blood spurted from the wound as he began to choke on his own blood. His eyes met mine, the panic and fear as bright as the blood that stained his front.

"A coward's last act of desperation," the man said as Fundus fell forward, dead.

He pulled my blade from the flesh and wiped it clean on the dead man's shirt, glancing at the hilt. He looked at it again, more closely, and slowly, his eyes lifted to me.

"I thank you for your hospitality, sir," I said carefully, realizing he recognized me, perhaps not as the Queen, but at the very least a member of royal high-standing, "but I must be moving on, now."

He gripped the blade and offered the hilt to me and his eyes locked onto my wedding ring, the thin iron band set with a blue sapphire. His brow furrowed and my heart hammered. I didn't exactly know the implications of being identified as Queen of Tachá to someone that didn't understand my situation, not to mention I'd just taken a man's life in front of him. Grabbing my pack from beside the bed, I turned and left the room without a backward glance, Kona followed silently behind, a white shadow. Down the stairs, I moved quickly around the bartop and out the door. I headed straight for my horse, saddling her with a growing unease.

I left the city and didn't look back, eager to quell the unusual anxiety that had grown around me. Kona's eyes and ears were scanning the area for me and I focused now on the Wall, seemingly never getting closer despite the hours spent riding toward it. I recalled Ylsa's advice to seek out Winchester, and wondered how long it would take to find him in a city that was so much bigger than Frostholm. Hours passed as I rode; Kona strayed from the path, off to hunt food for herself. I knew she'd return when she had a full belly or when I called for her, whichever came first, and by the time the sun began to set, I pulled Astrid off the road and sought shelter in a grove of thick trees. Fire came first; shelter was my bedroll. It was a cloudless night, and the snow glittered against the moonlight. The fire crackled and popped as I lay staring up at the constellations, reciting them quietly as I had been taught, and my eyes grew heavy. Kona buried her nose in the thick fur of her tail and she closed her eyes, but I knew her ears would stay alert to anything that dared approach.

I STOOD SURROUNDED by blackened snow, colder than my mind could process, stretching for as far as my eyes could see. The ground crunched under my boots, the snow turned to ash, frozen and brittle. I lifted my eyes and storm clouds swirled overhead, sliced by streaks and flashes of scarlet lightning.

"This isn't real," I whispered, grinding the palms of my hands into my eyes.

The breeze picked up and the scent of iron and blood surrounded me; the smell of death. The ground rumbled behind me and I whirled around. Rising out of the scorched earth, a gnarled, twisted tree unfurled, its branches reaching out as if in agony. At the base of the tree, a massive serpent lay, carved of stone, wrapped around the base of the trunk, eyes hollow and fangs bared. Buried between where the boughs of the tree split, a dagger's hilt glittered. I neared against my better judgment and my fingers trembled as they closed around the cold hilt. I freed the dagger as if it had been waiting for someone to pull it loose and I brought it close to inspect its detail.

The hilt was carved into a serpent's body, the craftsmanship like nothing I'd ever seen. The pommel of the dagger was a serpent's head, its carved eyes glassy and blind. As the moonlight caught the scales crafted on the hilt, they shimmered like dragon scales. I watched in awe as the hues shifted: red, green, blue, black, and white, glowing bright one moment and dark the next. Curved like a snake's fang, the blade itself was dark and smooth, but I knew it wasn't made of iron or steel.

This...this was something else entirely.

As I gripped it, it seemed to pulse, imitating my own heartbeat. I raised the blade, catching the reflection of the moon, and saw a figure behind me as the wind ceased. The world itself seemed to hold its breath as I slowly turned, meeting the eyes of my husband...a strangely younger version of him. Sorrow filled his gaze and a heavy crown sat atop his brow, the royalty emanating from him unfamiliar in his youthful presence.

"You know what this blade is," he said in a hollow voice, as if it were carried in from the wind. "It pierces not the body, but fate."

As I glanced at the dagger he spoke of, I realized that the pommel of the dagger had stretched and contorted, the mouth of the snake's head now latched around my wrist, a shackle that had no key. Ragnar knelt in front of me, his eyes void of fear or hatred, but welled with love. His armor, stained with countless battles, was cracked down the middle, revealing a stretch of pale, scarred flesh beneath. I knew the stories behind those scars, he'd whispered them to me as I had traced them with a delicate finger in the safety and comfort of our *bedroom, long ago. Lifting my hand to trace them again, my willpower failed me as I buried the blade into the soft hollow of his throat, the place that had once been kissed by my lips. Blood poured from Ragnar's fatal wound, but it flowed darker than night and sizzled as it burned the earth.*

I woke up soaked to my bones in sweat, violently shaking with ragged breath. I tore at my wrist, expecting to find the snake-pommel clamped around my wrist, but found nothing. No blood, no dagger, no dead husband, nothing. But the memory, all too vivid in the forefront of my mind, lingered. The Serpent's Fang had sought me out, found me, and seared itself into my mind. I *knew* beyond the shadow of a doubt that the dagger had been forged for my hand and my hand alone. I rested my head back on my makeshift pillow and stared up at the stars, counting the stars in each constellation to help me drift back to sleep.

The voice rumbled low and deep, like distant thunder. Not from around me, nor beneath, but a voice that came from between the stars themselves, falling into the deepest crevices of my mind. The power and authority that carried the words rattled my senses and the world around me blurred.

"You have felt its power over you. It was forged to break you, to bend you to their will, to kill the king through his greatest weakness."

Ragnar had no weakness that I knew of, and as if I'd spoken it aloud, the voice answered, from within me and all around me.

"You are his greatest weakness, Queen of Tachá. You are

the only one who can deliver the killing blow, but this is not your destiny, this is not your fate. My power exceeds theirs. What they have written in an iron pen I can sweep away. Continue on your quest. Seek out those who would guide you."

"Who are you?" I whispered to the night sky as the voice continued, ignoring my question.

"Your choice lies in the fork in the road. Choose carefully. If you let the serpent drink from your hand, if you stay on the path they've carved for you, you will damn the man you love. Buried beneath steel, gunpowder, lies, and forgotten blood, lies your divergence. Fight for the power to keep Ragnar alive. Fight, bleed, and fall, but Ragnar must live."

The temperature plummeted and I shuddered as the stars blinked out, as if something massive had blocked them out for a split second. I squeezed my eyes shut, blinking hard as I stared back. The stars twinkled as they had the night prior, as if they would the next night. There were no words I possessed to even try, but I knew that continuing to Enguard meant Ragnar's survival. Whatever waited for me there would have the answers I needed.

CHAPTER 12
REFUGEES AT THE WALL

I slept very little; my consciousness seeing shadows and hearing whispers in the corners of my mind, while Kona paced the rest of the night, growling in the darkness, sensing my unease. We got an early start and rode in silence until the birds sang the dawn to life and we watched the deer leap through the snowy expanse. Every step closer to the Wall seemed in vain; it just never seemed to grow any bigger. Astrid nickered and sneezed, shaking her head, and I patted her neck.

"We'll stay a full night's rest at the Wall, okay?" I told her, understanding that she was weary of walking, though my weight added nothing to her back. "Maybe I'll have you stay at the Wall. It's awfully warm south of the Wall, I think. I don't want to risk you getting overheated."

I knew she didn't understand me, but I also knew that she was a Tacháan mare, bred and built for the coldest winters. The warmth of Thyuland would not be good for her, and I loved her enough to leave her home. Kona, though, would fight and bite her way out of anything to stay at my side; I wouldn't even try to contain her to the North.

The sun sat in the highest point of the sky and I walked ahead of Astrid, taking a break for a few miles to ease her back and stretch my legs. Astrid walked lazily beside me, her reins tied neatly to the horn of her saddle, and Kona explored ahead of us. Astrid let out a squeal when Kona returned suddenly, her ears high and eyes bright as I grabbed hold of her reins. *Someone was coming.* Hooves and heavy wheels sounded after a few minutes and I pulled my hood up, continuing along with the least amount of suspicion I could summon. I appeared like a member of the Hunter's Guild, and it wasn't a lie. Before marrying the king, I was a very well-respected Captain of the Guild, and that's who I was right now. I kept my head down, not in a submissive way, but in a manner that exuded zero interest in communication, and as the pair of horses neared, I could see the wooden wagon pulled behind them. I led Astrid to the side of the road and allowed them to pass by, and the driver, a man with dark green eyes and layered head-to-toe with warm clothing, gave an appreciative nod, his face and hands, olive-hued and covered with goosebumps. The passengers, three women and five small children, sat huddled in the back, covered with furs and blankets. They continued toward Frostholm, and I saw that they were unmistakably elven, their cold, reddened ears pointed sharply. As a half-elf, my own ears pointed slightly, but not enough to mistake me for anything but a half-elf/human. I wondered what had brought the elves to Tachá, their warm-blooded constitutions holding a natural dislike for these frigid lands.

I continued on and at last, the Wall appeared in the

distance as I had imagined it. The Northern hunters who had traveled throughout Tachá had regaled us with stories of the immensity of the Wall, but to see it with my own eyes was another thing. Still so many miles from its base, I was breathless at its immensity, unable to see either end of it as it stretched on for what seemed the entirety of the border. Immovable, impassable, and impossible to breach, the Wall was one of Tachá's oldest and greatest defenses, but it hadn't been approached in wartime in hundreds of years. Another wagon approached, with a horse and rider leading the way. A few lengths behind it, yet another wagon followed. As the rider approached, astride a long-legged black gelding, I raised my hand in greeting.

"What brings you so far north, traveler?" I called, as cheerfully as I could muster.

Hopping down from his horse and pulling his hood off, the wood elf shook a head of messy blond hair and gave a crooked grin. He held out a hand and I shook it.

"Freedom," he replied with simplicity.

"What do you mean?"

"Thyuland is full of darkening whispers. My friends, family, and I are no longer safe nor welcome in our home-lands. We seek asylum, protection, from the King of Tachá. It is said that Tachá is as cold as ice, but her heart is warm to those who seek her embrace. Will you tell me if it's true?"

I smiled, genuinely proud of my husband's quiet efforts of allowing refugees into our lands. "It is true, newcomer. Tachá is a cold mistress, but she is as loyal as you have heard. I bid you welcome, you and your companions."

Seemingly appearing out of nowhere, a blonde

halfling woman stepped out from behind the elf, her nose and cheeks red with cold.

"Is it safe here or not?" she asked bluntly, her arms crossed defensively.

"Safe from what, exactly? We have wild wolf packs, yetis, uglabjorn, bears, wildcats, spiders, and more. That's not including the human monsters either," I added, thinking back to the man I'd killed in my rented tavern room.

"Do you have genocidal, egotistical, *psychotic* armies of high elves going from town to town burning and cutting down the women and children after they've rounded up the men they've captured to enslave?" the halfling asked darkly, stalling what thoughts I had in my mind.

Stunned speechless, I glanced at the wood elf, who gave a confirming nod. I let out a lungful of air sharply, resting my hands on my hips. The halfling gave a shrug and the wood elf sighed.

"My companion is a little...on edge," he said. "I'm Leo, this is Freya, we're leading these people away from Thyu-land. Our choices were either the frozen North or the desert South. I think we chose wisely."

"You chose wisely, indeed. A few hours from here is a town called Frostholm, but the main city, Sitica, is where the king resides. Seek an audience with him and his coun-cil, and tell him everything that you've told me. No mysteries or subterfuge, speak plainly and clearly. He will make sure you're safe."

"And *you* can confirm this?" Freya said with a smirk. "Who are *you* that a king would hear *us* simply because you said so?"

I pinched the bridge of my nose. Here and now, I was

not the Queen of Tachá hearing tales of genocide south of the Wall, I was merely a Huntress passing by. Freya stared at me curiously, her arms crossed as she watched me curiously. Tall for a halfling, she wore confidence and furs as she watched me with hazel eyes. Her bright golden hair, tied messily on top of her head, was level with the hilt of my sword, and I had a feeling that her size and stature didn't stop her from doing whatever she wanted. The daggers tied to her waist and the leather bracers on her arms that I knew held hidden daggers sharpened my eyes.

"If you held an audience with King Ragnar, what would you say to convince him that you speak the truth?" I asked.

"I would tell of the things we have seen with our own eyes and the stories of the few survivors left. The eyewitness accounts of scorched towns, missing men, and murdered children. Something is happening...and it's just the beginning," she said, the urgency and dampened fear in her tone emerging. "No one else is going to do a damn thing, but I won't just watch innocent people be burned alive and enslaved."

I shuddered and I didn't doubt a single word she said, but there was no way I could tell her who I really was.

"Tell King Ragnar that Val sent you."

"Val? Just that, no name, no town you hail from? No parentage?" Leo chortled and shook his head a little. "He's supposed to know one name out of thousands and know that you're the one who sent us? I'm not sure how you do things up in the north, but where I hail from, it's -"

"My name is all you need."

He stopped laughing and Freya cocked her head. Her

eyes dropped to my neck, then to my gloved hands. I knew she was searching for evidence of an heirloom amulet or a signet ring, but when she found none, she didn't look disappointed , but pleased, as if something had been confirmed.

"Okay," Freya said, as if in simple agreement. "We'll be on our way, then."

Grabbing hold of Leo's sleeve, she herded him toward the horse and hopped into the almost indiscernible spot behind him. I blinked as she seemed to become invisible against him. As the horse took a few steps, she appeared again, turning to face me.

"Many thanks, your Grace," she said quietly, offering up a grin and a wink.

Stunned, I simply inclined my head to her and continued walking with Astrid and Kona, the distance between us growing as the sun continued to move in the sky, marking the hours as they passed.

THE STORIES from the other hunters had done nothing to justify the breathtaking immensity of the Great Wall of Valthor. Its sheer presence commanded authority as it protected our lands from coast to coast. The massive stretch of steel, ice, stone, and magic, the Wall acted as a dividing line between the land of Tachá and Thyuland, home of the elves.

"This is it," I said as Kona pricked her ear toward my voice. "I don't know what we're going to do if the guards recognize me, or if they refuse to let me through. I don't think Ragnar has alerted the guards at the Wall quite this quickly. I don't think he'd trust the information sent with a crow."

As we neared, slowly, but not slowly enough to arouse suspicion, and as we drew close enough to the outer gate, a guard, cold, tired, and absolutely miserable, stopped us with a raised hand that was quickly dropped to his side. Inspiration blossomed as I realized it was shift change, the end of a long twelve-hour shift of standing guard where hardly nothing ever happened. The guards of the Wall made sure any merchants passing through had properly certified documentation, and made sure all cargo was accounted for, so a lone woman passing through could either interest them greatly or bore them to tears. I hoped for the latter. The guard groaned as he stretched his back and concealed a yawn.

"Yes, I have business south, but I need lodging for my mare," I stated.

"You and every other Northerner," he said with a laugh. "Our horses just don't fare well in that kind of heat. Or humidity. Or sun. Come to think of it, most Tacháans don't fare well, either."

"I'll have to muddle through, I suppose," I replied, "I'll have to unstitch my fur from my armor."

"Or sell it," he suggested. "Say it's real direwolf fur and those idiotic elven folk will buy it for triple its worth."

A wave of unease swept over me as his eyes wandered toward the wolf at my side and I smiled politely, thanking him as I headed toward the long line of stables. A boy stood kicking a frozen, dried ball of horse dung and I caught his attention. Handing my reins over to him, I paused as Astrid watched me with confusion in her eyes.

"You'll stay here until I come back," I said to her,

smoothing her mane and scratching gently under her jaw. "I'll send word for Floki to come get you if I'm not back by the next full moon."

"Should I send word to your husband, my lady, after a fortnight?" the quiet stable boy beside me asked.

"No. If I don't return after a full fortnight, send my horse to Floki Oakhand in Sitica. In the meantime, her name is Astrid, and she likes apples and honeyed oats."

"Yes, my lady," the boy said, bowing low to me.

I smiled and inclined my head to him, earning a wide grin from the boy as he tightened his grip on Astrid's reins.

Leaving my horse and keeping Kona close to my side, I headed to the next checkpoint toward the Wall. A guard stood at attention, his eyes staring straight ahead in armor that was either brand new or shined meticulously, and as I drew near, I could see the slight wear at the leather straps. I groaned internally and Kona sneezed. The guard redirected his gaze to me and held a hand out straight. I wondered if this was a facade or if he truly took *this* job, guard duty at the second entry point, so seriously.

"Business south, miss?"

I cocked my head as if I didn't understand him. I carried only my pack, my swords, and a bow that paired with a loaded quiver.

"Papers?" he asked, holding out a gloved hand.

"*Lát mik ganga fram,*" I said, demanding passage in the language of the natural-born Tacháans.

He squinted his eyes a little, recognizing the dialect but not the words, and I shook my head, gesturing to the gate as if I were pressed for time.

"*Erendi hefi ek þar*," I said slowly, gesturing over the gate and miming with my hands that I had business past the Wall. "*Lát mik ganga fram.*"

The man was growing frustrated and I feigned impatience, which was easy to do given the urgency I had to move through the long passage. Grumbling a few vulgarities under his breath, he signaled me through and swore at me under his breath, telling me to '*learn the damn language if I reside here.*' As I passed him, I stopped and turned around to face him, my arms crossed as I glared.

"That language was the tongue of our native lands," I said sharply as he paled. "You speak the common tongue that touches everyone's lips, but few are those who Tachá herself has blessed with her words."

I continued on, my anger fading with each step. Kona was within arm's reach of me, and finally, we stood in the very short line of travelers waiting for the gate to open. A young man stood in front of me, still and unmoving. Kona sniffed the air around him and whined. He jumped and whirled around, crying out in surprised fear at the sight of the white wolf behind him.

Kona glanced at me, unsure of what to do, and laid her ears back as the man, wrapped in furs from head to toe, rested a gloved hand on the ornate hilt of his sword. He immediately raised his hands in surrender and her ears perked up. Curiously, he lowered his hand again until it settled on his sword. Kona's eyes zeroed in on his hand, and it wasn't until his fingers began to curl around the hilt that she wrinkled her nose and snarled.

"Smart dog, miss," the man said, removing his hands from his weapons and smiling as Kona relaxed. "Very smart.

"Thank you, but she's not a dog," I corrected. "She's a Tacháan wolf."

His eyes, already a bright emerald green, brightened even more and he marveled with a quiet gasp.

"I've never seen one so close, and so well behaved," he said quietly. "May I approach her? We have a while until the gate opens, and I-I'd love to study her."

"*Study* her?" I repeated, mentally noting his weapons and the locations of mine, just in case he were to try something stupid.

He dropped his head and groaned.

"My deepest apologies," he said, standing and offering his hand. "I'm Mikhail, I'm a student researcher with the College of Enguard. I'm here to study the fauna and flora of the Tacháan lands."

"Oh?" I mused, knowing the dangerous mission he had. "How's that going for you? I'm Val."

"Nice to meet you, Val. It...well, it's not going anywhere, unfortunately. I've nearly died every encounter. Your vegetation seems to be as deadly as the beasts here! It's a wonder you Tacháans are still alive!"

I laughed and shook my head.

"I suppose I wonder the same about you Southerners, how you can survive in such sweltering temperatures! It's a wonder you all haven't melted into puddles!"

The chains, bigger than any I'd ever seen, shifted suddenly and began to rise with the immensely powerful magic and brute strength. I could feel the thick magic in the air, and Mikhail could too, judging by his shudder.

"Is it always like that?" he asked, thumbing toward the gate.

I shrugged. "Don't know. This is my first time through."

He raised a brow. "Really? You've never been through the gate? You've never been South before? How have you lived your life up here all this time?"

I smiled gently. "Tachá is much larger than you could imagine. She has lands that have yet to be explored, named, or tread on. You'll never explore all of her, nor will I."

"Well, Thyuland is uncovered, every last inch, thanks to the elven folk, and it's all been explored and documented by many. Here's hoping you'll find something new. Until then, may I study your wolf? I would appreciate taking some measurements, and taking notes on her."

I glanced at Kona, she licked her snout and sighed as I gave permission.

Carefully, Mikhail removed a measuring tape from one of the multiple pockets sewn into the interior of his coat and recorded Kona's length, the size of her paws, her height, and then as he knelt by her head, he hesitated, looking at her muzzle.

"Uh, may I see her teeth?" he stammered, inches away from them.

"Kona, *bera tǫnnur*," I commanded, as Kona wrinkled her snout, exposing her white fangs.

Mikhail lost his balance and scrambled backward at the terrifying sight and I chuckled.

"I simply told her to bear her teeth for you," I explained. "You'll need to get much closer if you want to study them."

Despite the fear plainly on his face, he approached my white wolf, who I *knew* was amused. With trembling hands he measured her fangs, took note of her gum color, and when Kona yawned widely, he quickly counted her teeth, noting and sketching a rough picture of her teeth in his notebook. He asked Kona directly if he could see the bottom of her paw, and she glanced at me for approval.

"*Já*," I said with a nod.

Kona sat on her haunches and lifted her paw in the air. Mikhail laughed joyfully and pulled a small jar from another pocket.

"It's just ink," he explained to us both, "I'd like to take an impression of her paw."

He painted the bottom of her paw pad with the black ink and opened his notebook flat to an empty page, gently directing Kona's massive paw to the page. Pressing delicately, he made sure her entire paw was positioned on the page, only just big enough to hold her entire paw. Her head tilted as she watched Mikhail manipulate her paw onto the paper.

"Why is it so large?" he asked, gesturing to her paw and wiping the excess ink off the insulated paw pad with snow and a cloth.

"To help her travel in the snow, they can act like snowshoes in deeper snow, but the fur between her toes keeps her feet warm and silent when she stalks."

"I can imagine," he said, beaming with joy as Kona allowed him to scratch her ears. "She's more fur and muscle than anything else, weather-proofing and power?"

"Yes, she's practically waterproof, and her under-coating insulates her against the harshest of cold. She's ecstatic in a blizzard."

"Well, I hope she'll be safe in the heat of Thyuland," Mikhail said, standing and dusting off his pants with his hands. "The gates are open enough now to pass through. Are you ready?"

I stared at the gate, massive yet minuscule in comparison to the Great Wall of Valthor.

"Ready or not, we're going."

CHAPTER 13
THE WALL

The massive wooden gate hung above our heads, continuing to rise slowly as we followed the small group traveling through. The guard shifts had changed over, and as I spied the uptight soldier, he caught my eye and sneered as he passed by. Thanking him for nothing with a loud "Þakka þér!" I waved as he scoffed. Mikhail glanced at me curiously as Kona's growl rumbled low.

"I just told him thank you, that's all," I reassured him with a grin. "He's not having a great day. I may have made it worse."

We followed the wagon ahead of us on foot, loaded with furs, hides, and barrels of Tacháan wine made with the sweet berries that grew in the bitter cold of the north. For the most part we walked in step with each other through the massive expanse of a tunnel. I noticed Mikhail beginning to sweat around his temples despite the frigid air and I raised a brow.

"You struggle with enclosed spaces?" I asked as he nodded.

"That obvious, eh?" he said, grimacing, though I'm sure he meant that as a smile.

I smiled sympathetically and he pulled at his collar, sweat beading down his neck. Kona's nose stayed to the ground as she took in every scent she could, and step after step, the torches that brought light to the pitch black became a beacon to reach.

"Tell me about your research. What interested you in Tachá in the first place? It's not normally the first choice for anyone from the South," I said, hoping to distract him enough from his phobia.

Through a few deep breaths, he told me about his upbringing in a high-born household. His father had been a highly respected noble high-elf of Gray Tide, a city on the western coast of Thyuland, and Mikhail's eldest brother was the Commander in the City Guard, followed closely by the next two brothers in the family tree, and as Mikhail put it, *"next in line for the honorary death sentence."* He had two more brothers and three sisters. He was the youngest by five years.

"That's a big family," I said, "I'm sure your mother enjoyed having all of you, even if you didn't get along all the time."

"My mother died a long time ago," he said quietly.

I offered my condolences and asked how old he was when she passed. He shook his head sadly. "I took her life as she gave me mine. My father never let me forget it. My earliest memory is him telling me that I murdered his wife and didn't have the decency to die with her."

A pit formed in my stomach mixed with rage and heartache.

"You were a child, an infant," I stammered. "That

couldn't have been your fault. Surely your father knows that and-"

"Knows and doesn't care. I'm cursed because of it. I'm a constant reminder of what happened."

"I'm sorry."

"I'm not," he said, straightening his back and clenching his jaw. "If it hadn't been for Father's outright hatred and dismissal of me, I'd be just another grunt in a Thyuland uniform. That life is *not* the life for me. Instead, when I became old enough, I traveled to the college in Enguard and took up a position as the assistant to the instructor of the botanical research lab to pay for my classes. I was the one that cleaned up after the experiments exploded. I learned quickly, and the instructor took notice of me after a while. I mean, it didn't help that I look the way I do."

I cocked my head, gesturing to him. "Looking... different?"

He forced a smile and reached for his hat. As he pulled it off his head, curly locks of dark auburn hair only partially concealed a pair of horns as dark as onyx and curled in elongated spirals.

"You were born cursed," I murmured. "That doesn't mean you're the reason for the curse, you know. Let's keep moving. I can see daylight, I think. What made you decide on studying botany?"

A bright light seemed to emanate from him as he spoke of his passion for learning more and more, and as he became distracted from the claustrophobic tunnel, he was able to share with me the specifics of his journey to Tachá.

"It would have been a failed mission, you know," he said with an appreciative smile. "You and Kona, well, especially Kona, saved my journey. I bet they haven't been nose-to-nose with a Tacháan wolf! Thank you again for allowing me to study her. We have very little on the world of Tachá past the cities. I mean, your horses are even different!"

I laughed. "Yes, they are. That's why I had to leave mine at the Wall. I wasn't willing to allow her to suffer in the heat."

"So I have a question, then," he asked as the light of the next torch illuminated his curious face. "If Tachá is so cold and Thyuland is so warm, why doesn't the Wall melt?"

"Magic and steel," I guessed. "It's not something I've thought much about, it just doesn't melt. I think if it ever did, something would be very, very wrong."

The next three torches passed in a comfortable silence, and I noticed my own mild discomfort in my furs. Within the next few minutes, the temperature climbed noticeably.

"We're getting close to the end," Mikhail said brightly. "When you can smell the forests, then we're there."

I wasn't sure what that meant, but I knew I wasn't going to be able to wear my fur-lined armor much longer. The first city I came into I would have to alter my armor for something more climate-appropriate. Unstitching the sewn-in furs would take hours, but it would be the best way to remove them.

"Are you headed back to Enguard?" I asked Mikhail as a light sparked in his eyes. "I'd like to accompany you there if I could, I have someone to meet there."

"I'd be honored," he said.

Selfishly, I knew I would be less conspicuous if I was

traveling with another person, and much less as a woman traveling alone. Traveling with someone like Mikhail would be different.

The Cursed Children, I had learned long ago, were born from pure selfishness, out of a corrupted wish, prayer, or demand. I wasn't about to pry for more information, but I knew that the Cursed Children went one of two ways: they either embraced the Darkness of the curse, or they rejected it and lived as normally as possible...despite having demonic horns, sharper-than-normal teeth, sometimes forked tongues and tails. If he wanted to share more, I would be there.

In the distance, what seemed like a distance impossible to measure, the bright light of day shined from the tunnel's exit. I swallowed hard and my heart began to beat a little harder as the outline of the gate became distinct. Kona's ears were forward, all of her attention on the gate's opening, growing larger and larger with every step we took.

"We'll be fine," Mikhail reassured, "I'll keep you safe. My position with the College protects us, and mostly, people leave me alone if they get a good look at me. I'm not dangerous, but no one really knows that. Except for you."

I knew my wolf's teeth and my sword's sharpened edges would be of more protection than Mikhail understood. He carried a shortsword on his belt, but I wasn't sure how adept he was with it. I could see how stiff the unworked leather was on his belt.

"Listen," he murmured as he pointed to his sharply-tipped ear beneath the mop of hair.

Birds sang songs foreign to my ears and the wind rustled leaves of trees that were not covered in weighted snow and ice. Grasses whispered greetings in the wind and I smiled. I rested a hand on Kona's head and inhaled deeply. The air itself was warm and bright, as if embracing me with its rays. The wagon jostled across the gate's crossing and we followed suit. I pretended not to notice Mikhail pulling his hood over his head to hide his horns. The sun's warmth washed over me and I closed my eyes, blinded by its intensity and inhaling as deeply as I could. I opened my eyes and counted the different shades of green that surrounded me. Pale green tendrils of vines hung from trees that grew up and out, trunks thick and full of vitality and broad leaves bigger than my hand. The outer court of the gateyard held elves, mostly wood elves, I noticed, manning the checkpoints, their eyes curious and watchful as we trekked through. Giving a polite nod, they allowed us to pass as Mikhail flashed a brooch, an ornate golden crest decorated with intricate filigree from the inside of his jacket, and I suppressed a grin when he held his head a little higher, nodding to the elves as we walked past. Their eyes watched Kona carefully, however they didn't reach for their weapons' hilts. Through the last guard post, the road lay before us wide, winding, and flanked by lush, thick forests. Mikhail glanced at me and grinned.

"Welcome to Thyuland."

CHAPTER 14
GHOULS IN THE GLOOM

Roosters sounded at dawn's arrival and I woke with the crowing. I was packed and halfway done with breakfast by the time that Mikhail stumbled down the stairs.

"We're leaving as soon as I finish eating," I said, taking a spoonful of sweetened porridge. "Get something to eat quickly. We have to cover a lot of ground today. It may be wise to get a pair of horses if we want to reach Haverdale by nightfall."

Mikhail nodded, his mouth already full of a chunk of bread, and slurped a bowl of thinned gruel down quickly. As we headed toward the door, all of our gear in hand, I paused by the woman wiping the bar.

"Do you know where we could get a pair of horses? We're headed to Enguard, but we plan to stay over in Haverdale for a while," I asked.

She frowned and shook her head. "You may have more willing elves to help you elsewhere. The stable-master here is...unsympathetic."

I held in my groan and thanked her, leaving the inn

on foot with Mikhail in tow. He sputtered as soon as the door was closed and Kona sat patiently near the gate. Her ears perked up as soon as she saw me and I rested my hand on her head as Mikhail swore, loudly.

"Keep your opinions to yourself," I said, keeping my voice low but commanding. "We will discuss this in a much more private area. Understood?"

He fell silent at once and merely nodded, his head hung low. We walked quietly for a quarter of a mile before he cleared his throat.

"Go ahead, Mikhail," I said gently, "ask your questions."

"Where to even begin?" he said, spitting on the ground as we continued. "I knew that the elves didn't like the people of Tachá, but I guess seeing it with my own eyes is a totally different experience. Why are they like that?"

I shrugged, not allowing the behavior to affect me. I was the Queen of Tachá, a Huntress of the North, wife of Ragnar Varggson. I feared nothing and no one.

"They believe what they want to believe," I said simply. "If their king has told them that Ragnar is a beast, warring just for the sake of bloodshed, that his men are almost as bloodthirsty as he is, and that his Queen is *just* as vicious, let them. Let them believe what they want. It doesn't change the fact that it's a lie. We are gentle folk, *but* we will fight to the bloody death to protect ours."

Mikhail was quiet, nodding softly as I patted his back. "I apologize for speaking so sharply to you earlier. It was for your protection. We were being overheard by more than a few ears."

He stayed quiet, his brow furrowed as if in deep thought, and as we walked, a wagon approached from behind us with a few horses tied behind it with a rider. Straying to the side of the road to allow it to pass us by, I glanced up at the wagon and a flicker of recognition drew my eyes to the rider. A tall, blonde wood elf gave a grin as he pulled the steed to the side of the road and hopped off the wagon.

"Leo!" I called brightly, looking around for his companion, Freya. "How nice to see a friendly face! Is Freya with you?"

"Right behind you," she said brightly, giggling as she startled Mikhail. "I'm sure it goes without saying that we're the only friendly faces you've come across since the Wall, yes?"

"Yes, indeed. This is Mikhail, he's...a student from the College in Enguard. We're traveling together-"

"For *his* safety, I'm sure," Freya said again with a wicked laugh as she turned to Mikhail. "How long did you last in Tachá's icy grasp?"

"It wasn't that bad," he lied, a flushed heat creeping into his face. "I just..."

"It's okay, kid," Leo said with a sympathetic grin, "good on you. We never left the road or the cities because of the stories. If you ventured into the Frozen Wilds on purpose, then you've got some serious bravery in you."

"Or stupidity," Freya added, receiving a smack in her shoulder from Leo. "Sorry."

Leo patted Mikhail's shoulder, and as he did, his bracer snagged the hood of Mikhail's cloak. As the thin hood was pulled down, Mikhail scrambled to cover his horns, flushing with shame. As Leo saw the horns, shining in the bright sunlight, he moved Freya behind him protectively and rested a hand on the hilt of his sword. Mikhail's head dropped, and my heart sank. This was not the first time someone had reacted like this to him. Freya looked not at Leo, nor Mikhail, but her eyes were locked on mine. Reading me as easily as a book, she stepped between her companion and Mikhail.

"Forgive us," she said gently to the boy, a tone I hadn't heard from her. "We assumed the worst of you. I'm sorry. We're not going to hurt you."

Leo visibly relaxed and extended his hand, the one that had previously rested on his sword, ready to draw, and shook Mikhail's hand.

"Old haunts," he said, "we've run into a handful of Cursed Ones that *really* went to the dark parts of magic. They're pretty savage when they want to be."

"I'm not like that, though," Mikhail said, defeated and sullen. "I've never hurt anyone, and I don't want to! I've-I've never even used my sword before!"

"It's okay," Freya soothed, "we believe you. You don't have to be scared of us, we're not going to let anything happen to you. Do you know how this happened to you?"

Mikhail gave a little nod. "I know how it happens."

"And you know it's not your fault," I added.

Visibly uncomfortable, Mikhail nodded and stared at his feet, his jaw clenched as his chin trembled, the threat of tears close.

"Alright, glad we cleared that up," I said, redirecting the conversation away from poor Mikhail, "what brings you two back south again?"

"More refugees," Leo answered, his eyes softened to the young man beside him, "as more of the Thyuland folk hear the stories of what's happening, the faster they want out. They're paying us treasure troves and it's easy gold in the pockets."

"If you'd care for a few more pieces, would you be

willing to purchase a couple horses for us? No one will sell to us, no matter how much we offer."

"Well I shouldn't be surprised," Freya snorted. "You look *just like* the textbook Tacháan woman, you know. All you need is fur sticking out of your armor!"

"She just removed that last night, actually," Mikhail said with a chuckle.

Freya chortled and Mikhail's mood improved once the target of conversation was off of him and his appearance.

"Take *our* horses, we'll toss our packs in the wagon and use your gold to buy new. It would be an honor to serve you."

He bowed to me, and I knew that my secret had been relayed. I returned the bow and held out my hand. He shook it and beamed. Freya sidled up beside him and shot me a wink with her surprisingly respectful bow. Leo gave a sharp whistle and the horses perked up, shaking out their manes and stamping their hooves in the dirt.

"I thank you for your horses *and* your discretion," I added softly as Mikhail turned away to pick out a horse.

"The boy doesn't know who you are, does he?" Freya said quietly. "Is that for your protection or his? Why are you out here without an entire army to protect you?"

"I have business to attend to in Enguard. Hopefully someone there will have the answers I seek."

"But to what end?" Leo asked. "What could make you leave your duties? Your king?"

"Your husband," Freya added, searching my face with furrowed brows as she cocked her head. "Why, though? Leo, what was the only thing that made you leave my side when we were in that infected city out east? That city with the contamination?"

"You mean when you were in danger of *literally* dying in my arms if I didn't leave?" Leo asked dryly. "Why do you ask? You were contaminated and you needed a healing draught. I went to go find it."

"Did you want to leave me?" she asked.

Leo scoffed. "No, it nearly killed me to leave you, even though you were with Soren and Bo, I still didn't want to leave you. But I did, and I got back to you, just in the nick of time, too."

Freya looked at me, searching my eyes and offering a sad smile as she patted my hand. She understood why I had left, not the specifics, but she knew.

"Whatever we can do to help, please," she pledged to me quietly. "We will always come to the aid of the Wolf Queen of Tachá."

I thanked her and Leo, and gave them a pouch of a hundred gold and a small bag of precious gemstones worth much more. I had plenty and I didn't foresee being able to spend much in Thyuland. They headed to the wagon, and in a practiced, fluid motion, Leo grabbed Freya's hands and she sailed through the air, landing like a cat in the wagon. Leo climbed into the driver's seat next to his companion and kissed her as the wagon lurched forward. Mikhail sighed as they disappeared and waited while I mounted the chestnut colored mare.

"Lucky running into some friends of yours," Mikhail said, "but you know that you paid way too much for the horses, right?"

"I paid normal price," I said, "the rest was theirs to do what they will. Let's keep moving."

We rode in a comfortable silence and soon our horses fell in step with each other, the rhythmic clopping of hooves making me drowsy. We rode through the sun's rotation, and I tossed Mikhail a chunk of dried beef and an apple.

"If we're lucky, we'll reach Haverdale in a couple days," I said between bites, "I don't think we'll have much luck staying in an actual inn tonight, but the skies are clear in case we sleep outside again."

"Is it safe?" Mikhail asked. "Sleeping outside?"

"Probably safer than sleeping in a tavern owned by a bunch of hateful high elves," I shrugged. "Either way, we sleep with our blades close by again."

"*Again?*" he stammered. "You-you sleep with your swords?"

"I sleep armed well enough that three weapons are always within reach. You should, too. Cowards attack those who are sleeping, and they don't fight fair."

"That's awful," he murmured as I agreed with a nod.

By dusk we could see the firelight of a small town ahead, and as we approached the gates, I pulled my horse to a stop. Thick woods surrounded us on either side, and though we could both see in the dark, something still felt...off.

"Do you want to risk going through this town?" Mikhail asked after a moment. "What could happen? What if someone tries to fight us?"

I bit my lip. It wasn't the fighting I worried about, it was the rare chance that someone was going to see me and not only recognize the Tacháan color of my armor, but see my face and somehow know that I was the Queen. As I considered how to weigh my options, Mikhail inhaled, sniffing the air.

"Do you smell that?" he asked. "Like...something died nearby? Ugh, it's awful!"

I glanced at Kona and realized her eyes were locked

on something in the shadows, something my half-elf eyes couldn't even register in the night. I spoke her name and she didn't respond. A deep, threatening growl rumbled from her throat and I dismounted my horse, nocking an arrow into my readied bow.

"Where is it?" I asked her.

Her teeth seemed to glow in the night as a small section of the treeline shifted.

"Mikhail, take my horse and get back. Don't let the horses bolt, okay?" I ordered.

Like an explosion, a trio of ghouls rushed from the trees, their slavering maws dripping with foamy saliva. I drew back my bowstring, anchored it on my cheek, and focused my shot, landing an arrow into the chest of one of the creatures. The force of the blow knocked it back and it lost its footing, tumbling over as another of my arrows sank into its shoulder.

"Finish it, Kona," I commanded as she rushed towards it, dodging the claws of another ghoul as she passed it by.

I dropped my bow and gripped the hilts of my swords as the two remaining ghouls reached me. Dodging a swipe, I raked my blades into the throat of the monster as the other crawled behind me. I felt the claws drag against my armor, slashing my sword against it as its roar was cut off mid-screech. I whirled around and severed the remaining rotted flesh as the ghoul's head rolled away toward Mikhail. I landed a kick to its chest and heard bones crack. In the distance, Kona tore out the throat of the ghoul with my arrows lodged deep in it. Burying my sword into the head of the ghoul in front of me, it twitched violently and fell down flat in front of me. I severed its head for good measure, and turned to Mikhail.

"Are you okay?" I asked as he nodded in response. "Good, bring me a tinderbox and the flint, please."

Kona dragged a dead ghoul by its leg, puncture marks from her fangs dotting its entire corpse, and I piled the corpses on top of each other as Mikhail offered the box with a shaky hand. My hands were slippery with the saliva and blood of the undead, and I struggled to open the box. Mikhail waved his hands over me and the slimy residue vanished. I thanked him, pulled my arrows free from the shredded ghoul, and lit a small ball of dried grass, tossing it on the pile of decayed corpses. Igniting immediately, black smoke curled upward, disappearing into the night sky, and the acrid smell of burnt death filled our noses. Mounting our horses, we trotted away, hoping that the scent wouldn't attract more.

"Where did those things come from?" Mikhail asked as we traveled along the road.

"Probably a shallow grave in the woods," I said with a shrug. "Ghouls aren't made from the corpses of those with good intentions. We did the city a favor by burning them, too."

"Would they have come back?"

"No, but the scent may have attracted more, or something worse."

"You didn't even get a scratch on you, though," Mikhail marveled "Kona did well, too! Have you fought many of those...ghouls before?"

"Yes and no," I replied, digging in my memories of the Guild's smaller jobs from my younger years. "Ghoul packs were trivial in my guild, so the pups, I mean, the new recruits, would be assigned to take out smaller groups of ghouls when they popped up. I didn't have Kona then, so it was usually me, high up in a tree, firing off flaming arrows while the ghouls tried to climb the trees to get me."

"Did they ever get close?"

I grinned and nodded. "Once or twice, but I got better."

We rode onward through the night, bypassing a few little towns along the road, and I regaled him with tales of my first jobs as a pup of the Tacháan Hunter's Guild. I realized quickly that Mikhail had no hands-on experience dealing with these creatures, only an impressive amount of book-sense, and wondered why his college instructors had turned him loose into such a dangerous country as Tachá. Surely they had known he wouldn't have survived long without someone intervening. Or had they? Had they sent him to die in a frozen wilderness?

CHAPTER 15
THE RAGING WOLF OF WAR

We walked on and on and Kona panted heavily while sweat gathered on my forehead.

"We'll find lodgings soon, and we'll figure out how to cool you both down," Mikhail assured us. "You both look miserable."

I wiped the sweat from my forehead and trekked on with a nod. The sun was beginning to set, and the temperature and humidity lessened, but not by much. We came across a small town with a tavern, and as we stepped inside, we were stopped immediately.

"No beasts," the tavernkeeper said, turning up his nose as high as his pointed ears. "Outside with 'om."

A shiver crawled up my spine as I cast my eyes around the room full of elves that stared at us in disgust, as if we'd offended them in the moments we'd been inside.

"My wolf will stay outside. Is there a stable nearby?"

The high elf turned to me, his chin long and sharp and his eyes narrowed as he grimaced.

"*You*, Tacháan she-wolf," he sneered, "*you* are the beast. I do not allow beasts within my establishment."

I paled and then flushed, embarrassed and suddenly keenly aware of the armed elven men in the room. Mikhail held a hand up, a peaceful gesture, and rested it on the bartop as he shared a forced laugh.

"Please, gentle sir," he said, "she is my companion and we have traveled far. Lodgings for the night are the only thing we seek-"

"Keep seeking. The she-wolf is not welcome here," he snarled, reaching under the counter. "Soon, you will not be either."

I grabbed Mikhail's arm and pulled him toward the door as a pair of men emerged from the back, failing to conceal long knives beneath bar rags.

"We need to leave," I urged quietly in his ear. "*Now.*"

Outside the tavern, I wiped my boots on the doorstep and spat in the dirt. I led Mikhail back toward the road and we continued on the road as dusk grew to night. I buried the emotions that were fluttering around my throat, begging to escape in a scream of fury and injustice, swallowing hard instead. The insects of the night woke and sang loudly, trilling in my ears.

"Hey, Val, wait a minute!" Mikhail cried out as we stopped. "That's not right! They can't turn us away just because you're Tacháan! That's completely asinine! They didn't even know about *me*! I can understand that they would turn *me* away, but *you*?"

"It's his place of business that he can do as he wishes," I said through a clenched jaw. "It's not the first time I've been treated that way, though that's the first time as a Tacháan. We'll camp in a grove, come on."

"Wait, *outside*?" he balked. "No way, we can't camp outside, we'll get eaten!"

"Potentially eaten by a beast or certainly stabbed in our sleep, which would you prefer?" I said as I whirled around to face him. "Those elves are not happy that a Tacháan is walking on their soil and I have a feeling I will not be welcome at any inn we happen upon. I'm very surprised that you're shocked by this, you being so differently regarded in an elven world."

"Who ever said I was shocked?"

I shrugged, "I just assumed. You have every reason to be expectant of cruelty and unjust treatment, but your kindness exceeds that of most Cursed Ones I've encountered."

"Yeah, I get that," he said as we left the safety of the road toward a wide clearing. "I sometimes think my father would have been more accepting if I'd just gone along with the whole evil-cursed thing, but I didn't think that my mother would have liked that."

"That's awful, he sounds like a monster," I said as we reached a small clearing, safe for slumber. "I'm glad that you're focusing on your mother's kindness and mercy that runs through your veins, and thankfully not your father's hatred and disdain."

We gathered a handful of sticks and logs for a small fire and I filled my pockets with dried moss and grasses for the kindling. Spreading our bedrolls around the space I cleared for a campfire, Mikhail watched as I struck the tinder twice, creating a thin plume of smoke. I spied the flame and gently blew, cupping my hands around it protectively. It grew and I nestled it inside the dried sticks, and in a matter of seconds we had a roaring fire. I turned to Kona and gave her a smile.

"Find a rabbit," I told her.

She recognized the words and took off into the woods, disappearing in the greenery.

"Will she?"

"Oh, yes. It'll take her a moment to find the scent in such a different world, but she'll find us a coney or two. While we wait, you and I can find fresh water."

We found a creek of clear, moving water, and I filled my two waterskins. Digging in the bottom of my bag, I pulled out a small pot and filled it with water to boil over the fire. Kona came trotting out of the woods with a rabbit clamped in her mouth, her eyes bright with hunt. I took it from her and as it wriggled, trying to escape its fate, Mikhail exclaimed.

"She didn't kill it?" he exclaimed. "How did she not kill it?"

"Because a Tacháan wolf knows that once blood has been spilled, it clings to the life-taker and the scent will spread. Once the scent of blood permeates the air, things are much more difficult to hunt. If she were to pierce the rabbit's skin, the scent of its blood would alert every animal in the area and they would flee."

I took the rabbit and killed it with a quick snap to its neck as Mikhail watched curiously.

"Have you ever done this before?" I asked quietly as I removed the head from the body, setting it aside and having the two forefeet join it.

Mikhail shook his head slowly, his eyes locked on the rabbit's head.

"We...we had people to do that for us," he stammered. "Cooks, hunters, the like."

"Come sit next to me and I'll explain to you what I'm

doing, then, if Kona comes with another you can try your hand at some of it."

He sat studiously and drank in every word as I explained the skinning process, how to remove a rabbit's pelt in one piece, how much pressure was needed, and how deep to cut. He grew slack-jawed and green as I split the coney's breast and removed the innards, and I pretended to be oblivious to it. I couldn't recall the first game I'd killed and dressed, but I knew I had most likely been sick while doing it, so I wasn't about to shame him for it.

"Do you know about the plant life around here? Are there any wild roots or tubers nearby?" I asked as he perked up.

"Oh yes, yes, I'll find something to boil with the meat!" he exclaimed, creating a soft ball of light that glowed from a small rock in his hand as he dashed into the woods.

I smiled and finished preparing the meat, and a wave of longing for my husband washed over me without any warning. I sat in the grass as the water came to a rolling boil and looked up at the stars. The same constellations glittered down at me as those in the night skies of Tachá, and despite my attempts to blink away tears, they rolled down my cheeks as I yearned for the embrace of Ragnar. I hid my head in my hands as the aching refused to cease, and after a moment, a cold nose bumped my arm. Kona had returned without another rabbit, but she had been brought back to me by my unconscious call. She laid beside me and rested her head on my bent knees, and I dropped my head as I wiped away the tears.

"We'll go home as soon as I figure this out," I whispered to her. "I'd rather we not have left in the first place, but I just can't take the chance of hurting him. I wish he could understand it all."

Kona stayed as silent as the night, and a glow came from the treeline beside us a few moments later. Emerging victorious, Mikhail presented his arms of leafy greens, thin potato-like tubers, and a couple of thick carrots. He cleaned them and chopped them, tossing them into the pot with the meat, and stirred it all around. We ate in a hushed silence, appreciating the chorus of crickets around us. I enjoyed sleeping under the stars, the safety and reassurance of my blades within reach and my wolf at my feet, Mikhail tossed and turned on his bedroll, and I counted the stars until I slept.

WE WOKE WITH THE SUN, gathered our camp and doused the embers of the fire, and continued south on the road. It was silent for roughly half of a mile.

"May I pick your mind regarding a few of the creatures I encountered in Tachá?" Mikhail blurted, as if his self-control had fizzled out.

"Of course, I'll do my best to answer your questions. Go ahead."

"I came across tales of a hybrid creature of sorts," he said, "travelers claim it had the feathered head of an unnaturally large owl, big eyes and a sharp beak, and the body-*and temperament*! of a massive bear. Have you heard of this creature?"

"Yes, and you should have, as well. We call them Uglabjorn, they're very common around the world. In fact, they favor the climate here more than my homelands. In Tachá, they have acclimated to the cold and snow, growing their feathers and fur thick and white for camouflage. They're easy enough to track and kill, but unless they're preparing for the colder, longer winters, they'll leave you alone if you show it fire and fearlessness. The yeti are not so docile."

"I beg your pardon, the *yeti*?" he stammered, nearly tripping over a rut embedded in the road from a heavy wagon wheel.

"Oh, yes," I explained, recalling my encounter with the yeti back home before finding the Hunter's Guild again. "Experts in camouflage, stalking, and the art of surprise, a yeti pack will follow you back to your camp and eat you before your traveling companions wake up."

"I don't think I'm equipped for the wilds of Tachá," he muttered softly.

I patted his shoulder and grinned. "You're just new to her secrets. You never should have been allowed to traverse the wilderness alone, though. I'm very surprised your superiors allowed it."

"They encouraged it, actually," he said, downcast and doubtful. "They said it wasn't as bad as the Northerners claimed; that the Tacháans said it was so rough and wild to keep everyone else out."

"And your thoughts on that?"

Mikhail shook his head. "King Ragnar has always allowed refugees in, right? Why would he do that if it was so uninhabitable?"

"He has stated very plainly, '*Tachá is a land of plenty, a land of safety to those who can survive her cold.*' Any refugees that come in are always welcome with open arms. They are expected to work, eat, and live alongside us Tacháans. Tachá is a mother to many, regardless of her children's birthplaces."

"That's honorable of him. He doesn't seem so eloquent, though. From what we hear in Thyuland, he is a raging wolf of war. If the rumors are true of him, I struggle to see him give such an elegant speech of homecoming and acceptance. Does he have a Queen?"

I carefully considered myself and the words I would speak next. I couldn't give away who I was, it was bad enough that the halfling woman, Freya, had figured me out so quickly, but I was positive that she'd simply guessed right, and my shock had given her confirmation.

"He does have a Queen," I said truthfully, shifting the subject a little. "Did you know that customarily, in Tachá, it is tradition for the women to govern and rule in lieu of their husbands? Would you like to take a guess as to why?"

He seemed surprised and I grinned as he sputtered for reasoning. He let his arms fall, slapping his sides as he laughed.

"It's so contrary to Thyuland," he exclaimed. "King Rofellos rules with an iron fist, his Queen is rarely ever seen, much less asked her opinion of matters of the kingdom. Please, tell me why are the Tacháans this way?"

"Because we view the traditional roles a little differently. The men of Tachá traditionally go to war without hesitation, including the king. *Especially* the king," I said with a smirk. "So, with the men away to war, the women cannot be expected to simply pick up where they left off without a moment's notice. However, if the women *and* the men had equal say in matters of politics, war, and the like, both would be equally as educated, capable, and trustworthy to make decisions for the best of Tachá's people. So while the king gets to be a, how did you put it... a *raging wolf of war*? He'd appreciate that sentiment, by the way. His Queen leads the people, with the full trust and power of Tachá."

"So...correct me if I'm wrong, but...is the Queen more powerful than her King?"

I laughed brightly, never having looked at my position that way.

"Technically, yes, but Ragnar and his Queen are very similar, yet very different. She was not born royal, which gives her an advantage in dealing with her very stubborn husband...or so I've heard."

As the sun rose to its highest peak, we continued, finally pausing at a crossroads at dusk. One lonely inn sat at the corner, and my coin was accepted. As we took our rooms, I peeked out the window and saw Kona's bright white fur seemingly glowing in the dark, breathing a little easier knowing she was safe in the stables, even if I did have to pay a little extra. I removed all of my armor, wiped the sweat off my forehead, and began the arduous process of removing the fur lining from the pieces. It took upwards of an hour or two to do it right, but soon the furs were tucked carefully into the bottom of my bag and my head finally settled onto a goose-down pillow.

CHAPTER 16

WHISPERS IN THE SILENT GROVE

We woke to birdsong from our made campsite and continued riding almost immediately, entering a thick forest as a much-needed shortcut. Surrounded on both sides by overhanging trees, shrouded with green and brown mottled vines, the trail became too narrow to ride side by side on, and I took point as we continued. Kona weaved her way ahead of me and trotted ahead, her bright white fur keeping her in my eyesight. Peering deep into the woods, I noticed birds of all kinds, some I could recognize and others I depended on Mikhail to identify for me. As his confidence grew, the hood of his cloak fell back and stayed pooled around his shoulders. Mikhail was incredibly intelligent, able to not only tell me what kind of bird had flown in front of me, but also which song belonged to each, if it was endangered, common, or if it was magically adept. He was a walking fount of knowledge, like I had never seen.

"Where did you learn all of this?" I asked after he had educated me about the seventh different bird species.

"Well, I had to do something to stay out of my

father's way," he said dully. "I wasn't good at holding a sword, I'm decent at spellcasting, but he didn't view that in a way that wasn't because I'm Cursed. The art of learning everything I could became my passion. Every day I committed to learning and fully understanding something new. I couldn't best my brothers or sisters with anything but my mind, and I wanted to be the best. I needed to be."

"What did your father say?"

Mikhail hesitated, as if shame had filled his throat. "He said he couldn't see the point of having a son unable to defend himself with a mind that couldn't even harness Elven magic. He gave me an ultimatum. Become worthy of his surname or he would banish me. I left the next morning."

"How long have you been gone?"

"It'll be four years in two weeks and three days."

"I'm sorry."

He gave a shrug and pointed to a small red bird, its tail plumage almost iridescent and almost pulsating a bright red glow, nearly as long as my sword's blade. "That one is incredibly dangerous. You can tell by the tail and the way it's so brightly hued, but it is famed for its ability to mimic the human voice. They'd be great companions if the oils from its feathers didn't melt your skin off."

I took note of the stunningly beautiful bird and Mikhail continued pointing out to me the different species of birds, insects, and small creatures. The trail thinned more, with intermittent patches of grass and tree roots crossing our path, and we carefully continued, especially wary after one of the tree roots seemed to move as we neared. Kona stayed next to me, and as the overhanging boughs sank lower and lower, we were forced to continue on foot, leading our horses through the trail's faded, almost indiscernible path.

"Do you know where you're going?" Mikhail called, stepping over a root.

"Yes, Mikhail, just follow me and don't stray off my path, okay?" I answered, an intuitive urgency to get out of this forest as quickly as possible rearing in my mind. "We need to keep moving."

A thick vine crossed the path, too thick and awkwardly placed to lead the mare around. I took out my sword and sliced deep into it as it thrashed wildly, spurting greenish black goo from the wound.

Mikhail shouted and the horses screamed, and as I turned to him, a thick green vine curled around his waist and began to lift him up off the ground. He beat at it with his fists and as I ran toward him, from the corner of my eye, I saw another thick vine shoot out towards me. Slashing at it with my blade, I managed to cut into it, but it simply retreated and sent another, this time with yet another aimed for my swordhand.

"It's an Engulfer!" Mikhail cried, the panic in his voice clear as birdsong. "We're going to die!"

"We're not going to die," I growled, focusing on my target. "What do you know about it? Tell me everything!"

The vines came from one location, I assumed that was the body of the Engulfer, and two shot out toward me, one connecting hard with my stomach as I lost my breath and the other took my feet from under me. I rolled away, narrowly missing its impact as it slammed vines bearing three inch long thorns into the ground where I had been only a split second earlier. I screamed Mikhail's name and he stammered over his words.

"Engulfers are made of angry forestry," he shouted. "The carving out of the trail through the forest probably birthed it! Its only focus is to grow and absorb any who would bring harm to the forest. It consumes its prey by absorbing it into its body and dissolving it with botanical acids. People don't survive these, Val. We're gonna die here!"

"Oh, like hell we are," I growled, calling for my white wolf.

Kona snarled as she bit through the vines that had restrained my wrists, and as she shook them violently, the entire forest seemed to shudder. Willing the magic I possessed into my blade, I struck the vine against the ground and thorny vines of my own burst from the ground, ensnaring the vines and burying the thorns deep into it. Unable to retract its vines without shredding it against my magical entrapment, the body shifted into full view. It towered over me, and a mass of small, glittery eyes shined from its center near an oddly shaped beak of a mouth. Freeing myself from the grasping vines, I rushed to rescue Mikhail and found Kona already tearing at the vines, spitting out the remnants. With a few well-placed slashes, I was able to cut Mikhail loose.

"Get the tinderbox, get some oil, get *anything* we can use to burn this thing," I ordered, watching him take off his pack and dig frantically inside of it.

"Here, here, use this!" he shouted, holding out a small scroll, tied with a piece of singed twine. "Open it, read it, and do what it says!"

"I'm not a wizard," I snarled, swinging at an approaching vine near Mikhail's throat. "I don't know that kind of magic!"

"You don't have to! Just *read* it and do what it tells you!" he screamed back, ducking from a shooting vine.

I pulled the singed twine off with my teeth, unfurling the small scroll with haste. Written in small, intricate script, the words told me to simply speak my request at my intended target. I locked my gaze onto the Engulfer and snarled a simple phrase, putting my intention of burning this thing to ashes into my native tongue.

"*Brenna bál!*"

Fire erupted from the beak of the Engulfer and quickly spread down every vine, flames licking and biting as it screeched and screamed. I grabbed Mikhail by his collar and pulled him past the writhing mass of fiery tendrils, Kona was close on my heels as we followed the hoofprints in the soil. The acrid stench rose as the squealing stopped, and the air in the forest seemed to lift as the sun peeked through the leaves of the trees. We found the horses in a sunny meadow, drinking from a small creek.

"What was that about dying?" I asked Mikhail playfully.

He grinned and shook his head. "I really thought we were going to," he said breathlessly. "Never been so glad to be wrong."

We drank deeply at the creek with our horses, Kona lapped up water, rolled in the long grass, and chased a small rodent playfully. She returned, crunching the remains of whatever she caught, and I checked her for injuries. With no injuries on any of us, we mounted our horses again and I turned in my saddle to lock eyes with Mikhail.

"We're on the last leg of the journey before Haverdale," I said, "we have a good long road ahead of us but I think we need to just get there as soon as possible. We'll spend at least two days and rest up before heading to Enguard."

"I agree," Mikhail admitted. "Maybe we can stick to the road, too? Where the ghouls and Engulfers don't traipse?"

I laughed and pulled the reins to the southwest, where I knew the road lay. "Sure. Also, what's the story behind that scroll?"

Mikhail raised a brow and I blinked hard. Our horses climbed the small incline to the road and dust formed around their hooves.

"You had a magical scroll in your bag that just so happened to be exactly what we needed? Did you steal it? Mikhail, explain," I demanded. "From the start, don't miss a detail. Where did you get that?"

"Get it? No, I made it. I crafted it and a few others like it, on my travels up here."

"I don't understand," I stammered, pinching the bridge of my nose as I tried to maintain my patience. "Can you talk me through the process?"

"Sort of," he said with a shrug. "For my basic scrolls, I just weaved the magic into the paper, carefully so it doesn't ignite, and then I just imbue whatever components I need into the ink, and I roll it up...and there it is. Unroll, read, and boom. Don't you have teachers like that up in the North?"

"We do, they're very well-educated and good at what they craft, but my question is how you knew to select *that* scroll, Mikhail. Why that specific scroll?"

He fell silent and after a moment, sighed and slapped his legs.

"I don't know," he said after a moment. "I dug in my

bag and knew that if I didn't get exactly the right one, we'd die. I didn't want to face my gods with your blood on my hands."

"Well, I don't know what kind of magic that was, but I'm very grateful for it," I said earnestly. "Thank you, Mikhail."

He gave an awkward smile and I realized that he had not been on the receiving end of gratitude in a very long time, if ever. We rode quietly for a while until dusk had settled around us. In the distance to the east, a small town lay protected by a grove of trees, shrubbery, and intermittent torchlight. Surrounded by a quiet hush amid the intermittent sound of crickets, I pulled the hood of my cloak up as a hooded figure waited patiently for us at the path.

"Please, if you're looking for lodging, we have vacancies," he said with a deep bow and a pleasant smile. "If you would, just follow the winding path into the heart of the grove. You'll find a stable for your horse, a meal for your bellies, and a pillow for your heads."

"That would be very refreshing," I replied, "your generosity is very appreciated."

Mikhail and I followed the simple directions the man provided, Kona trotted beside me. Luck was on my side as a shower of cool rain fell from thick, heavy clouds above, ensuring my hood stayed covering my ears and we were met with a friendly wave under a lean-to that served as a makeshift stable.

"I'll care for your horses," a tall man called from the din of the rainfall, taking our horses as we dismounted and grabbed our gear. "You two go get dried off in the tavern and grab a hot meal. Tell Twyyla that I sent you in! Your wolf is free to join you, Northerner!"

I thanked him, appreciative of the kindness, and he waved us away, leading our horses to a rack full of hay. Kona stayed close and lifted her nose, catching the scent of roasting meat at the same time I did. We entered the tavern's main door, finding it warm, welcoming, and half-full, with about a dozen men and a few women at the moment. A thin, dark haired woman appeared from a doorway and smiled sweetly.

"The stablemaster said my companion could come in," I said politely. "We just need a night's stay."

"Your wolf is more than welcome, Lady of the North," she said, offering a polite bow. "Please, take a seat anywhere. You are most welcome here. Your hood obscures nothing from us, either, Mikhail, son of Lord Mistbrooke of Gray Tide. We see you, Cursed One."

Mikhail gasped softly and nodded, almost apologetically, sitting at the nearest table and watching the woman carefully. I sat across from him and Kona took her place at my feet underneath the table, a little cramped but probably more comfortable than the drenched outdoors. Mikhail was quiet, keeping his head down, and I cleared my throat.

"Well? What is it that's got you so quiet?" I asked as a plate full of warm bread and a dipping oil was set between us.

"How did they know me?" he murmured. "I don't know how they knew where you're from, either. I don't know if I trust these people. We should go."

"You need not be afraid," the dark-haired woman said, seeming to appear from nowhere. "If anyone is trusted to know your identity, it'd be us. But like I said, you're safe here."

"Where is here?" I asked.

"The Silent Grove. A place where whispers come to rest," she said with a knowing smile, "where secrets come to be buried, and where highly-sought figures come to sleep soundly."

"That's the most non-answer I've ever heard," Mikhail said through a mouthful of bread. "This oil is divine, though. Is this imbued with garlic and thyme?"

"My name is Twyyla," she said, inclining her head as she switched from the common tongue and spoke Nord-maarian, almost fluently. "I'm very pleased to make your acquaintance, my Lady. How does your traveling companion *not* know you are the Queen of the North?"

Mikhail's eyes glazed over a bit as they bounced from me to her and back again as he listened to the native language of the Tacháans, absently dipping his bread rind in the oil.

"He is safer with his ignorance," I replied smoothly, keeping my voice conversational in my native language. "How is it that you knew? I've been here for such a short time."

"My scouts reported the ashen remains of an Engulfer a ways north, and two riders headed south with a Tacháan wolf. One of the riders: a blonde woman in Tacháan blue. With the whispers of the runaway Queen, the missing Queen, or the devoured Queen, it wasn't difficult to put two and two together."

"The devoured Queen? What, are there rumors that Lady swallowed me whole?" I said, failing to hide my irritation as little as it was.

Twyyla chuckled and gave a shrug. "Rumors are rumors, whispers are whispers, but truth lies in them all, no matter how small."

"I suppose," I said quietly. "But for right now, the

truth is that we need rest for the night. Enguard is my destination, we're hoping that someone will have answers to the questions I have."

Twyyla paled slightly and shook her head. "Avoid Enguard, Highness. Danger lies in wait for you."

"Why do you think that?"

In the common tongue, she spoke slowly, carefully, as if picking her words from a den of vipers.

"There are...some...in Enguard who would see you fail," she whispered.

"Who knows my quest?" I asked quietly.

"Very, very few. Those who would see you fail are those who have set this path in motion. They have carved it into the very stone of the earth. I fear it cannot be undone. The power that is held by them is greatly feared by all."

"Who are they?"

"That's just it, I don't know. I have a contact who *may* have more information," she said. "I suggest you go to him straight away."

"His name?"

"Mr. Winchester," she replied. "If he does not have the answers to the questions you seek, I fear none will."

CHAPTER 17
A ROYAL PROCLAMATION

The next morning, I broke bread with Mikhail, still sleepy with his hair in wild curls, and informed him of the details that Twyyla and I had shared. He was a little quieter than usual, and as we each took our leave, accepting small packages of wrapped breads, dried meats, and a small bottle of the oil sweetly gifted to Mikhail, I watched him, his focus far from the road in front of us as we quietly left the safety of the Silent Grove.

"So, who is Mr. Winchester?" Mikhail asked as we rode.

"I don't know," I admitted, "but I was told by someone I trust entirely to see him and Twyyla said to see him, too. He's supposed to have the answers I need."

"Maybe..." he trailed off, his mind far away again.

I caught glances of him as we continued toward Haverdale, and by the time the sun was beginning to set, casting our shadows far, he still wrestled with something unspoken.

"Mikhail," I said gently, "what's wrong?"

"Nothing, really," he said with a sheepish grin. "Just… well, I'm thinking about my father, that's all."

"Care to share?"

"Not really. No one needs to be downtrodden," he said with a sad smile.

"He'll come around," I reassured. "You're going to do great things, and I have a good gut feeling that you're going to make him very proud one day. Your mind is your strongest weapon, and you've trained it very well. Use it wisely and you'll make him proud. Opportunity will come, you just need to wait and be patient."

He murmured a quiet thanks and we continued in a silence that grew until shouts rose in the distance behind us. Kona turned and lowered her head, growling softly, and I pulled back on the reins, listening carefully. The hairs on the back of my neck stood up and Kona took a step backward.

"Get off the road," I commanded.

We quickly and quietly led our horses off the road and found cover behind a line of thick trees a distance away. As we let the horses graze, we watched as a group of eight dwarves rode past, yelling and laughing loudly.

"Where do you suppose they're going?" Mikhail asked in wonder.

"I'd rather not ask them," I replied. "The faster we get to Haverdale the better, at this rate. Who knows who else is on this road."

After a few moments, allowing the horses to nibble up the rest of the sweet clover patch, we resumed our journey, reaching the edge of Haverdale as the last light left the sky. The tall wooden walls of Haverdale were dotted with armed sentries, strolling from tower to tower, and as we approached, the gatekeeper opened the small window as the guards watched carefully from above.

"My companion and I seek lodging for the night," I said clearly. "We're passing through to Enguard tomorrow."

His brow furrowed with a muddled confusion.

"Not going to Gray Tide with the others, eh?"

"No, sir, our business lies elsewhere," I replied politely, curious about his assumption.

"Alright, then," he said, closing the window and signaling to someone hidden behind the gate. "Best of luck finding a bed. Stables are available if nothing else is."

The gates creaked open, pulled by two strong men and a series of pulleys, and we rode inside with Kona close by. We reached the biggest inn and as we tied our horses and opened the door, a room packed with well-dressed high elves looked down their noses at us.

"No room for you, blood traitors," someone barked from the dimly lit corner. "Be gone from our sight!"

As they started throwing food and drinks still in flagons toward us, we hastily left, narrowly escaping. The next tavern a few blocks further into the town was met with similar greetings, and I glanced at Mikhail as we approached the third.

"If someone throws something at us in here, I'm throwing it back," I warned. "I'd like you to stay with the horses in case it goes sideways, okay?"

Mikhail nodded and breathed a heavy sigh of relief as he tugged his hood up and over his horns. He held the reins tightly as Kona followed me toward the wooden door of the inn. I could already hear the raucous laughter and shouts from the other side of the entrance. Bracing for impact, I opened the door and slipped inside, my eyes scanning the room for flying tableware.

"Sorry about the noise," the barkeep half-shouted from the bar. "Need a room?"

I nodded and held up two fingers; he shouted and mimed that only one was available, and I accepted it with a nod. Handing me a key, he pointed at the stairs in the back of the room and leaned over the counter.

"Last room on the left!" he shouted over the din.

"Thank you," I said, nearly shouting in the man's face as I waved my hand around. "What's going on here? Why is everyone so loud and...drunk?"

The man laughed. "You've not been around many dwarves, have you?"

I shook my head and scanned the room, finding it mostly full of heavily bearded dwarves carrying flagons, flasks, and in the rear of the room, I saw a dwarf drinking heartily from a wooden bucket. I thanked the man again and headed out to retrieve Mikhail and Kona.

"Keep your hood up and your head down," I instructed, "and stay close."

Navigating through the sea of dwarves on the right side and a band of men, elves, and a few halflings and gnomes mixed in, we managed to weave our way to the stairs. Mikhail paused halfway up the stairs and squinted at something or someone across the room. I urged him to keep going, eager to not draw any suspicion, and we reached the room without interruption. The room held one bed, and Mikhail stammered as his eyes darted from the lone bed to me.

"Absolutely not," I said. "I'm sleeping on the floor next to the door in case anyone tries anything funny. Take the bed or Kona will."

I made a makeshift bed out of my bedroll and the pillow I stole from under Mikhail's head, and lay in front of the door itself with a dagger under my pillow and my sword within reach, nestled under my bedroll. Through the floorboards, the party grew louder and more raucous, until the laughs eventually turned into snarls and curses.

"Are we safe here?" Mikhail asked hesitantly.

"Better locked in here than down there in the middle of it," I said, drawing away from the door and tucking a chair under the knob as I reset my bedroll under the window, hidden in the shadows.

THE RAISED voices waxed and waned between anger and drunken merriment, and shortly before dawn arrived, I was able to sleep for a few hours. I left Mikhail to sleep and descended the stairs, finding a handful of dwarves and two of the halflings from last night bruised, beaten, and tired. Beside them, a small group of half-elves and round-eared men sat, all eating in comfortable silence. Their eyes all locked onto me as I came into view, and I took a seat at a table. A dark-haired woman wearing an apron around her thick waist brought me a small platter of meats, cheeses, and breads, inquiring if I wanted coffee, ale, or both. I requested both and she gave a nod as the eyes still watched me, unwavering. I swallowed a bite and raised my gaze, locking onto each of their eyes, slowly and directly as I silently challenged each one of them. One by one, they lowered their gazes into their drinks or plates, and after the last one averted his eyes, I returned to my breakfast. Mikhail descended the wooden stairs just as I was nearly finished mopping up the sausage juice with the crust of bread.

As he walked past the tables, a few of the dwarves spoke to each other in what I thought was Dwarvish, but soon I realized my knowledge of the Dwarven language must be severely limited. Mikhail sat across from me and accepted a plate and a mug from the woman, his eyes bright from his rest.

"Morning, Val," he said, tearing into the meat. "That was the best night's sleep I've gotten in a long time!"

"Uh-huh, sure," I said, ignoring the sharp pain that plagued my back from the hardwood floor and the mental fatigue from keeping watch for most of the night.

I was distracted enough by the frustration that the effortful years I'd spent learning to read, write, and speak the Dwarven language had apparently been for nothing, and Mikhail waved his hand in front of my face.

"Sorry," I murmured, "what is it?"

"*What is it?*" he repeated with astonishment. "I've *never* seen you distracted, not even a little!"

"Well, I consider myself...*well educated* when it comes to foreign languages," I said hesitantly, "but I'm wondering when I apparently stopped understanding Dwarvish."

Mikhail laughed brightly and shook his head. "It's not you, not at all. Basic Dwarvish is the standard of learning, but the regional dialects are for advanced students, usually the noble families or those who travel around the world. Those dwarves are speaking the Deephammer dialect. They reside in the deepest of the mines, where the dwarves have dug and mined further than any of their forefathers...well, they're not exactly social, being busy digging and all."

"Deephammer?" I murmured, astonished. "I thought that was a dead language."

"Most people think that," Mikhail said. "I have an affinity for dead or rare languages. The ones that are particularly difficult or rarely heard, I enjoy the mental challenge."

"You learn almost-dead languages...for the mere challenge of it?" I said quietly, gesturing discreetly toward the dwarves. "So you can tell me what they're saying?"

"Absolutely," he whispered. "They're discussing what drinks will be at the wedding, and if they'll be comparable to their homeland's meads."

"Whose wedding?"

He turned his head a little to listen and his brows raised as I waited impatiently. He gave a quiet, astonished laugh of disbelief and shook his head.

"That can't be true...hang on, stay here," he said suddenly, rising from the table and dashing to the wall.

I, and every other person in the room, watched curiously as he plucked an official-looking proclamation from a gold-painted nail and slowly scanned it before returning with it in his hand. Placing it in front of me, I read it carefully and kept my face neutral as thoughts raced through my mind. This wasn't just a wedding.

"Do you know what this means?" Mikhail whispered excitedly. "This isn't a mere wedding between two elvenfolk, Val! This is a giant, political power play!"

Impressed with Mikhail's sudden passionate explanations of the joining of two powerful, ancient families of Fareland, I listened patiently as he explained how intriguing the marriage of Prince Azran *Ra'zír* of Ibria, son of the Great Pharaoh Tekhmet, and the Princess Valeria Vael'Quinalis, youngest daughter of Rofellos, the Magnificent Elven King of Thyuland, truly was. When I asked why, he paused for a moment, as if waiting for the punchline.

"Val, everyone knows that Rofellos is a little...*preferential* toward the high elves," he said, choosing his words very carefully as we sat in the Thyuland inn. "This event is going to be in the history books, a political alliance and a moment where the intertwining of...wait, this is...Val, can we go? *Please?* Oh, this is a massive chapter in the history and sociopolitical climate of Fareland! Everyone is going to be there, I bet even this Mr. Winchester, too! If he's anything like you said, he'll be there, too. He wouldn't miss an event this huge."

"Why do you think that?"

"Because there are a lot of folk coming from the ends of the world, dragonborn from Ibria, probably some Tacháan royals, and I'm almost positive every single high elf in Thyuland will be in attendance. I wonder where it'll be held, they're going to need a massive temple," he said, trailing off in thought.

A small tendril of doubtfulness crept up my spine, clawing its way up to the forefront of my mind: something wasn't right. Rofellos was a proud highborn elf, his lineage untainted, vividly recalling the smug letter he had sent along with the wedding dress...before Ragnar had ripped it off my body. Why would he give his blessing for his youngest daughter to wed an Ibrian prince whose elven blood was mixed with the scales of a dragonborn? Despite my reservations about the wedding itself, with as much publicity as this was going to bring, it was foolish to think Mr. Winchester wouldn't be there.

"How far is it to Gray Tide?" I asked Mikhail, whose eyes lit up.

"It's a three-day ride," he said, already having the mileage worked out in his head. "It's only a couple hours to Enguard, *but*, if Mr. Winchester goes to Gray Tide, he may already be there and we would have to wait until he decided to come back. Depending on the lengthiness of the celebrations afterward, we could be waiting here for upwards of a month!"

"Then it's settled," I said with a heavy sigh. "We ride for Gray Tide."

CHAPTER 18

THE PRICE OF ACCEPTANCE

Mikhail

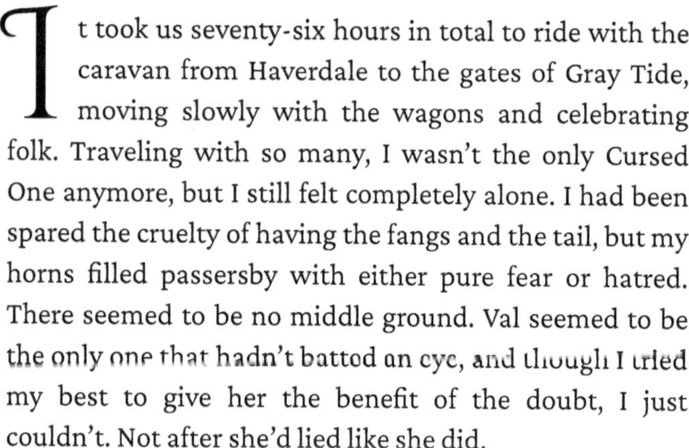

It took us seventy-six hours in total to ride with the caravan from Haverdale to the gates of Gray Tide, moving slowly with the wagons and celebrating folk. Traveling with so many, I wasn't the only Cursed One anymore, but I still felt completely alone. I had been spared the cruelty of having the fangs and the tail, but my horns filled passersby with either pure fear or hatred. There seemed to be no middle ground. Val seemed to be the only one that hadn't batted an eye, and though I tried my best to give her the benefit of the doubt, I just couldn't. Not after she'd lied like she did.

I supposed it wasn't her fault that she missed the fact that I understood Nordmaarian, perhaps not fluently, but maybe she was too distracted with her conversation with Twyyla to realize. As we rode into the city, the usually packed streets were overrun with people, making our horses panicked and restless. As we stabled them, I watched Val carefully as I pulled my hood up securely, her eyes scanning the crowds as if she were waiting, watching for someone specific. The knot that had formed in my gut had only grown since finding out that my traveling companion was the Wolf Queen herself. She had played the part of the Huntress, kind yet fierce, almost too well. I wouldn't have believed it if I hadn't heard it from her own lips. My father, my brothers, and even a few of the professors at the College had shared their stories of the Warlord and his vicious wife. Ragnar Varggson was formidable, without a doubt. The legendary stories transforming him into a beast that drank the blood of his enemies were greatly exaggerated. The stories of his wife, the Huntress-turned-Queen, were not as numerous as Ragnar's, but were always consistent in detail. I knew that she had been orphaned at a young age, shipped off to the Ironclaw Hunter's Guild of Tachá, risen through the ranks with her natural skill and determination, and had somehow caught the eye of the Tacháan king.

"Let's find a place to bed down for the night," Val said, almost shouting over the noise of the crowd around us.

I nodded and followed, nearly tripping over the wolf between us. As Val called out politely to move aside, her voice was drowned out and I scoffed to myself, wondering how far she could be pushed before the she-wolf bit back and drew blood. It was a long walk, closer and closer to my father's property, before we found lodging, a crowded tavern with non-elves. Val paid for the room and we headed upstairs almost immediately.

"I'm a little hungry," I lied, dropping my pack on my bed. "I'm going to head down and grab a bite to eat."

She nodded absently and I slipped out the door, heading down the stairs and maneuvering between the crowd until I was able to get to the door. Washed in warm sunshine, my shoulders dropped as the tension I'd been holding lifted. I turned north from the entrance and began walking, weaving between people, carts, animals, and wagons. The side streets were far less crowded, and I was glad of it. I knew those back alleys much better, aware of which ones held less-than-savory residents and which would be completely empty, and as memories of my bullied adolescent years returned, I held my head higher, knowing I was stronger than I had been before I left.

I hadn't lied to Val. My father had unofficially banished me from his sight until I became worthy to stand in his presence again. As a child, I had hoped the absence of my cursed horns would be enough, and as I had been caught stealing a small saw from the horsemaster, my father had laughed. *"You thought removing those things on the top of your head would make anyone forget what you really are?"* My heart had been crushed, and I knew that my father's acceptance would have to be earned with much more than that.

Today that would change. My future would never be the same, and my eagerness to please my father, to have him finally accept me as his son, had only grown. The street curved and I hopped through the grove of trees that sat between the common street and my family's private lane and began walking toward the house. Seated at the top of one of the hills of Gray Tide, Mistbrooke Manor overlooked the bustling city below and watched the rolling sea on the western coast. As the largest domicile in the city, my father had outfitted the manor with an elegance that rivaled King Rofellos' own, and as I approached the doors, a halfling emerged quietly, bowing her head as she spoke.

"The Master would like to see you immediately, my Lord," she said quietly, her face turned down to her feet as her straw-colored hair, tied on top of her head in a neat knot, wobbled.

Father had not allowed the servants to look upon the elves, and it had never sat right with me. Her eyes stared intently at my boots.

"What is your name?"

She jumped as I addressed her. "B-Belinda, my Lord."

"Thank you, Belinda. Is my father in his study?"

She nodded, stammering through her words and I thanked her. I pretended not to notice her flinch unconsciously as I held out a copper piece to her. She accepted it with wide eyes and fled. As the halfling vanished, I wondered absently if Val's halfling friend, Freya, knew who Val really was. I surmised not. If Freya knew that she was speaking with the Ice-Hearted Queen of Tachá, she probably wouldn't have been so informal to her, and neither did Leo know, by that calculation. Val must have some serious self-control not to rip them to shreds like the stories said.

My father's servants, half-elves that had accepted their place in his manor, stood outside his study, and blinked hard when they saw me, dropping their gaze instantly.

"Welcome back, my Lord," they said together, bowing as they ushered me into the room.

I gave a nod and stepped inside, my eyes resting on my father for the first time in so many years. He looked exactly the same, as if a day hadn't passed. I waited for him to give permission to approach, and after a few minutes, he folded his fingers together and raised his head.

"Approach."

I obeyed and bowed, using every ounce of my royal upbringing to prove that I hadn't forgotten myself on my time away.

"Father, I have come home with a gift for you," I said, clearing my throat and gathering my courage to look him in the eye.

"What could you possibly give me that I could not obtain myself?" he said with a sneer. "Your very presence is a curse. I should never have let you set foot in Grey Tide again."

I had hoped he had been watching for my return, and I fought to keep a smile off my face.

"Your servants have reported truly," I said carefully, choosing my words with wisdom. "Have they also reported the one who travels with me?"

"A woman in blue. You've picked up a Northern whore," he scoffed with utter disgust. "You dare to come into my presence when you've lowered yourself enough to share a bed with a dog! Be gone, you insolent-"

"I have brought you the Queen of Tachá, Father," I said firmly, standing tall. "She travels anonymously and believes I do not know her true identity. She believes I am her ally."

He was silent as he stared, boring into my eyes as if he were searching for deceit.

"Bring her to me. Unharmed," he growled slowly after a long moment of silence. "I would like to...have a *conversation* with the Wardog's bitch. If you deliver her to me, I will reconsider your status as my son."

I swallowed, fully aware that Val wasn't going to visit my home for dinner, especially with everything I'd said about my father to her. I'd do whatever it took to bring her home to Father, but I was no match for her if it came down to strength and agility. As if reading my mind, Father reached into his desk drawer and pulled out a tiny vial of pale pink liquid. He set it at the edge of his desk and I grasped it carefully, the thin glass cool to the touch.

"In her drink," Father said. "You'll have only a few minutes until the magic takes effect."

"Father, she's half-elf," I stammered, afraid of angering him. "She won't fall easily."

"Do you think I haven't taken that into consideration? Get out of my sight, and don't return empty-handed."

I RETURNED and found Val at a table, eating heartily with a group of halflings and half-elves, all bearing a silver brooch on their cloaks of two silver wolf heads, biting each side of the fabric. It seemed vaguely familiar, but I couldn't put my finger on it, not with my mission at hand. The conversation faded as the group departed and Val turned back to her meal, gesturing for me to sit.

"You've been gone a while," she said, her eyes holding no suspicion. "This is your hometown, right? You must have a lot of people to see and talk to here."

I nodded, wondering how I was going to pull this off, and took a deep breath. Clearing my mind, I focused on the first part. Val needed to drink. She currently had less than half of her ale left. As I mentally crafted a master plan, I absently nodded and participated in the menial conversation. Val was explaining who the group that had been around her was, but my focus was elsewhere.

I knew what I had to do.

"I'll grab another round for us," I offered, rising and heading toward the barmaid.

I held up two fingers to the woman and she nodded, filling two flagons to the top. With a swiftness that defied my trembling fingers, the vial was emptied into the flagon while the barmaid's back was turned, and grasping it in my left hand I returned to the table, actively drinking from the flagon in my right hand.

Val thanked me and drank deeply. We talked of the upcoming nuptials, playfully wagering a copper piece if the bride or groom fled from the temple. A shadow of doubt crept up my spine. *Surely this woman wasn't so horrific. Val wasn't dangerous to me, right?* My warring thoughts were interrupted when a bar fight broke out between two dwarves and five elves. As the fight drew close, Val drained her ale and dodged a thrown plate that shattered against the wall behind her.

"Should we leave?" I asked as she smiled, as if amused by the blows and blood.

"Not unless you want to. I won't allow you to be hurt, Mikhail," she replied.

As an elf was slammed bodily into the tabletop next to us, I jumped as Val stood to her feet, grabbing the dwarf by the beard as she snarled at them. I knew then, without a doubt, that Valérikka Varggson, the Cruel Queen of the North, had been hiding her true nature from me this whole time. I was ashamed to doubt those that tried to teach me the truth, and I knew I was doing the right thing. Val pushed the dwarf away and turned to me, her eyes a fiery blue.

"We should leave now," I stammered.

Her gaze turned from an icy blue to a dull, foggy hue for a split second, and she stood up straight.

"We should leave now," she repeated, her tone echoing in my ears as she began to leave the tavern.

"Wait!" I called, and watched as she stopped in her tracks.

I paled and swallowed hard. I moved myself to stand in front of her and met her eyes, empty of the fierceness that I was almost used to seeing.

"Follow me, and do not speak," I commanded her.

I turned and headed for the door, and she followed obediently. She didn't speak a word, she didn't hesitate or falter. She didn't even cough or clear her throat. She just obeyed. Father employed the most talented mages in the city, some of them almost as talented as he was, but I knew that this vial contained his favorite potion. The Draught of Complacency had been his favored tactic of learning secrets and plots, and his final command before the draught's end was burned into my mind. *You will forget this conversation and greet me with a bow.* They always bowed low to my father, rarely of their own accord.

My HAMMERING heartbeat drowned out the sounds of our steps as we approached the Manor, and Belinda allowed us inside. I noticed a bandage on the halfling's fingers but paid no attention as my feet drew me closer to Father's study. The half elves drew back as I approached with Val close behind, her expression blank as she waited for the next command. Val still wore her Tacháan armor, fitted snugly to her figure, her twin swords tied to her back and her daggers hidden beneath her bracers. Without a doubt, she was one of the fiercest, most intimidating creatures I'd encountered, and as I entered my father's study, a fleeting look of surprise crossed his face.

"I didn't think you could actually do it," he muttered, his face neutral as he pulled out a small vial from his desk. "Tell her to sit down."

"Sit down in the chair," I stammered, my confidence scrambling to stay present.

Val blinked and sat in the ornately carved wooden chair, her blank eyes looking ahead. Father smiled and I tried to hide my shudder.

"Follow me," he said, his eyes darting to me with a hunger that chilled me to the bone. "Bring the bitch."

He opened a door that had been magically concealed, and the stone staircase led downward in a tight spiral.

"Follow my father," I ordered Val, as she stood from the chair and followed him, her face void of awareness.

I tailed after them, and the scent of damp stone filled me with fear. I knew where we were going, though I'd never taken this route myself. Winding tunnels drew us deeper under the estate, and the torches no longer lined the wall, leaving us in total darkness. With elven blood we could still see, but as we continued, the air itself grew heavy and thick. A wooden door at the end of the tunnel served as a barrier, and though I was used to doors opening well enough in advance for my father to maintain his pace, this one did not move. He took out a knife and slashed his palm, placing the bloody wound against the door's face. The lock disengaged loudly and the door opened, revealing a small room, windowless and bare of furnishings. Val walked in after Father and I was able to slip inside before the door slammed shut. Val stood motionless as Father circled her. Taller than the average high-elf, Lord Dorian Mistbrooke ruled his city with a sense of justice that always seemed to be in favor of the high elves. His overcoat clung to him, custom-tailored and enchanted with things I would never know. Reaching inside his coat, he produced a small vial and the bright pink liquid inside turned my stomach.

"A concentrated dose of Complacency will loosen your tongue," Father muttered, taking a fistful of her blonde hair in his hands as he wrenched her head up. "We won't have as much time, but you'll have no fight in you."

"I'm sure she'll tell you what you want to know," I answered, swallowing hard as his spine stiffened.

"I don't *care* what you're sure of," he snapped. "This she-wolf will spill her guts or I'll spill them on the floor, it's *your* choice. Which would you prefer, hmm?"

He opened her mouth and poured the liquid into her mouth, and waited until she swallowed it. Val blinked, her eyes growing foggy again as she inhaled deeply, waiting for her command. Father stood in front of her and pulled a small book from his pocket. Throwing it toward me, he watched as I flinched, not bothering to hide his smirk.

"Record everything. Do *not* miss a word."

I nodded, my neat script recording the date and time by habit. I watched carefully as Father reared back, striking Val across the cheek as he began his interrogation.

"State your name."

"Valérikka Varggson."

"Are you the Queen of Tachá?"

"Yes."

Father turned to me. "You finally did something worthwhile."

"Where is the King? Where is Ragnar?"

"I don't know."

The blow delivered to her stomach doubled her over as she gasped for air, the strike sending the wind from her lungs.

"A true Tacháan wolf. Why are you in Thyuland?"

"To find help…"

"Why would I ever help you?"

"Not you…I know you would never help."

"Why travel so far from your beloved wolf-king? And alone? Are you alone?"

"I have to find help. I am alone."

"Help with what?"

"The dream…I have to stop it."

"You Tacháan bastards are so irritating with your vagueness and lack of clarity!"

Father approached Val, nearly nose to nose as he bent in front of her, screaming as spit flew with his words.

"WHO IS HELPING YOU?! WHAT ARE YOU SO AFRAID OF?! TELL ME!"

"No one is helping me. I fear myself…"

He paused and turned to me. "Where is her bag? Bring it to me now!"

"It's at the inn we're staying at, at the bottom of the hill."

Fury radiated from him as he pulled a satchel from another pocket, snarling an incantation and throwing the contents in the corner of the room.

"Fetch it, now," he seethed, the swirling portal revealing the basement of the inn.

I stepped through it and ran immediately to the room, throwing open the door and finding Kona snarling as I entered.

"Easy, girl," I whispered, spying Val's bag near her armor in a corner of the room.

I waved my hand and it rose, the weight of the bag straining my mind, and as soon as it was in my hand, I turned to leave. Kona's ears flattered and her lips curled, fangs bared as she lowered her head. My heart hammered and I pulled a pinch of sand from my pocket, blowing it at her, commanding her to sleep. Growling as she wavered, her paws unsteady as she fell, she closed her eyes and fell into a magical slumber. I dashed downstairs and jogged through the portal to find Val's ears and nose stained with blood.

"What did you do?" I stammered, unable to stop myself.

"A little mind-flaying is just as effective as a physical assault," my father smirked. "Fruitless, though. She's not concealing anything. Her bag? Dump it."

My hands trembled as I poured the contents, neatly packed rations, bandages and herbal salves, fish hooks, a length of rope, a flask of oil, and a dagger. The fur that had previously lined her armor fell atop the items. Father kicked through it and paused, his eyes on Val. She was trembling, her mouth agape in a silent scream as her eyes locked on the dagger.

"Interesting," he murmured, picking up the dagger and twirling it between his fingers as he drew closer to Val.

"What's wrong with her?" I asked, her voice void of any sound.

"I commanded her to be silent. You may continue the

documentation of this interrogation," he said flippantly as I scrambled to open the book.

Her eyes were wide with fear as a single tear slid down her cheek.

"This is yours, I assume. Who are you going to kill? Speak!"

"No one. I will not use it. I will not."

Her breath came in ragged gasps, and I could hear the wheezing that came with a bruised windpipe. I remembered that pain, and I found myself rubbing at my throat without realizing it. Father's grip was always unbreakable. My pen was poised to record when I saw Father inspect the black dagger closely. Val hung her head as she groaned, her body swaying gently. I knew she was waking up from the effects of the Complacency Draught.

"Where did you get this? Who gave this to you?"

"No one. It came to me."

Father held it in his hands as if it were precious, and exhaled sharply as he turned to me, fiery rage in his eyes. Faster than I could react, he grabbed my horn and wrenched it, showing no mercy as I cried out from the searing pain.

"You idiot," he seethed in my ear, "you absolute waste of space, do you know what you've done? Do you? Pray to the gods and ask them for mercy, you shall receive none from me! Hope that you've only delayed the Queen Mother's plan for this one!"

"I don't understand, Father, what's happening?"

He released me with a shove and I landed hard next to Val's bag, her things still scattered.

"You brought her to me to try and earn your way back to the family, and you may have just destroyed my legacy!" he shouted, the walls thundering his echoing shout.

"King Rofellos will never welcome me into his halls if you ruin the plan that The Mother has laid out! You bring dishonor to this family! Leave these halls, leave this place and if you ever step foot here again, I will personally separate your head from your shoulders!"

I scrambled to collect Val's things, trying to put everything back the way I thought it should go, and as I picked up the black dagger, I shuddered as the tiny, almost imperceptible Mark of the Mother caught my eye. I shoved the dagger in the bag and buried it with all of her other things and turned to see my father pouring a bright pink potion down her throat and grabbing her by the hair, their noses almost touching as he towered over her.

"You were never here," he spoke firmly, clearly. "You have no memory of this place. You will forget. You will attend the wedding, to see the historical event in person. You will continue on with the orders you have been given."

He turned to glance at me, disgust filling his eyes.

"You will erase any memory of Mikhail from your mind. You will not know his name, nor his face. He is no one to you, just a Cursed One you must avoid. You will return to the tavern where you came from, you will sleep in the bed you paid for, and you will rise the next morning with no knowledge of this."

My head hung as I mourned, knowing my father's power over Val's mind. I was worse than dead to her, I was to have never existed. A punishment my father relished in, from the way his lips curled up. He waved his hands over her and her wounds were healed, inside and out. Opening another portal to the tavern, he ushered her toward it.

"Go through the portal and go to your room. Sleep

and wake at dawn with no memory as you have been told. Go," he said, pointing as she turned and walked obediently.

She didn't even look back at me, fully under my father's power. The portal closed and he turned to me.

"Leave the city," he ordered me with a calm tone that exuded its deadly undertone, "leave immediately or I will hunt you down like a dog and cut you into pieces. You are not my son. I cast you out. You have no family. You have no one. Be gone from my sight forever."

I dropped my gaze and began walking, my mind racing as I started down the long, dark tunnel. I would never see Val again. I would never get the chance to apologize, to try to explain why. I wished I could, but my wishes had never come to fruition...why would they start now?

CHAPTER 19

THE CHAIN WHISPERS

*S*tanding *beneath a black sky, the wind howled in torrents around me and lightning tore across the expanse. At the heart of a storm, beneath my feet was not earth or rock, but iron. Heavy iron chains stretched in all directions, groaning with tension as they threatened to buckle and bind. I knew without knowing that the eyes that lay upon me were ancient, older than the sands of time, but I felt no fear, even when the figures began to close in.*

Through the swirling darkness around me appeared a faceless figure clad in gold. The Cleric's god is silent but the path is clear. He walked through the storm with his eyes fixed on me. A voice whispered in my ear, 'He follows the light, but the light will lead him to you.'

From the corner of my eye another figure approached. I whirled around and the Cleric vanished. This figure was clothed in living bark and vines, the wind circled around her like a wolf mother curled around her pup. The Druid's hands trembled in awe as they reached toward the chains at my feet. She had followed the echoes of a screaming forest to its source, and a whisper rang softly, 'The wild bends to fate, fate yields to you.'

Another figure appeared from the shadows, a blood-stained blade at his side and his armor cracked and worn from countless, unnamed battles. He did not speak, but knelt and laid his weapon at my feet, not in surrender, but in recognition. The whispered voice spoke in my ear again, 'Steel remembers its master, even when the hand forgets.'

The figures stood, at my left, my right, and directly in front of me, and the wind died. The chains grew still and the three looked to me, their eyes burning with a passion, not of worship or awe, but of connection. We were bound together by fate, by bond, and by something my mind couldn't comprehend. From within and all around, a voice growled, 'You will not stand alone when the world breaks.'

I woke drenched in sweat, and as consciousness returned, the whispering of chains faded. The room stopped spinning and I sat up as the dream faded from the forefront of my mind. My temples pounded as I stood. I didn't realize how much I must have drunk last night. Catching up with hunters from the Hunter's Guilds of Thyuland and Ibria had apparently led to more and more ale, but it had been a relief to be able to introduce myself as Val, Captain of the Ironclaw Guild again.

Kona groaned and yawned as she stretched on the floor, rising and shaking from her nose to her tail and then stretching again. I dressed, picked up my bag, and paused, my mind foggy as I pressed my palms against my eyes. I sat at a table with Kona under my feet, eating a breakfast of potatoes nestled under a couple fried eggs, and I let my mind wander back to the dream that had woken me with such a shock. I couldn't recall the faces of the figures, but I focused on the words that had been whispered, wondering absently what they meant. A few of the hunters from last night tipped their heads to me as they headed toward the door, and one of them paused by my table.

"If you don't leave now, you're not going to get a good spot, you know," he said with a grin.

My confusion must have been apparent, he picked up my coffee and sniffed it with exaggerated motions.

"You haven't changed your mind, have you?" he mused.

"About what? What exactly did we discuss last night?"

"Last night?" he laughed, "you're funny this early, Val. Come on, you said you were going to the wedding."

My confusion must have shown, his face fell. He cocked his head as he sat across from me.

"Val...that was three days ago. The wedding is today. Where have you been?"

"Wait, what? That's not possible," I scoffed. "Yesterday afternoon, we sat at this same table, we had drinks...and then, I don't exactly remember. But, we were here just yesterday."

The others drew closer to us, exchanging glances of confusion and worry. A woman approached and inclined her head.

"Shae, tell him," I said. "Tell him we were just here last night."

She shook her head without breaking her gaze from mine. "It's been days. We thought you had left the tavern. Do you need to see a healer?"

"No, I must have just slept harder than I thought," I lied, "I'm okay, I'll head to the wedding in a few minutes."

"Want us to wait for you?"

"No, but I'll find you there," I murmured, "thank you. It was really nice catching up with you all. Take care."

As the group departed, I closed my eyes. My body was weak, and Kona was lying on the floor, whining softly. What had happened to me? How had the last three days suddenly vanished from my mind? My head throbbed the more I thought about it and I groaned, rubbing my temples. One of the serving girls brought me a platter of breakfast, most of which I gave to Kona, her drool dampening the leg of my pants.

I returned to my room with Kona at my heels, both of us with bellies full of sausages, eggs, and potatoes. As I straightened my tunic, smoothing out a stray crease, I frowned. I would have preferred to wear a gown suitable for a royal wedding, but as I paused, I remembered that I had stepped away from my throne. I hung up my armor, shining the scuffs out and straightening the buckles and braces, and donned a deep blue dress, simple but still one of my favorites, and fastened my dark blue cloak, marking which Hunter's Guild I called home.

My swords were sheathed, placed beside my armor, but I ensured my small daggers were hidden in my belt; one was lashed to my thigh, just in case. Weddings of high-importance always drew danger, and I was nothing if not prepared for the worst. A whine came from behind me, and I glanced at my white wolf.

"There's no way you can come, Kona. You have to stay," I commanded. "You can stay in the stables, otherwise you'll be locked in the room, all by yourself."

My hair hung in the traditional Tacháan way, the

intricate braids woven throughout my loose hair, and though I would have liked to have gemstones laid into the thick plaits for the occasion, I had neither the stones nor the second pair of hands needed. In the back of my mind, it would have drawn unwanted attention, and a Huntress did not wear such things, either. Dressed in the only gown I had packed, I descended the stairs with Kona at my side, and the bartender raised a hand to give me pause.

"She will be safe in our stables, my lady," he offered. "We would be honored to have her as company."

I thanked them and Kona followed slowly, glancing over her shoulder at me as if she were worried. With such a highly attended event, I had no doubt that the security would be increased, that there would be a presence of armed guards every few feet, and that it was the rest of the city, left nearly empty, that I was concerned about.

I vanished into the crowd of wedding celebrants, from the ends of every world, and as the crowd neared the Temple of Apollo, the crowd funneled through a portal that teemed with illusion magic. After the attendees had passed through, they were directed to the left, the right, or forward. I noticed many of the lesser-valued shuffled to the far left. The unattractive, the poorly dressed, the lame, and the sickly were all ushered to the rear, outside the temple, nearly on the outskirts. They wouldn't be able to see or hear a thing, and I hated the injustice and prejudice of it all. Shuffling forward, I was sorted and was ushered into the temple itself, while the elderly gnome couple that had been leaning on their staves as we waited were snubbed to the side. Disappointment veiled their expressions, the excitement gone as realization dawned.

"That couple is with me, they're my assistants," I lied, pointing to the couple. "They accompany me."

"My lady, these two...gnomes are yours?" the elf confirmed, the unconscious grimace on his face infuriating me.

I flipped the switch and turned on every royal attitude I hated to use.

"You dare question my statement? I will *not* repeat myself," I snarled, my head held high as I turned, snapping my fingers at the couple. "Come, you two! You must record every detail as I command!"

The elf muttered his apologies, still mildly suspicious but allowing the very confused gnomes through. As soon as we were out of earshot, they reached up to touch my hand to catch my attention.

"Thank you, my dear lady," the small woman said, tears in her eyes. "We will never forget this selflessness. You have our gratitude and our service."

"Nonsense," I smiled quietly, "you're much too excited for the nuptials to be stuck in the back. Enjoy yourselves."

Weaving in and out of the crowd, nimbly bypassing larger humanoids, the couple were able to sneak through and grab seats that were incredibly close, where they would be able to see everything they wanted. I made my way forward and found a seat beside a man with coiffed yellow hair who looked bored out of his mind. I sat and he turned toward me, flashing a smile and sitting up a little straighter as he introduced himself as *Thaddeus Raccuglian, the Fourth of his Name, of the Great City of Erythos*. I groaned, smiling politely, introducing myself with my first name, and he inclined his head, leaning forward as he not-too-subtly attempted to peek down my bodice.

"A breath of fresh air is your beauty to behold, my lady," he said, the silvery tone of his voice repulsive to my ears. "I'm surprised to find a woman of your beauty clad in such a simple dress and not a gown that would summon a suitable dancing partner afterwards. And the color, though bringing a sparkle to your eyes, makes you look like one of those brutish Northerners! Perhaps we could find another color more suitable, to bring out the gold of your hair?"

His smile was wide, as if he'd practiced it to perfection, and I plastered a polite smile on my face, turning to the person on the other side of me. The high elf glanced at me once and groaned, muttering about wolves with the sheep under his breath. I wondered to myself how many shared his sentiments. I supposed I did look a little wild, with my Northern hair and my blue dress, but I was assured of my own safety with my hidden daggers. Thaddeus opened his mouth to speak again and was interrupted by the great bells of the Temple ringing across the town, the deep tones resonating in my chest as the entire congregation stood. Clothed in silken robes of gold, their strides so smooth they seemed to be floating, the clerics of Apollo lit the ceremonial torches, the flames casting an unnaturally warm, divine glow across the white marble floor and walls. The last bell rang out, carrying its song through the air as it stilled, and the silence that followed was almost overwhelming. Thick plumes of fragrant smoke curled into the air and dissipated, leaving the lingering scent of Apollo's sacred incense floating with the salty coastal air. Bannermen clad in the red and gold hues of Ibria walked alongside bannermen of Thyuland, the gold and green banners waving with the breeze. As they marched, their steps magically muted, the men parted as Thyuland stood to one side while Ibria lined the other.

From the entryway, a large pair of Ibrian flags, the scarlet hue offset by bright gold filigree, so bright that some shielded their eyes, led the way as the Prince marched close behind. As he passed by the aisle I stood in, he strode with an elegance and ferocity that reflected in his proud heritage. As he stood at the altar, his olive toned skin was marred by the deep red dragon scales that covered half of his face, the dominant blood of the dragon seeming to burst from him as it crept down the side of his neck, disappearing beneath the collar of his golden wedding tunic. Prince Azran Ra'zír waited for his betrothed, his eyes calm and curious while his posture became stiff and unmoving under the watchful eye of his father, Pharoah Tekhmet.

I glanced around the room, seeing nobles, warriors, and emissaries of every kind standing at attention in the temple's massive expanse, clad in fine silks, polished armor, and all eager to witness to history. A hushed whisper caught my ear and my attention was drawn back to the front where a high elf took his place behind a golden altar. High Cleric Lysander of Apollo stood tall, radiating a soft golden light as he lifted his hands high. A warm golden light swept over the crowd, the Blessing of Apollo engulfing the crowd as the doors to the temple opened wide. Clothed in white silk, two slender figures carried poles of laurels and golden olive branches, shrouded with the anonymity of golden masks that covered their faces. Behind the pair, the Princess emerged, walking through the draped greenery in a dazzling, luminous gown of silver silk embroidered with green, elvish runes delicately woven in with what I knew was enchanted thread. Princess Valeria Vael'Quinalis floated down the aisle soundlessly, her every step graceful and light, almost divine. Her veil covered her completely, shimmering and sparkling like the morning dew as it draped her figure. The length of the aisle was walked to the sounds of a quiet elven choir and a pair of harps, in a synchrony that left me breathless at its beauty, and as I redirected my gaze to the hopefully-happy couple, my mind wandered to my own wedding, the memory sweet and rich. At the High Cleric's bidding, we took our seats and I wondered what Ragnar's thoughts of the event would be. The political power play as well as the wedding itself would be laughable to him, and I smiled sadly, missing what I knew would be whispered insults to the elven king in my ear.

The High Cleric raised a hand and a reverent silence fell over the crowd.

"Honored guests and citizens of our great country. We gather under the watchful gaze of Apollo, who shines his divine light upon this sacred day. Today we witness the union of not only two souls, but we herald the forging of an unbreakable bond between two nations. This bond shall surpass the sands of time and the tides of fate. Prince Azran Ra'zír, heir to the throne of Ibria herself, do you swear to honor, to protect the Princess Valeria Vael'Quinalis, through light and shadow, through storms and calm seas, in the name of your gods and ours, and in the sight of every soul that bears witness?"

"I swear it. I swear by my blood, my honor, and my kingdom," he answered confidently, his voice reaching to the edges of the temple as a gentle smile pulled at the corner of his mouth.

I knew that though this marriage was a politically-motivated event, perhaps the Prince hoped to love his bride. The High Cleric turned to the veiled bride and spoke to her.

"Princess Valeria Vael'Quinalis, daughter of the Great King Rofellos, do you swear to stand beside the Prince Azran Ra'zír in times of prosperity and in times of hardship, in the joyful moments as well as the sorrowful, and do you swear to honor him with your words and deeds?"

The High Cleric paused for her answer but silence filled the space.

"Princess?" the High Cleric whispered, clearing his throat quietly.

The emptiness lingered and the crowd shifted uncomfortably as hushed whispers rose. An icy chill swept through the temple, unnaturally sharp as if winter had descended in an instant, a breath of cold in the midst of summer. The torches flickered and the golden glow faded as a heavy weight of stillness settled over the room, as if the very air in our lungs were being stolen away. The High Cleric stepped forward and reached for the edges of her veil. Prince Azran averted his gaze, his respectful gesture touching as he turned away. The High Cleric cried out to Apollo and staggered backward as the veil was pulled free, revealing a woman...but not Princess Valeria. In her place was a twisted, horrific figure, transparent and ghastly. I covered my mouth in horror as the banshee opened her mouth in a silent wail, her once-radiant elven face now a visage of rage and sorrow. Hollow eyes filled with unfathomable grief and fury, and her decayed form flickered in and out of translucency, the beautiful gown now a ragged, rotted death shroud.

She screamed. A sound made by no living thing, it cut through the body and soul like an icy knife. The stained glass windows of the temple shattered, exploding shards of colored glass over the crowd, and chaos erupted. The wedding guests stampeded toward the door, some assisting others, some trampling others. My eyes locked onto the gnome couple toward the front, they were frozen in fear, cowering under the seats. I leapt over the chair and Thaddeus grabbed my wrist.

"What are you doing! Run!" he shouted, his eyes wide with fright.

I wrenched my arm away and continued to the gnomes, ducking and dodging panicked elves, screaming and fleeing. I reached them and caught a much closer sight of the banshee, fear lodged itself in my throat, tangled with a scream, and I swallowed hard.

I gathered the gnomes under each arm and dashed to the nearest window, the glass slippery as it crunched under my feet. I gently tossed them out the window and watched as they were able to run to safety before turning my eyes back to the banshee. She unleashed another scream and the torches burned an eerie blue before snuffing out, drenching the room in the dim natural light from outside, still unnaturally cold as my breath became visible. The banshee turned to the Prince, glaring with sunken, soulless eyes, and her rotted hand clasped around his throat, her long, sharp fingernails digging into his neck. As she gripped it, the Prince's flesh began to rot under her hold, the necrotic, cloying scent of dead flesh spreading throughout the temple. An arrow sang through the air, sent from the light crossbow of a dark-haired elven woman dressed in a breathtaking green gown. Her mark sailed wide, missing the banshee, and I covered my ears as the banshee unleashed another wailing scream, fighting the urge to flee. Her wail was cut short as a thicker crossbow bolt caught her in the shoulder, throwing her backward as her grip released. The Prince fell, his knees cracking on the cold, white marble. He was dead before he hit the floor, the necrotic energy having eaten away at his life from within with black veins that devoured.

A human man, his shaggy dark hair obscuring most of his face, shouldered his crossbow as he grabbed up an abandoned sword from the marble floor. I reached instinctively for my swords, their absence sorely missed, and I spied a guard, trampled to death from the crowds. I muttered an apology as I grabbed the two swords from the body and rushed toward the banshee. She swiped at me, her long nails coated with the Prince's blood, and I dodged, ducking out of the way as a massive warhammer connected with the banshee's head. Knocking the monster against a bust of Apollo, a dwarf rushed toward me, waving me out of the way as he picked up his hammer again. The banshee returned faster than the dwarf anticipated, and I turned into the incoming attack, slashing the swords across the banshee's middle as her shroud hung in tattered ribbons. Blood hadn't been drawn with the injuries that had been delivered, but an ethereal ooze began to drip from the wounds as she swung hard at the dwarf, sending him flying backward into the heavy pews of the temple.

The pews rocked and fell, broken under the force of the dwarf, and with a mighty roar, the dwarf stood, planted his feet, and heaved the pew across the aisle.

"Y'unholy *bastard*!" he cried, picking up his hammer and running alongside the dark-haired warrior, both rushing toward the banshee.

Spying a bow next to a guard's corpse, I grabbed the quiver and stood nearby the elf, her sharp eyes focused on the banshee as she fired another arrow into it. I drew back, anchoring the arrow's fletching to my cheek, and released, the arrow hitting its mark as the banshee wailed. The dwarf staggered, his hands covering his ears as he dropped his hammer, and the human vaulted himself backward to avoid the razor-sharp nails that raked wildly. The elf released an arrow as the banshee screamed, and her aim faltered. Her arrow sank into the backside of the dwarf, who roared in pain and anger as he turned to her, their faces equally shocked.

"Watch yer aim, would ye?" he bellowed.

He channeled the pain and began to glow a deep golden hue, his hand clutching the holy symbol around his neck. The power radiated from the center of the dwarf, enchanting his weapon with holy power as he raised it above his head. The human slashed at the banshee's arm and severed one of her hands. It rolled away and began rotting, decaying into bone and dust in a matter of seconds. Screeching and distracted by the wound, the banshee never saw the hammer falling upon her head. Crushing it into a pulpy mass of ooze and bone shards, the divinely blessed hammer fell once with precision, and the dark, dim atmosphere cleared as the temperature seemed to return to its normal warmth. The elf and I drew closer to the sludgey remains, and an incorporeal form rose from the tattered shroud, hissing softly, *'He...lied...to...me...'* before dissolving into nothing.

CHAPTER 20
A PARTY FORETOLD

The dwarf raised a brow to me, turning his gaze to the human, and finally the elf, and he let out a guttural sound that I supposed was a laugh. Reaching behind, he gripped the shaft of the arrow that still stuck from his rear end, yanking it free with a roar.

"I believe this belongs to you, lass," he said with a groan, holding out the arrow to the elf.

The elf dropped her gaze, blushed deeply, and gave an elegant curtsy. "My apologies to you, it was not my intention. I am Althaea Galanodel. Are...are you in need of healing, sir?"

"Thorric Shattershield, at yer service. And dinna you worry, lass," Thorric said with a chuckle. "But thank you for the offer to heal. Now, though, may I ask when in the world did the beauty turn into a beast?"

I turned to the banshee's remains and saw that the human had turned to the Prince's body, examining the necrotic wounds carefully.

"What do you observe, sir?" I asked as I crouched next to him.

His eyes were as dark as his hair, and they held an apprehension and flicker of what I thought was recognition. He shook his head and pointed to the black veins that had crawled up the dragonborn prince's neck.

"This sort of creature doesn't have the sense to plan an attack like this," he muttered darkly. "This was a political assassination."

An icy pit formed in my stomach and I studied the man carefully.

"Which factions could have done this?" I asked calmly. "Who can harness the banshee and manipulate her?"

He opened his mouth and promptly closed it, as if he had stopped himself from answering. He gave a shrug and stood, adjusting the collar of his tunic, and sighed.

"Her spirit spoke to us," he said quietly. "*He lied to me. I have a good gut feeling for who she was talking about.*"

"Who?" Althaea asked curiously.

"Never mind that right now," I interrupted. "We need to check for injured people and get them to the healers."

Althaea and Thorric took the left side of the room, and the man and I took the right, sifting through shattered glass, broken statues, and lifeless bodies. Checking a thin elven woman for any signs of life, the man reached out and closed her eyes solemnly as he found none.

"Who are you?" I asked as we moved to the next victim.

"Morrak. Don't have a surname anymore. Gave it up a long time ago," he murmured. "You?"

"Val," I replied. "My surname is...complicated."

Morrak looked at my clothing and my hair, nodding. "A Tacháan woman...armed to the teeth and able to confidently defend herself and others…you're a Huntress, aren't you? You gave up your surname when you joined."

"Yes," I replied, nearing the pew that Thorric had thrown.

A tiny squeak came from underneath and Morrak instantly leapt into action, clearing the rubble from the source of the sound and calling out. Together, we uncovered a gnome, his dark, curly hair coated with dust and glass. Coughing and brushing the debris from his tailored tunic and trousers, he finally looked up and met our faces. Smiling broadly with joy, he hugged me, squeezing tightly, and moved to hug Morrak, who remained motionless, uncomfortable with the gnome's affection.

"Th-thank you so much for saving me!" he cried out. "I'm Phil-lip, owner and operator of Phil-lip's Family Jewels, the finest connoisseur of gems and rocks for every occasion!"

Morrak grimaced for the slightest moment before moving on to seek out other survivors.

"Are you injured, Phillip?" I asked, relieved to see him shake his head as he straightened his suspenders. "Why don't we get you to a healer, just in case. I'd hate to see you injured and not be aware."

"What an incredibly kind thing to say," he murmured, patting my hand lovingly. "It's Phil-*lip*, by the way. It's a very proud family name. Allow me to lead the way, my lady!"

Phil-lip took four steps, tripped over a chunk of marble, and face-planted with a sharp slap that echoed through the temple. He jumped up and continued as if nothing had happened, and I saw Morrak hide a grin as we passed. The survivors were carried and escorted out of the temple, and as we left, I saw the High Cleric Lysander seated on a makeshift cot, staring blankly at the ground, his head wrapped in a bandage stained with healing salve and blood. I knelt by his side, meeting his eyes with a deadly seriousness.

"Did you know?" I asked quietly.

He shook his head and his face contorted with grief. "I didn't know, but I should have. She wasn't...I should have known..."

"What does *that* mean?" Althaea whispered from behind me, the others with her.

"Ye have a holy duty to your god to speak the truth about this," Thorric growled. "Answer the lady, now."

The High Cleric stammered and wept as he spoke. "Princess Valeria, that *wasn't her!* I know that girl, I've known her since birth...and that creature was *not* her! Where is she?"

"What should you have known?" Althaea asked firmly, zeroing in on the High Cleric as her hands glowed softly.

"She...she never wanted to be married. Especially not to a man so far away," he replied, choking back a shameful sob. "I thought it...odd...that our King would allow his youngest daughter to marry someone of..."

"An impure bloodline?" Morrak snarled darkly as the High Cleric's eyes gave away his guilt. "Everyone knows Rofellos wouldn't sully his pure lineage like that, even for a political power move like gaining Ibria. Nah, he knew what was going on. I'd even say he planned it."

I glanced around and saw a few guards and healers pause at the name of their King, and as Morrak spat on the ground, a few of the guards began to move closer, very, very slowly, listening intently. I nudged Morrak and he followed my eyes to the armed men eavesdropping, and gave a subtle nod.

"But *that*," he continued carefully, "that would be absolutely ludicrous. No one in the great land of Thyuland would ever accuse the King of murdering the Prince of Ibria under the guise of marriage and unity. Crazy, totally crazy."

"Okay, you've made your point," I muttered. "Let's get out of here. Is there a place?"

"Oh, please, my new friends!" came a voice from behind us, revealing Phil-lip the gnome, clean as a whistle and beaming. "And more friends! I have seen you defend, fight, and rescue, and I know that it's you that I've been searching for...you're exactly who I need right now."

Thorric raised a quizzical brow and cleared his throat as Althaea cocked her head, curious as the gnome wrung his hands anxiously. Sputtering helplessly, he took a steadying breath and addressed us.

"Please, I need help. I don't know who you all are, but you fought against that monster. You stood your ground, and didn't run away like everyone else. Join me for dinner tonight at dusk, at The Salty Seagull. I'll make it worth your while, even if it's just a warm seat and a strong drink. If you're able to help me, though, I'll make it a reward far greater than alo," he pleaded.

As he patted his pocket, the faint yet distinct clink of valuables echoed from his pocket. He bowed to us, and retreated into the city, far away from the ruined Temple of Apollo.

CHAPTER 21

THE MINES OF GRAY TIDE

Dusk settled over the town, an eerie calm after the horrific events that had transpired, and as I approached the door of The Salty Seagull, a small tavern at the coastal edge of town, the smell of seawater and smoke enveloped me. Morrak appeared from the shadows and paused as he caught sight of Kona, a silent ghost behind me.

"I knew I was right about you," he said with a small grin. "A Tacháan wolf *and* the blue armor confirm it."

"This is Kona, she's a gift from my husband," I said as he reached out and rubbed the top of her head fearlessly.

Inside, we met Phil-lip, who greeted us excitedly with tight hugs at a table he had reserved, and called the bartender over.

"Drinks for my new friends, Barth!" he cried to the half-elf behind the bar, who eyed us curiously as he set two steins of ale in front of us.

The locals were quiet in the tavern, whispering and muttering about the events of the day, and as I took notice of those seated on the barstools, I noticed a very obvious absence of elves. Thorric and Althaea joined us only moments later, and as ales were brought, Phil-lip cleared his throat. Althaea garnered attention with her elven beauty, and as glances continued, whispers began, fingers pointing toward our party. As Phil-lip thanked us for coming, Althaea gave him her full attention, and smiled sweetly. Phil-lip blushed and a large figure approached. With tusks that grew from his bottom jaw, jutting out his bottom lip, an orc sauntered over to us, full of ale and bad ideas. He staggered just enough that I knew he wasn't much of a threat, and Phil-lip paused as he approached.

"Y'ain't welcome here, she-elf," he growled, the green tinge of his flesh deepening. "Go on before we throw you out on your bony arse!"

"You will not lay a hand on the lady," Thorric replied, his eyes glistening with the thrill of a fight. "This'll be your only chance to return t'your seat."

"A dwarf defendin' a she-elf?" the orc laughed sardonically. "She must have you under her spell, t'be sure."

Althaea's eyes connected with the orc and she held his attention. "I will take my leave after I have dinner with our new friend. You will leave us now. I have no quarrel with you."

The orc blinked with heavy eyes and spat on the floor, but turned away, returning to his seat where Barth the bartender set another mug of ale in front of him. Althaea turned to Phil-lip and smiled.

"Phil-lip," she asked, carefully placing the pause between syllables in his name. "What do you need our help with? How may we be of service?"

"I think...no, I *know*, my friend and her workers are in

trouble. She and her crew come to Gray Tide every two weeks. Every two weeks, without fail. She's never missed or been late with a delivery in over three years! But now... I haven't heard from her for over two and a half weeks. No sign of them, no messages. Nothing. I'm worried about her."

Phil-lip's joyful exuberance was gone, replaced by a gut-wrenching anxiety that brought a sharp ache to my heart.

"I've sent letters, I even asked, I begged the city guards to help me, to look for them, but they shrugged it off and didn't even make a report. Please, I know I'm small. Too small to be of any real help to my friend, but you four? You could have ran or hid from that monster that attacked, but you all fought it, together, being strangers! Please, help me find my friend. She works the mines, she finds me rocks and gems to sell while she works, and I *know* she's still alive. Please, just let me know if she's okay."

Phil-lip's voice trailed off as he wept quietly, and my heart broke. Althaea brushed a tear away and Thorric's forehead creased with deep thought. Morrak cleared his throat and drained his mug.

"Why would a gnome delve into the mines?" he asked quizzically.

"A *gnome* wouldn't," Phil-lip answered, "but Thora Coppervein is a mountain dwarf, with beautiful long, chestnut hair that turns red in the sunlight. She's one of my very best friends. She likes gems almost as much as I do!"

"A dwarf in need? Why didn't you say so? When do we leave, Phillip?" Thorric said.

"Phil-*lip*. Best to leave at first light, the mines are

quite a few hours walk east," Phil-lip said with a sniffle, rummaging through his pockets and pulling out a gleaming red gemstone. "Any news of her and this is yours. I'll give it to you now in good faith."

Thorric's and Morrak's eyes lit up, and as both of them reached for it, Morrak's fingers wrapped around it first. I had no desire for the gemstone, and from the looks of it, neither did Althaea.

"You have a deal, Phil-lip," Thorric said, keeping his eyes on the gemstone as Morrak tossed it from palm to palm. "We'll find your friend."

As promised, Phil-lip purchased our meals and drinks and we ate our fill, Thorric out-drinking us by leagues. I left The Salty Seagull and Kona followed close behind as we returned to our room at the inn, across town, where a pillow had never looked so inviting.

MORRAK WAITED at the eastern gate, seated beneath a leafy tree as he fidgeted with a long piece of grass. He noticed me coming and stiffened slightly as Kona approached boldly, sniffing him curiously. Nose to nose, they examined each other closely until Kona sneezed unexpectedly.

"She likes you," I laughed as he wiped his face clean.

"I'd hate to see what she'd do if she didn't," he muttered, failing to hide a playful grin as he scratched behind her ears.

A few moments passed and Althaea and Thorric joined us, the elf appearing from the dim morning light with silent footsteps while the heavy-footed dwarf was heard before he was seen. Thorric led the way with a steady pace east, winding north along the mountain pass, and Kona's ears laid flat as she growled. The ground seemed to shake under our feet as something massive approached.

"What do we do?" Althaea asked, finding nowhere to hide.

"We stand and face whoever's approaching," Thorric said, stomping his feet and pulling his warhammer from his back.

Morrak drew a one-handed battle axe and strapped his shield to his left forearm and Althaea produced a light crossbow, loading a bolt and steadying her breathing.

"*Fylgja*," I commanded Kona, drawing my swords as she oriented to my side.

I drew my twin swords and set my stance, waiting alongside my new companions as we spanned the road. The rumbling grew stronger and Kona gave a whine, surprising me as she sat down.

The source of the quaking rounded the curve, the group of mounted men approaching quickly. The sun shined brightly enough that I couldn't make out the flags that the bannermen carried. By the time they were close enough for me to see, they had already seen us, very clearly.

"Val...those people coming," Morrak said under his breath, "uh, aren't they *your* people? Why do you look so nervous?"

"Long story," I muttered as I replaced my swords on my back, "but you'll find out soon enough."

Morrak eyed me curiously and replaced his axe, but kept his shield arm up. Thorric backpedaled to our side and Althaea, unwilling to be left on her own, scurried to us. We stepped off the road and Thorric swore under his breath as he turned toward the winding path that the mountain pass formed. Over one hundred men, clad in the dusty blue of the Tacháan country, marched behind two men on horseback. They approached and my heart hammered behind my chest as they came to a pause. Hooves stomped impatiently as they stood, and I swallowed the lump in my throat and met my husband's gaze.

"Far from home you are, Huntress," Ragnar spoke evenly, veiling his emotions from his face. "Keep your shield up, *Min Kona*, the crows are near."

My breath caught in my throat as my husband spoke the loving name he'd given me, followed by the Tacháan words of warning: a war was coming. Beside Ragnar rode his eldest son, Bjorn, a blond, fairer version of his father, blessed with patience and the calm intellect that his late mother possessed. I straightened my back and inclined my head to Ragnar, bringing my fist to my chest.

"Strength to you, my King," I said, Bjorn rolling his eyes at the traditional gesture.

Ragnar eyed my companions carefully and silently moved on. He didn't look back, not once, but I watched, my heart aching as I longed for him, wishing I could explain everything. I set my jaw, clenching my teeth as the last of the men passed by, glancing at me with mixtures of curiosity, faint recognition, and apprehension. The soldiers saw a Tacháan Huntress carefully watching their King and Commander, but they passed by without a word. Thorric moved first, and I followed quietly as we continued up the mountain. Why would he have ridden south? Surely, I knew, it wasn't to find me, and that had been all but confirmed when he warned of an impending war. Whose war, though?

It wasn't until I smelled the death and decay in the thin air that my focus returned to the present reality.

Mixed with the scent of the earth, it was a sobering moment.

"No tracks, no birds singing, no bugs flying...it seems calm and quiet," Morrak commented quietly. "They're definitely dead in there."

"Gracious, you awful thing!" Althaea snapped, "that's a terrible thing to say! Such luck that Phillip isn't here!"

"Phil-*lip*," Morrak mumbled absently under his breath, crouching at the mouth of the mines.

Thorric gave a shrug that made it seem like he agreed with Morrak, and as we paused outside the mouth of the mines, Thorric inhaled deeply.

"It smells like a goblin's arse down the left and smells like a heap of dead goblins' arses down the right," the dwarf said, sighing. "Let's head right."

"*Toward* the worst thing I've ever smelled in my life?" Althaea asked as Thorric nodded.

Stepping inside the mine, the temperature around us dropped and I shivered, but not from the cold. Kona lifted her nose and sniffed the air, the foreign smells intriguing and almost overwhelming her. We continued, following the iron tracks for the missing mine carts, carefully following the narrow tunnel and ready for danger, and we rounded the corner. The tunnel opened into a cavern that had halfway collapsed, and cold torches lay on the dark walls and as Morrak fumbled blindly. Althaea produced a ball of light in her hand, sending it toward him. The light illuminated the room, and among the chunks of rock, earth, and mineral, we found the bodies. Thorric gave a soft groan, the kinship of dwarven folk strongly knit as he mourned, and slowly, carefully, we unearthed the corpses. We found six bodies in total. Morrak crouched next to the nearest body and peered carefully, using the ball of light that Althaea had created.

"Look at this," he said quietly, pointing to the belly of a dwarf, slashed open. "This wasn't done by the cave-in, this was a claw...a big one."

He measured with his hand and deduced that four claws had raked the dwarf's middle, spilling his insides. Morrak moved on to the next, pieced together, and sighed heavily. With a great respect for the fallen, Morrak explained the wounds and manners of death, some being torn apart, some slashed, and clawed, some of them too mangled to determine the cause of death. He reached inside the coat pocket of a dwarf whose head was crushed under a fallen column, and pulled out a small, hand-drawn portrait of a dwarf child and a woman. Morrak's jaw clenched hard as he pocketed it carefully.

"Search them. Maybe we can find out who they are and notify their families," I said gently, watching Morrak as he glanced up at me with a grateful nod.

Althaea knelt next to a fallen dwarf, his arms positioned beside him, torn free from their sockets, and she lifted a blood-spattered pendant from his neck.

"A Follower of Brokkr and Sindri," Thorric said thickly, gesturing to the hammer-and-forge symbol on the pendant. "These dwarves served him well. They deserve an honorable burial."

"We shall see that they get it," Althaea said, returning to the body and squinting at the hand. "What's this?"

She pulled a swatch of tattered fabric that had been hastily tucked into the sleeve of one of the severed arms, and as she flattened it out, we all drew close to inspect it. Burned into the cloth was a crude design, a trio of snakes, their raised heads forming a triangle of sorts. Morrak paled, and stood as he took a step backward, mumbling about the sight of the bodies. I didn't confront him on the lie, but he met my eyes and knew, but now wasn't the time for a confrontation.

I uncovered a note in a dwarf's pocket, written neatly in Dwarvish, *'Remember Thora's tea! Equal parts mugwort & mint for her headache!'* and found a handful of obsidian pieces, the dark surface polished smooth. In yet another pocket, a letter home was half-finished, written in a man's blocky hand.

Don't know quite when we'll be done with this dig, love. It's been mined dry as bone, but orders remain to continue. That elf-king Rofellos has ordered us to dig until something worthwhile is found. Don't know what that means, but I suppose I'll miss Gerra's birthday. I'm sorry, love, give her a kiss from her papa.

The letter cut off, and looked as if it had been hastily shoved back in the pocket. I read the letter aloud and Thorric cocked his head.

"Ordered to mine a dead mine? Odd. But here, I wonder what this unlocks," Thorric murmured absently, holding up an iron keyring, two long, elaborately carved iron keys dangling from it.

Half-buried in rubble lay a dwarven axe, the hickory wood handle carved with dwarvish runes covered in blood. Gingerly, I pulled it free and Thorric swore under his breath as the shattered axe head lay nearby.

"Thorric," I asked in a whisper, "what could break a weapon forged by dwarven magic?"

"Nothin' good," he growled. "These dwarves were killed without even being able to draw their weapons, and a cave-in didn't kill 'em. Keep your eyes open, let's keep moving. We haven't found Phillip's friend's body yet."

"Phil-*lip*," Althaea gently corrected as we continued, finding nothing else of note in the cavern.

The keys matched a wooden door, half-covered by a fallen pillar as it lay flat on the ground, and as we peered through the dark doorway, Althaea's ball of light revealed the sleeping barracks, empty.

"I suppose now we're gonna head down that dank, dark, deadly mineshaft over there?" Morrak said with a heavy sigh, pointing to the tunnel across the room.

"Yep," Thorric replied, gripping the handle of his hammer tightly as he led the way.

The mines were cold, much cooler than they should have been, and a growing sense of dread crept into my mind. As we continued, Kona began to growl, a deep rumble as her hackles stood tall on her back. Weapons were drawn as we squinted, and Althaea flicked her wrist. The ball of light shot down the mineshaft. A shadow, as massive as it was fast, shot across our view at the end of the shaft.

"Was...was that thing *watching us*?" Althaea asked breathlessly. "Waiting for us to get closer?"

"Did anyone get a good look at it?" Thorric asked as we shook our heads.

"It was too fast," I muttered. "Kona barely got a sense for it before it moved, too. It...it moved so fast."

Fear crawled between us and I adjusted my grip on my bow, making sure my arrow was nocked. "Kona, stay behind me." We continued, Thorric led the way and Morrak and I held our bows steady, squinting in the dim light for any source of movement.

"Remember, we're also looking for Thora, so make sure your aim is true to this beast," Thorric said quietly.

Despite his whisper, Thorric's voice echoed down the mineshaft, and disappeared in the distance. He let out a soft grunt as his foot connected with a loose piece of gravel, sending it flying against the iron tracks, and as we reached end of the straight length of tunnel, I positioned myself with my bow pulled back and ready, and gave Thorric a nod as he gripped his warhammer. I stepped out and aimed for anything my elven eyes could see, but saw nothing, alive or dead. I lowered my bow and we continued, slowly and silently. We came to another bend in the mines and mentally prepared, this time, Morrak took the step, his crossbow readied as his brow furrowed with concentration. It was waiting for us, this time. Kona snarled just before it emerged, giving us a split second to avoid the surprise attack. Swiping wildly at us with four-inch long claws, a massive werewolf stood tall, hunched over as its head grazed the top of the mineshaft, furious as it missed its target. I realized that its wrists had been clamped with iron manacles, remnants of what had been once a secure chain clung to each side.

"Don't let it bite at ya!" Thorric shouted as he swung his hammer at the beast's chest, covered in a thick, black fur.

Morrak fired his crossbow and the bolt hit the werewolf squarely in the shoulder. It screamed and swiped at it, but redirected its rage immediately to Morrak.

"*Að baki!*" I shouted to Kona, quickly swapping my bow for my swords.

Kona darted nimbly at my command to attack from behind and grabbed hold of its leg in her teeth, clamping down fiercely as it screamed. Thorric dodged a claw as my sword sang through the air, slashing at its chest and belly as blood poured.

"Víkja, Kona," I commanded, keeping my eyes on the creature.

Kona returned to my side, waiting for her next opportunity, and Thorric swung his hammer to the side of its head; its roar cut short as it was knocked off balance, catching and scratching the wall of the mineshaft. Long, jagged claw marks marred the rock wall, and I shuddered. Shaking its head, it snarled and foamy saliva mixed with blood dripped from its jaws. It roared, a bone-chilling sound that rattled loose rocks from above, raining dust and gravel on us, and it turned and fled.

"After it! We can't let it escape!" Thorric shouted as he turned to give chase.

Dodging and nimbly darting ahead, Morrak took the lead.

"I got 'em," he called, his eyes locked on the massive beast.

Its claws scratched the walls as it rounded the corner, rocks fell in our path and dust fell in our eyes, but Morrak wasn't slowed. He leapt over the rocks, launching himself past the turn and firing just before he slammed into the rocky walls of the mineshaft's tunnel. The crossbow bolt hit the werewolf in the back, and the beast turned, wheezing from what I know was a punctured lung, and roared. Morrak loaded another bolt as rocks and dirt hailed over us, and as the beast lunged, the fighter set his aim and pulled the trigger. Time seemed to slow as the bolt shot forward through the raining sediment, burying itself into the beast's throat. Howling and screaming in volumes that I feared would cave in the tunnel, it scrambled backward and collapsed in a heap, dead. Morrak approached, his weapon reloaded, and gave it a nudge with his boot to make sure, and nodded to us as we stood in the tunnel. As we approached, the smell of the beast made my eyes water, and I stepped over its corpse, realizing that it had tried to escape back to the room it had once been shackled in. Thick chains had been reinforced into the very foundation of the earth, yet this thing had still broken free. The entrance to the massive room had been broken apart, and piles of rubble, stone, and what was once perhaps a wooden door, lay in front of us.

"Nice shot, lad," Thorric said, clapping Morrak on the shoulder.

We entered the room, carefully stepping over the rubble, and a soft groan sounded from under the rubble. Althaea and I uncovered the source of the sound; quickly and carefully we revealed a dwarven woman, her long red hair ashen and covered in dust, dirt, and blood. Helping her to her feet, Althaea healed her with a gentle hand that glowed a warm, soft light.

"Thank you, adventurers," she said, taking in a full lungful of air. "I can breathe again! Where's the monster? Did it flee from the mines?"

"He didn't get too far," Morrak said, shouldering his crossbow. "You must be Thora Coppervein."

"I am, and *you* are?" she said, her face knitted with suspicion.

"Friends of Phillip," Thorric said. "Er, sorry, Phil-*lip*. He sent us to find you."

Thora beamed and laughed. "Well done, my good friend, Phil-lip. Let's get the hell outta this place before the thing that crawled from that sarcophagus comes back and attacks us!"

"The...the what, now?" Thorric asked, following Thora's finger as she pointed into the darkness.

Morrak grabbed a torch from the wall, cold, bare, and full of stringy cobwebs, and held it out to Thora's flint and steel, striking it flawlessly. With the torch bearing enough light to illuminate the entire room, the others drew closer to the massive stone tomb, its lid lying against the thick wall of the tomb. They didn't see the stone relief, etched in the wall of the earth with intricate detail, but I did. A massive portion of the wall had been divided into individually framed sections, revealing a story that lay under what had been a thick layer of dirt and dust.

On the far left, the first large image framed around a man, standing tall, strong, and regal, as he reigned above the world with a confidence I was all-too familiar with. His armor was thick and lined with fur, and swirling around him were delicate snowflakes, etched carefully in the stone. The man was Tacháan, but I wondered how they had captured his features so well. From the tiny furrow between his brows when he was focused, to the battle scars on his hands, identifying my husband was simple. Figures surrounded him, bowing reverently all around him. My eyes continued to the next panel, where Ragnar was mid-fall, a grimace of shock and pain carved in his features. Buried in his back was the hilt of a dagger, wielded by a beautiful woman with long hair, dressed in the traditional Tacháan formal attire with a delicate jeweled crown upon her head.

The chilling realization struck like a bolt of lightning: my nightmares were more than just that. They were foretold.

CHAPTER 22

CONVERSATIONS BETWEEN KINGS

Someone was calling my name, but all I could hear were the echoes from my nightmare: the soft gasp Ragnar had uttered as his blood poured, the faint gurgles and choking wheezes as he struggled to breathe, and the faint hissing that came from the dagger in my hand, buried in his throat.

Morrak approached me; I could see him as if he were at the end of a dark tunnel, and he rested his hands on my shoulders. He knelt and I realized that I had fallen to my knees. He locked eyes with me, and a flicker of some recognition lit his gaze. He spoke gently, quietly, soothing words that helped me to find the air in the dank cavern. His words fell on my ears and I focused on them, obeying his gentle orders to stand and feel the packed dirt under my feet, to listen to the sound of his voice, to smell the moisture in the mines around us. I inhaled deeply and exhaled shakily, and Morrak nodded.

"Chin up, Val," he said quietly. "It happens to us all. Keep your feet on the ground and keep moving forward. Hear?"

I nodded, swallowing hard as I redirected my attention to the others, who were now studying the giant stone relief, a mixture of fear and wonder in their faces. I didn't dare look at the carving of myself and Ragnar, so I focused my attention on the ones that followed. At the center of the next panel, a robed figure stood with arms stretched out, flames surrounding and erupting from his hands. His face was shrouded in the sculpted folds of the robes, hiding his features, but at his feet, the figures that had been worshiping Ragnar were now bound with heavy chains.

"That one, there," Thora interrupted as she gestured toward the robed figure, "I think that's the one that crawled out of that sarcophagus."

"There's a body in that grave?" I asked as I drew closer.

Thora snorted. "Not anymore."

"What? What in the nine hells does *that* mean?" Thorric half-shouted. "What happened here? How did this all happen? Where did that great beast come from and how did you survive?"

"Maybe we can address that later," Althaea interrupted, earning an annoyed glance from Thorric. "We need to look deeper into *this*. This is a prophecy, but it's too vague for me to interpret. I've recorded the individual panels, but what do you all think? What am I missing?"

I took a deep breath and forced myself to see the stone reliefs as just that; carved stone. I took in the details of the Tacháan king as he stood powerfully atop the world, the betrayal of love, a robed wizard with slaves. The next ones were new, so I studied them carefully. A mountain of gold and precious gems lay under the feet of thousands as men climbed toward the top. Some were depicted as falling, sliding, or laying dead at the foot of the mountain, while others persevered and continued to gain. I shifted to the next stone relief to see the robed figure surrounded by carved runes as he performed a ritual, surrounded by flames. The next had turned the mountain of gold into a deep hole in the earth, those that had been climbing were now spiraling down the hole, scrambling to avoid demise. The last stone relief brought a shiver down my spine and took the breath from my lungs. Taking up most of the space, a monstrous beast stood, five scaly heads sprouting from its massive body. From each of its mouths, lined with teeth carved razor-sharp, the elements poured out from each; bolts of lightning, plumes of flame, acid spraying outward, shards of ice, and droplets of poison.

Thorric turned away, clasping the holy symbol hidden beneath his beard, muttering under his breath, and focused his attention on the contents of the empty tomb. He leaned inside, brushing the bottom with his hands as he scooped a handful of dust and fragile remnants of what may have been parchment into his empty alms box.

"Maybe a Mender can restore this," he suggested.

"Restore...the dirt? Sure," Morrak replied plainly with a shrug as he turned to Thora. "I think you need to tell us what happened here. How are *you* the only survivor?"

She paled. "The only survivor? No, no, no, that's not possible, I told them to run! I gave them orders to retreat...we were following orders."

"Whose orders?" I asked quietly, pulling a note from my bag. "This note says that you were told to dig, even though the mine was dry. Why would you do this?"

She hesitated and Thorric growled. "Our people were

massacred, cut down without a chance to fight back! How dare you-"

"It's not like that," she said, her throat thick with grief. "They weren't just orders, it was a threat. Stop digging and we all die. We didn't realize we'd dug too deep until...until we heard it growling."

"I'm guessing you're talking about our hairy little friend over there?" Thorric grumbled, waving his hammer toward the body of the beast.

Thora hung her head and sighed. "I led the excavation of the biggest cavern, and we followed the natural slope downward, and though the earth seemed to melt right under our hammers and pickaxes, we didn't mine anything but rock! Not a single gemstone, no gold dust... nothing. But we hoped that it was just another couple feet away. The earth fell away eventually and we broke through to this little clearing, and we saw the door. We were about spent, just exhausted after a full day of mining, and we stopped to rest, just to take a breather. The air was heavier than it is now...like we were breathing in mud, but as we approached the door, that's when the growling started. There was a little window, like an air vent, and I looked through. It was looking right at me, but it was chained to the wall. But it was waiting."

"Waiting for what?" Morrak asked, his arms crossed as he listened.

"I-I don't know," she admitted, continuing. "All I know is that I turned away to whisper to my men to quietly retreat, and when I looked back through the vent, I was nose-to-nose with it."

I swallowed hard, and Althaea covered her mouth as we waited for Thora to tell us what had happened.

Thorric shifted uncomfortably and Morrak's furrowed expression was marred as he clenched his jaw with anger.

"How did you survive?" Morrak asked quietly. "Your men are lying in *pieces* in the next room and you're somehow unscathed."

"What are you accusing me of?" Thora said, anger and red-hot grief lining her words as she spat them, her voice rising with every word. "D'ya think I sent my men to die? Or d'ya believe I hid like a scared mouse? Huh? Speak up!"

"That's enough, both of you," Althaea snapped with a surprising outburst. "Allow her to finish, Morrak."

Thora burned with anger and heartbreak as she opened her mouth to speak.

"I told them, I screamed at them, to run," she said, her anger melting into tears that began to fall from her eyes. "They were able to round the corner before it was able to break down the door. I held it as long as I could, but that thing tore it right off the hinges. It fell on me, I thought I was dead, and I hit my head on the ground and passed out. I woke up when one of you must have stepped on me."

"That would have been Kona," I said, as the wolf's ears twitched and her head cocked. "Sorry."

Thora nodded and she turned away from the stone carving and sarcophagus, kneeling at the side of the great beast. As we joined her, I took in a few details, and Morrak knelt by its monstrous head, inspecting a thick, iron collar around its neck. Pulling a short dirk from his boot, he wedged the blade between a thin hinge and pried it apart, where it fell with a clang that echoed through the room. Thorric shushed him as he took hold of one of the manacles that had bound the beast to the wall, lifting the heavy arm in the air.

"Take a look at this!" Thorric exclaimed. "These cuffs are so tight they've nearly grown into its skin. They have runes and glyphs imbued into them...and yet our friend here *still* broke free."

"This collar is something else, too," Morrak muttered. "I don't do that...magic stuff, so can somebody tell me what we're lookin' at here?"

He held the iron collar up and Althaea took it, her brow furrowed as she studied it before shaking her head.

"This is beyond me, at least here in this dank place," she said quietly, apologizing to the dwarves. "I'll need to study this further...but you can keep it in your bag, Morrak. Can we get out of here, please?"

She handed it back to him and brushed her hands off on her pants, shuddering. The room held nothing else of value, and we escorted Thora out of the room, the chilling prophecy etched into the very earth searing itself into my mind. Quietly, we navigated the winding mineshaft until we reached the cavern where Thora's companions lay. She rushed past us with surprising speed and knelt at their sides, weeping. Thorric approached and rested a hand on her shoulder.

"I've been taught the holy words, lass," he said softly. "We can bless them and lay them to rest."

"Not here," she asked thickly. "Not in *this* mine. It's cursed."

"Agreed," Thorric replied. "We'll take them to town and bury them with honor."

Thora thanked him, and as Thorric knelt at the head of each dwarf, he blessed them and placed small coins over their eyes from a small, golden pouch he had nestled inside his armor. We wrapped them in whatever kinds of cloth we could salvage from the mine and set them in a minecart as we marched in a solemn silence toward the entrance. Thora brought a cart and two sturdy ponies from a hidden meadow nearby, the makeshift safety for their ponies surrounded by thickets and heavy shrubs. She hitched the ponies as we transferred the bodies from the minecart to the wagon. Once everything was situated and secured, Thora began to lead the ponies down the path, and paused suddenly. She handed the reins to Thorric, who was behind her, and she turned to face the mouth of the mine. With a guttural shout, a ritualistic stomping of her boots, and a wave of her arms that was both graceful and full of anger and power, she shouted a curse at the mine. As quickly as she had stopped, she took up the reins again and didn't say another word until we left her in the gentle hands of the city's elderly dwarven cleric, Vorrald Runecrafter.

We returned to the Salty Seagull, worn, tired, and heavy-hearted, and as we dined and drank to the memories of the fallen, Thora joined us, with a joyful Phil-lip in tow. He let out a squeal of excitement as he saw us, rushing to hug each of us.

"My friends, I'm so glad you're back!" he said, accepting a mug of ale and holding high. "To my old friends, to my new friends, may our bond run deeper than the deepest mines, may our friendship stretch longer than the longest of rivers, and may our love span longer than the life of the elves!"

"Kinda weird, but okay," Morrak whispered to me as he drank the toast. "Also, did you know you're being watched by the group of men in the far corner?"

"No, describe them to me, subtly, please."

"They're city guards. Somebody beat 'em to hell and back. Uh-oh, one of 'em's headed this way," he murmured, taking a sip from his stein.

I braced and turned around, meeting the guard's eyes, and he held up his hands in a peaceful surrender.

"We don't want any more trouble, ma'am. *I* don't, at least," he said. "We just want all of you to leave."

"I've been...away on business, just got back today. What happened to your men?" I asked, nodding toward the bruised guards.

"That King of yours, the Wardog Ragnar," the man said, a mixture of fear and respect thick in his tone, "King Rofellos and the Wardog met behind closed doors...and I heard that during their...*conversation*, someone said somethin' untoward. Rofellos stormed right out, hopped on his horse, and took off, back to his Keep. Ragnar and his boy, Bjorn, carried out four guards, all beat to hell and knocked out cold. Ragnar just dropped 'em in front of the other guards. I heard from another guard that King Rofellos won't say what happened or what was said. But you Tacháan people are the problem, here. Leave our country or there's going to be trouble for you."

"Are you threatening me?" I asked, my voice dangerously calm.

"No, ma'am, just advising," he answered quickly, turning on his heel and returning to his table.

"I hope you ain't buying that load o'dung," a voice behind us said quietly.

The tall bartender, greenish tinge of his skin betraying his forest-born elven ancestors, glanced at me and wiped out an already clean mug as he continued working and speaking quietly to me.

"I've heard what really happened," he said. "Ragnar

confronted old Rolly about the wedding. I heard he thinks it was set up by Rofellos himself."

"Not exactly a stretch to the imagination," Morrak muttered with a subtle shrug.

"Well, whatever happened, there was a good ol' fashioned brawl in the Town Hall's meeting room, and Rofellos didn't stick around to get his hands dirty. The rumors are already flyin'."

"I can only imagine," I said, rolling my eyes and envisioning Ragnar's preferred type of diplomacy and the resulting bruises. "Regardless, what was the point of the meeting? Why would Ragnar meet with Rofellos? Those two hate each other."

"Rumors are that the Wardog's searching for his Queen. She's run from him, supposedly. You're from up there, you know anything about it?"

I shook my head. "I've been down this way a while," I lied as the barman sighed, disappointed to have no more gossip.

Morrak leaned in. "What do you really know?"

"I know I need to find out what happened between those two, but I can't explain."

"No need, I'm sure we need to talk to more than a few people to find out about this collar, and check up on the latest wedding news. We're basically heroes, you know."

I scoffed and Althaea leaned in.

"Morrak is right," she said with an air of astonishment. "Someone has spread wild stories that it was us who fought the banshee and saved so many people. Rumors are going around, alright."

"We're not heroes," Thorric growled, his eyes glazed over with a haunted grief, "we just happened to be there and we got lucky."

"Regardless of what we think of ourselves, the situation has taken a turn," I said, careful of how I chose my words. "Two kings conversed in the town hall, supposedly about the wedding. I think it would be a wise move to find out exactly what was said...and who swung first."

"I think we can guess the answer to that," Althaea said. "Ragnar is a soldier. He probably heard something he didn't like and knocked out the guards to prove a point."

"As a Tacháan, you *may* be right," I replied, "but if Bjorn was there, he's the one to keep Ragnar in check. Rofellos must have said something absolutely nefarious for Ragnar to swing, but the question is, why did he go after the guards and not Rofellos himself?"

"First thing in the morning," Thorric announced to us, "we'll head straight to the town square and find out who knows what. And then we'll make them talk."

THE ROOSTER loudly heralded dawn from outside the window, and Kona whined as she watched them perched on the fencepost as I donned a simple linen dress and a soft leather overdress.

"Fylgja, Kona. I'll get you something to eat, you wild thing," I said, patting my side as she trotted to my side.

Meeting Althaea at a table, the others soon joined, and I realized that for every three bites Morrak took, one more vanished underneath the table...into Kona's waiting jaws. Fully aware that I knew and mildly disapproved of feeding Kona under the table, Morrak locked eyes with me, a playful smirk on his face as he slowly lowered his hand under the table, a small chunk of sausage pinched between his fingers.

"Oops." He grinned, wiping his hand on his shirt.

"You're going to make her fat. She won't fight well if she can't move," I replied with a grin.

"Who do you think we need to find first?" Althaea interrupted. "I can't imagine many will be willing to speak so openly with us. Do we split up...pair off and hope for the best? I don't think a group of armed folk is very...inviting."

"That's not a bad idea, lass," Thorric grumbled as he lifted his empty stein to the passing barmaid as she took it for a refill. "We'll pair up and speak with townsfolk. Merchants hear everything, and so do the guards, for the right amount of coin."

Thorric and Althaea covered the southern half of the city square while Morrak, Kona, and I traipsed around the northern half. Morrak frustrated me as he seemed more interested in what the merchants were selling, touching and talking about everything except the matter at hand... but then it happened. As fluid and nonchalant as the conversations he had been holding, suddenly the topic had turned to Ragnar and Rofellos.

"I mean, if it were *me*, I wouldn't have let those savage men into the country at all, let alone into our town hall to have a sit-down with our king," the spice merchant said simply as he leaned against his wagon, laden with exotic spices.

"They're really as vicious as people say?" Morrak said, his challenge met with a solemn nod.

"Listen, I know that Rofellos sent four of his guards in prior to the meeting, like a while before, Rofellos went in, and then Ragnar and the other one went in right after.

Bjorn? Looked just like Ragnar. They were in there for an hour before Rofellos burst outta there, mad as a hornet. Little bit later, Ragnar and Bjorn come out, draggin' out the guards like sacks of grain!" he said, the hushed explanation growing louder as he continued. "Y'know what I heard him say? Heard it w' my own ears or I wouldn't have believed it. *'They slipped.'*" Can you believe that?"

He chortled under his breath and sighed, hands on his belt as he shook his head in disbelief.

"Why did Rofellos need additional guards if it was supposed to be a diplomatic conversation?" I asked.

"Did anyone else see what was going on inside?" Morrak asked, "you know, anyone that was still in the hall working a little late?"

The merchant shrugged. "Don't know, don't really care. I know what happened, and that's what I told ya. All that'd be in there would be the orphan, and I don't think he'd be anywhere near that."

"An orphan? A child?" I stammered, "why would a child be working in the town hall alone?"

The merchant looked at me, carefully scanning me, and chuckled gently. "The response of a woman, naturally, my Lady. The orphans work here, just like the widows do. Everyone contributes to the city's well-being. Luka is very grateful to have a quiet job where he can stay out of the public eye."

I met Morrak's glance and we quietly shifted away from the wagon of spices.

"Let's find that kid and make him tell us everything he knows," Morrak growled.

I stopped in my tracks and turned to Morrak in shock. "You...you don't have any experience with children, do you?"

"No, why?"

"How about I handle this one? If I don't make any headway, then I'll let you…interrogate the child," I said, waving to catch Thorric and Althaea's attention as they drew close.

Sharing the information we obtained, it became very clear that no one really knew what had happened inside the secured town hall. Everyone speculated and allowed the exaggerations to flow freely, but we all agreed that finding the orphan boy, Luka, was the most important. He may have seen or heard the happenings, we just needed to persuade him to share that with us.

CHAPTER 23

THE BRAVERY OF A BOY

As we neared the town hall, positioned opposite the market square, Kona drew closer to me as the crowds grew larger and louder. The entrance was guarded by elves wearing the shining gold armor of Thyuland's army, and I had a feeling we weren't going to be allowed to simply traipse inside.

"Let's find a less conspicuous way in," I murmured, taking a wide berth around the entrance toward a side street.

As we spied a back door, propped open by an overturned bucket, we waited, half-hidden in the shadows of the wall and the cluttered property, to see who would emerge.

"Who are you waiting for?" a soft voice came from right beside us, startling each of us.

A small boy, thin and hungry, stood next to Morrak as he watched the door with us. I knelt next to him and my eyes met his. One was a bright emerald green, the other a sapphire blue, with copper flecks matched the smattering of freckles across his face. I smiled and offered my hand.

As he shook it, I noticed how his small hands were calloused with years of work already. His hair was unkempt with golden blond curls, making his unique eyes pop with vibrancy.

"We're looking for someone who can help us find the truth," I said. "We've heard that some scary things happened very recently, and we know that some of those things really happened, but some didn't. We heard that you might know what really happened."

He nodded, and his eyes dropped to the ground, focusing on Kona's white paw. He wiped his nose with the back of his hand and sniffled.

"I-I don't wanna get in trouble, I don't wanna go to the dark room again," he mumbled, his little chin trembling with fear. "I didn't see anything, I didn't see anybody."

My heart ached as he wept, shaking with absolute terror, and I set my hand on his shoulder. He jumped and I drew my hand back, apologizing.

"We won't hurt you," I promised. "Are you Luka? I'm Val, these are my friends, Morrak, Althaea, and Thorric. And this is Kona. She would like to say hello to you."

The boy lifted his head, and nodded. "I'm Luka. Can I pet her?"

As if she already understood, Kona nuzzled her head into his open palm and his mouth split into a smile, the youthfulness returning to his gaunt face.

"What kind of dog is she?" Luka asked, his voice bright with joy.

"Oh, she's not a dog," I said with a grin. "She's a Tacháan wolf! Have you ever seen one before?"

Fear flickered on his face for only a split second before

he took her muzzle in both hands, planting a wet kiss on her nose. He laughed and looked at me with joy.

"She's not scary!" he exclaimed.

"Did someone tell you she was scary?" Althaea said, stooping down next to him with a warm smile.

He took a breath and turned to her, paling as he caught sight of her pointed, elongated ears, the tell-tale high elf's outward marker. He quickly shook his head and gave Kona a quick pat.

"I can't help you, I don't know anything. I didn't see anything, I have to get back to work," he stammered helplessly, his eyes firmly on the ground as he almost tripped over his feet as he walked quickly away.

I connected with his trauma immediately and called his name gently. He paused and turned around to look at me with eyes welled with tears.

"She's my friend, she won't hurt you, either," I said, holding my hand out to him, a peace offering I desperately hoped he would take. "We can keep you safe from the people that have you so scared."

His eyes darted back and forth as he battled his fears, and Kona approached him without hesitation. He wrapped his arms around her and muffled his cries in her coat, and Althaea returned to Thorric and Morrak, her hand covering her mouth as tears grew in her eyes. She mouthed her apologies to me and I nodded in understanding.

"Luka? My name is Valérikka," I said quietly, so only he could hear. "I need to ask you some really hard questions, because I need to make sure that my family is safe. Can you help me, please?"

He glanced up from Kona's fur, confused and a little curious, but the fear was still rampant.

"I promise I'll make sure that no one will know that you talked with us. I promise you'll be safe," I swore to him.

"Can Kona stay by me, please?"

"Of course she can."

He sniffled, wiped his runny nose on his sleeve, and took a breath. "Okay, I'm ready."

"Can you tell me what happened between Rofellos and Ragnar?"

He gave a tiny laugh. "Oh, he got so mad at him! I was in the back room making sure that the inkwells were full, if they're not I get in trouble. And there was all the stomping that the guards made and they came in and stood in the corners of the room, still like statues. Then Ragnar came in, with another man that kinda looked like him."

"That would have been Bjorn, his son," I said as he nodded.

"Ragnar spoke to him kinda quiet, but I couldn't understand what they were saying."

"They were speaking Nordmaarian. That's the language of Tachá. It's a beautiful language."

"Can you speak it?"

"*Ek tala Norðmarisku mjök vel,*" I replied, watching his eyes grow big. "Would you like to try?"

"Yes! Can I say something to Kona? Does she understand Nor...I forgot what it's called," he said, sheepish and excited.

"Tell her *Leggstu,*" I whispered in his ear.

"Kona...leg-stoo," Luka said, gasping as she laid down in front of him.

"Now, tell her *Góði hundr,*" I said, failing to hide the smile.

"G-Guh-goh-thee hoon-der!" he said as Kona's ears perked at the praise of being called a good dog, her tail wagging against the ground.

"What happened after Ragnar and Bjorn were in the room?" I asked as he continued to pet her. "Did Rofellos come in, too?"

As he picked up Kona's paw, setting it atop his own hand, he nodded.

"Yeah. They sat down at the big table and were nice for a little bit. It was quiet for a minute, and then Ragnar spoke. He said that he knew what Rofellos did, and that it was his fault. He said *a lot* of bad words. I hid so that they wouldn't see me, but I could still hear everything. Rofellos laughed at him and said that he didn't have any proof, but then Ragnar said some *more* bad words and said that *he* knew that Rofellos was working with the Trifecta. I don't know who that is, but Rofellos got mean after that. He said Ragnar was looking for monsters so that he wasn't the only one, and then Ragnar said that if he found proof that Rofellos was working with the Trifecta...he would do somethin' read bad."

"Did he say what he would do?" I asked gently as Luka sighed and nodded.

"He-he said that if Rofellos was working with the Trifecta people, then he would put his head on a spike. Are the Trifecta really bad men?"

"I...I don't know. But I *do* know this: Ragnar is a really good man and a very good king. If he says that the Trifecta are really bad, then they must be really, really bad. Ragnar doesn't lie, and he always protects his people."

"He's a good guy? He says a lot of bad words for a good guy," Luka said doubtfully.

"I know, and you're right. I'll tell him that he shouldn't say so many bad words when I see him next, okay?" I said as he nodded with a grin. "What happened next?"

"I peeked out into the room and I saw Rofellos stand up. He leaned over the table, and I couldn't see his face, but he said something to Ragnar...and he said a bad word so I can't say it, but he said it anyway. Ragnar stood up real fast and threw his chair. Bjorn got up fast, too, but that's because Rofellos snapped his fingers and the guards tried to beat them up. Rofellos just walked away but I don't know why Ragnar got so mad at what he said."

"Can you tell me what he said? Even if it has a bad word, you won't get in trouble for saying a bad word," I asked, a knot forming in my gut as Luka agreed.

"Rofellos looked at Ragnar and said, *"I'm gonna find that bitch of yours and kill her."*"

My stomach turned. I kept my face neutral so as to not scare Luka, but Kona's ears flattened. Did Rofellos truly know I was in his country, or was he simply baiting the Wardog with his notorious impatience, knowing that no one knew where his Queen was?

"Luka, you've been so helpful for us, we're going to be able to help a lot more people because of you," I said, the warmth in my heart for the orphan. "Do you have anyone that takes care of you?"

"No, Madam Grosbeak says I'm old enough to work and fend for myself, so it's just me."

"Would you like to be taken somewhere where you would be taken care of?"

Luka cocked his head and watched my face curiously. "I-I don't know, what does that mean?"

"I have friends that help take people from bad places and help them get to Tachá, where I'm from. There are families that would love to adopt you. Is that something that you'd like?"

"Leave Thyuland? Go where? With who? Will you be there?"

"You would leave Thyuland, yes, to go north, to Tachá where Ragnar is the king. My friends Freya and Leo will make sure that you get there safely, and I'll join you as soon as I can."

"When do we leave?" he said with a bright grin.

"Well, I can't leave quite yet, I'll have to write to my friends, but they make regular trips to the cities back and forth, so I'll tell them to keep an eye out for a brave boy named Luka. It might be a couple weeks, can you wait that long? I'll send the crow today if you'd like."

"Yes, please!" he cried, rushing forward and wrapping his arms around me.

A sniffle brought my attention to the rest of the party, where Thorric wiped a tear.

"Wha!?" he said, his voice breaking. "I'm not a heartless beast!"

I introduced Luka to Thorric, who knelt and shook his hand and patted his shoulder. Next, Morrak nodded toward him, and handed him a small knife.

"Stick this in your boot, kid," he said, kneeling to tuck it into Luka's boot and ruffling his messy hair. "Y'never know when you're gonna need to defend yourself."

Althaea held out her closed hand, and as she opened it, a flower, its petals alternating blue and green, fully blossomed. Luka's eyes grew wide and he gasped as she held it out to him. He accepted it and whispered his thanks, his eyes darting to her ears as she smiled sympathetically, knowing that she would need to give him space until he felt safe enough near her. My heart ached as I pondered what his past could have been like, and I sighed, watching him lavish attention on Kona. A requirement of the Hunter's Guild was to forsake all family ties, both past and future, which meant that children were not born into the Guild. I had accepted that I would never feel a child kicking in my womb, I would never suffer the birthing pains, nurse an infant, or see myself and my husband in their features. Despite my vow, Luka's innocence tugged at my heartstrings, and my vow remained intact with my ability as Queen of Tachá to send him to the safety of my home, inside the safety of the Keep.

"Val, we need to move, we've been here for too long already," Thorric said quietly as I nodded. "Send your letter, he'll be fine."

"Hear that?" I told Luka, "do everything you normally do, and I'll send my two friends to pick you up and take you to my hometown. Freya is a halfling, Leo is a wood elf, but I trust them wholeheartedly. You'll be safe with them, okay?"

He nodded and grinned. "I'll watch for them."

"Go on, back to your work, boy," Thorric said, patting his shoulder. "Tell no one that you've spoken with us, tell no one else what you saw between the kings, understand?"

The boy nodded. He knew what it would mean if someone knew he had first-hand knowledge, and we knew it, too. Luka ran down the street, pausing to grab a wooden box that he had stowed behind a broken cart. He vanished around the corner and I straightened.

"I need to get to a crow, now," I murmured, staring at the vacant street.

By the time the sun had set, the letter had been sealed and sent. It contained a detailed description of Luka and the importance of escorting him to safety, written in the language of the Halflings, a very uncommon, rarely written language, especially in Thyuland. I sent it with a smaller crow, her dark feathers seeming to glow iridescent in the light. Whispering the urgency into Freya's name, projecting the woman's features into the mind of the crow, I was confident that she would find her. Returning to the party, Kona and I found them eating at the table of the inn, and I speared a sausage to eat before Morrak could swipe it.

"I think I'd like to go back to that mine and study the prophecy wall a little more," Althaea suggested, "anyone like to come and help?"

"Sure, I want to inspect that beast, too," Morrak said. "Sooner, rather than later, before it really starts to stink, I mean."

"I have nothing to do until Freya and Leo get here, anyway," I said with a groan. "I'd like to keep busy and think more about that Trifecta group that Luka mentioned. It sounds *so* familiar."

As a group we left the inn, quietly pondering the events of the past 24 hours to ourselves. Heading toward the gate, I spied Luka, hard at work with a few other children, carrying firewood and stacking them carefully against a shop's sidewall. I smiled to myself, knowing that he would be safe and loved in Tachá, and I continued.

CHAPTER 24
AN UNEXPECTED MISSION

Marching closer to the mines brought a heavy, thick sense of dread into our bones with every step. We paused at a meadow, refilling our waterskins from the bubbling creek nearby, and we struggled to move forward, as if we were moving through a thick haze. As we began, a rustling in the trees nearby caught Kona's attention, and her deep growl alerted the rest of us as we drew weapons.

"Show yourself," Thorric growled, his hammer glowing faintly. "Now."

A mangled, unusual sound came from the higher branches of the evergreen trees, as if a man were trying and failing miserably to imitate an owl.

"Is-is someone up there?" Althaea asked. "We know you're not an owl."

"The hell I'm not!" the voice called angrily, scrambling as it made the poorly imitated owl hoots. "That's it, if I'm coming down there, I'm kicking someone's-"

"Kona, *gakkt at!*" I commanded, pointing at the tree as she began snarling at the base of the tree.

"Alright, alright!" the voice called, the panic forming a few breaks in the voice. "Call off the wolf and I'll come down."

"*Við hlið!*" I said.

Kona stopped immediately, giving a frustrated glance to the tree branches as she returned to my side, waiting with slavering jaws. A few leaves dropped, and after a moment, a heavy sigh announced the visitor. As soon as his talons gripped the bottom branch, I groaned as the tiny, snow-white teacup owl made his appearance.

"What are you doing here?" I barked at the miniature bird.

"Funnily enough, I could ask *you* the same question," he retorted sharply, snapping his little beak.

"Uh, you two know each other?" Morrak asked, a mild amusement on his face.

"Unfortunately," I replied dryly. "This is Axel, a rat with wings and a foul mouth."

"Wow," the owl replied, faking a distraught sniffle. "I thought we were friends. Comrades-in-arms. Life-long lovers!"

"Axel, why are you here?" I said, ready to strike if he were to reveal my identity.

"What, can't a guy just stop by to say hi?" he mused, fluffing his feathers and watching as a down feather the size of my fingernail floated to the grass.

I crossed my arms and Kona let out a deep rumbling growl. Axel swore in a chaotic, angry tongue that I knew as the language of the Nine Hells, and I shouted.

"None of that, Axel, not here," I warned. "Use Nordmaarian if you're going to be *that* vulgar. Understand? No one wants to hear that evil, not when we're already surrounded by it."

"Hence why I'm here, Val. I carry a very important letter from the King. Y'know, Ragnar, the King of Tachá. Are you familiar?" he said with a mocking tone.

I grit my teeth. "I'm familiar. Hand over the letter."

"*No*! You're just gonna *hurt* me!" he shouted, jumping from the branch, flapping wildly, and landing on Althaea's shoulder. "*She* doesn't look like she wants to kill me."

"He's awfully small, and kind of cute, too," Althaea said with a giggle. "He can't be *that* bad."

Axel side-stepped into the crook of her neck and made a tiny little chirping sound, and I rolled my eyes.

"Did you say you had a letter for us, wee bird?" Thorric asked.

Axel spread his wings and shook out his feathers, and a sealed parchment letter fell from his feathers. I didn't recognize that kind of magic and it must have shown on my face.

"Old birds *can* learn new tricks, y'know," Axel said. He folded his wings against his body as Thorric picked up and unsealed the envelope.

Axel glanced at me, his head twisted halfway around as Althaea turned to read over Thorric's head. I waited for Thorric to finish reading and Axel scoffed.

"*Þeir vita eigi hverr þú ert,*" the owl said in Nordmaarian, the curiosity clear in his hushed tone as he realized that my companions didn't know who I was.

I shook my head. "*Þeir vita eigi. Þeir mega eigi vita,*" I replied quietly.

He understood that my reply, '*they do not know, they cannot know,*' grew from a place of fear and protection, not selfishness or pride, and he hopped from Althaea's shoulder, soaring to cross the distance between us. I held out my arm and he landed, so weightless that it almost didn't register.

"Don't kill me and I'll keep your secret," he said quietly.

"Don't piss me off and I won't," I replied. I turned to Thorric, his brow deeply furrowed as he read the letter to himself.

"Well?" Morrak said expectantly, brandishing to the letter.

"We've been offered a job," Thorric said slowly, as if choosing his words carefully. "King Ragnar would like us to investigate an abandoned house to the north. He suspects there are Trifecta members holed up there and he wants them...displaced, and-"

"That's not what it says," Althaea interrupted, deftly swiping the letter from his hands and reading aloud. "*Whispers have reached my ears that a supposedly abandoned house to the north is being used to house Trifecta members. A four-hour walk north of Gray Tide will lead you there, just follow the coastal cliffs and you'll find it. Investigate what is happening, collect all evidence, and burn it to ashes, including anyone with a Trifecta brand. Look at their chest, that's how you'll know. Collect the evidence, and keep it safe until it can be delivered to safe hands. If you choose to accept the mission, whistle, and you will be compensated.*"

"That's it?" I asked.

"Not quite," Althaea said softly, handing the letter to me. "I think the last bit is for you."

Taking the letter, I read to the bottom and my breath caught in my throat. Written in firm, bold letters, unmistakably angry, I could almost hear his words as I read them. ***Valérikka. Your husband would like you to come home. Now.*** I swallowed hard and folded the letter back up, handing it back to Thorric.

"Your husband must have some strong ties with the King, eh?" Thorric chuckled.

"Something like that," I muttered, turning to Axel. "Tell us what you know about the Trifecta. Please."

"What's to tell?" he said with a stomp of his feathered feet. "They're an elite criminal faction that's elbow-deep in every single political, economic, and feudal instance in the countries of Thyuland and Ibria. It's only by Ragnar's threats and reputation that they haven't attempted to take Tachá. And the massive, magical wall helps with security, too. They're *horrible*, they're the worst of the worst sort of people."

"Who's the leader?" Thorric asked.

Axel turned his head and gave a laugh that sounded like an owl's hoot. "If *anyone* knew the answer to that question, do you think the Trifecta would be so untouchable? I thought you all were supposed to be smart. No one knows who it is or they'd be dead already. Pretty sure it ain't one person. It's three...hence their pretty little symbol."

"What's that look like?" I asked, my memory faintly recalling the discussions of the faction south. It had never been a true concern, not with how strong our forces were and how cold our lands were.

"No one outside of the organization knows for sure. And if they do, they're dead shortly after," Axel replied.

"Well, this is the second time we've stumbled across the Trifecta's mentions," Thorric said, catching our eyes. "If they get wind of us, regardless if we're in their business or not, we're targets. I say let's get ahead of them. Who wants to whistle?"

"Should probably be a Northerner..." Axel muttered, trailing off.

I rolled my eyes and gave a short, sharp whistle. A barking caw sounded in reply and a massive crow landed on a nearby branch, a small bag tied to its leg. Easily recognized as one of the castle crows, I approached fearlessly and took the bag from its leg. It was no larger than my waterskin and weighed nearly nothing. I handed the bag to Althaea and stroked the crow's beak, thanking it in my language for the gift. Althaea laughed suddenly, and I turned to see that she had opened the bag.

"You have to see this...it's amazing!" she cried, reaching her entire arm into the bag.

She pulled out four glass bottles, about the size of my palm, each holding a blood red liquid inside that would heal our wounds, and passed one to each of us. She murmured under her breath as she managed to free four pairs of boots from the bag, all sized specifically for each of us, and as I inspected it, I realized that these boots had been heavily enchanted to protect the wearer from the bitterest of cold. The thick treads that lined the soles would ensure our footing would be solid always, and I smiled, seeing a small wolf trinket tied to my laces. Althaea pulled out the last item; a smooth stone, as dark as night, polished to shine.

"What's that?" Morrak asked.

"That, lad, is a Sending Stone," Thorric said, holding out his hand as Althaea set the dark stone in the center of his palm. "It'll send whatever we speak, up to a few sentences. The stone glows and speaks my words, in my voice, to the twin stone in the other's possession."

Thorric gave it a tight squeeze and when he opened his hand, he leaned in and spoke. "This is Thorric. Message received. Mission accepted. Anything else we should know? How dangerous is this mission and how dangerous are the Trifecta?"

A few moments passed and Morrak scratched the back of his neck.

"So...we just wait?"

Althaea opened her mouth with what I guaranteed to be a sarcastic response, and the stone glowed in Thorric's hand. A rush of emotions flowed through me and I struggled to remain unaffected as my husband's voice rose from the stone.

"Trust no one. Shadows stir in Gray Tide. The Trifecta are unreasonable and merciless. Do not hesitate. Be careful."

I could hear the pleading in his voice. I bit the inside of my cheek and breathed steadily as I fought the urge to run back home, to wrap myself in his arms and stay under the warm blankets of our bed until someone else dealt with this. I braced myself and lifted my chin, and the fear in my companions was unmistakable. Thorric hadn't moved since Ragnar's voice ceased from the stone, Morrak ground his jaw, clenching it tight, and Althaea's hands trembled. Fear crept up my spine, threatening to strangle me. My husband knew that I was traveling with them, so he sent Axel to us for a reason. Was there more to this than an abandoned house and suspected evidence? Perhaps the evidence was too delicate or well hidden for his men to find, or perhaps it implicated Rofellos like he suspected.

"Are we ready for this?" I asked with an urgency in my tone. "Because if we are, we need to do this now. I don't know what's going on at that house, but I'm gonna find out. He chose us to do this. *Us.* Maybe it's because we're the closest in proximity, but maybe it's because he thinks we're capable of handling it."

"You're right, lass," Thorric said quietly, nodding in agreement. "Let's get going, then."

Axel cleared his throat and turned his head around, burying his beak in his feathers. He pulled out a small gold coin and sighed.

"Someone...someone needs to hold on to this. Can we stick it in someone's bag who we *know* isn't gonna spend it or lose it?" he asked, the coin muffling the words in his beak.

"Why not spend it?" Morrak asked. "Is it lucky? Valuable?"

"Not exactly," he mumbled, offering it to Althaea, who took it gently and Axel sighed heavily. "Please guard this coin with your life as it is tied to mine."

Althaea glanced at me and I gave her a small nod as Axel hung his head in shame. She tucked the coin into the bag that the crow had delivered, now secured to her belt. Donning Ragnar's gifted boots, we began the trek north, quietly marching. The sun had shifted significantly in the clear blue skies by the time the house appeared, a dark pinprick in the distance. Taking cover behind an outcropping of rocks and thorny bushes, we rested.

"How are we doing this?" Morrak asked. "That house is far from abandoned."

"How can y'tell that?" Thorric wondered.

Morrak pointed toward the house and shifted to the east. Barely discernible in the grass, rolling in waves from the cool ocean breeze, the faint trail of a wagon led to the house.

"Okay, we're going in there quiet. Is anyone gifted

with the subtlety of reconnaissance? My armor isn't exactly made for skulking," Thorric murmured as he patted the chain mail armor that surrounded his barrel chest.

"I mean, I could, but I really don't want to die for you all, not this early," Axel mumbled, flying to perch on a rock. "I'll stay here and watch everyone's stuff. I can't promise I won't eat a few rations."

"I'll go," I offered. "Someone will have to hold on to Kona."

"I'll go with you," Althaea said, "my armor was crafted from the softest leather, made for silence."

Thorric nodded and placed his hands on the tops of our heads, whispering a blessing over us. The magic trickled down from my head like warm liquid, enveloping me all the way to my toes. Althaea smiled and thanked him as we crept toward the house. Kona whined and Morrak rested his hand on her. I turned and summoned the authority I held over her, knowing she would bite anyone who tried to keep her from my side.

"Kona, *bíð*," I commanded her, raising my hand as she obeyed, staying where she was. "And don't eat the bird."

Althaea and I began the agonizingly slow journey, maneuvering a wide arc around the house, shrouded by the shadows of tall bushes. The grass that surrounded the house had grown up tall and tangled, and sneaking close was simpler than I had anticipated. Pressing ourselves against the foundation of the house, we deftly peeked inside the only window that wasn't broken and boarded up, spying a pair of figures seated at a table, a set of dice and a pile of coins between them. I noticed that the door was cracked open opposite the window, and a shadow passed by every minute or so. Miming with hand signals, we circled the rest of the house and discovered nothing new. Returning to the others, nearly invisible in the hiding spot we had chosen, we shared the information and Thorric sat, thinking.

"We have to assume that the house is filled with Trifecta, and we have to assume that they know we're coming."

"Stick together?" I suggested.

"Absolutely. Do not split the party," Thorric said, the glimmer of a haunting memory washing over his face for a moment. "We stay within sight of each other, and when the house is cleared, we stay within earshot. Don't let your guard down. Don't assume the house is empty. Don't separate yourself."

Agreed, we started toward the house, utilizing the same path that Althaea and I had taken. With the windows boarded up tightly, we were able to approach unseen, and as we steadied ourselves near the front entrance, Thorric turned and put his finger to his lips. I drew an arrow and nocked it, focused on the guard that had been patrolling. While making our way toward the north-eastern corner of the house where the gambling men were holed up, I knew we would encounter the patrolling guard. Killing him quickly and quietly would ensure we weren't discovered sooner than we wanted. Thorric turned the doorknob and opened the door wide, allowing me to enter the house with my bow readied. Kona was right behind me, and she understood the importance of our stealth. Her head had lowered and her paws were silent as she waited for me to make the first move. I crouched in the shadows and listened for the footsteps that approached, and the guard didn't even see me, not even when my arrow sank into his throat. It wasn't until he fell to his knees, gurgling and choking on his blood, that he met my eyes. The shock registered in a mixture of anger and fear as he grew ashen, falling to his side as he exhaled for the last time. I pulled at the man's shirt, checking the center of his blood stained chest, and found no mark of any kind, let alone a Trifecta identifier. Had I gotten it wrong? I paled and glanced at Morrak, who had joined me. He shook his head and pointed to the man's heart, reaching and pulling the soaked clothing away. He wiped the blood away from the area and my breath hitched.

"Is that..."

Morrak nodded. "The Mark of the Trifecta."

Branded by a hot iron, the angry pink scar appeared to be a few years old, and I peered closer to get a better view. A trio of snakes formed an open triangle, each snake biting the next as the jaws of the serpents formed the points of the triangle. A shiver ran down my spine and I glanced at Morrak, his face set, emotionless and void.

"He didn't choose this path," Morrak whispered, pulling him to the shadows.

We continued, with Morrak on my left with his crossbow loaded and Althaea directly behind me, Thorric trailed behind, moving slower than us in an effort to stay quiet. Hiding around a corner, we peeked at the staircase, finding no one around it. With the large entryway empty, I spied the door, opened only a few inches, and as I listened, I could hear the dice rolling.

"Ready?" Althaea whispered in my ear.

Morrak and I gave a nod and she approached the

door, reaching around to push it open. The door creaked and the men paused their game.

"Someone there?"

Chairs scraped the floor as heavy boots approached the door. The dull sliding of steel against the leather scabbards brought our senses to a sharpened focus, and as I steadied my aim, a crossbow bolt buried itself deep into the man's chest. He dropped, gasping as the second man yanked the door open, rushing out with his sword readied. Swinging wildly and desperate to live, the man was disarmed by a lateral swing of Thorric's hammer, and he fell to his knees, begging and blubbering.

Thorric hesitated and lowered his hammer, which had been leveled to kiss the man's cheek squarely. Morrak reloaded his crossbow as the man sobbed.

"P-please, please don't kill me," he said, spittle dripping down his lips as he bowed his head and hugged himself, rocking back and forth. "I'll tell you anything you want to know!"

Althaea lowered her bow and Thorric relaxed, nodding.

"Alright, tell us. Tell us everything about this house," Thorric said.

The man lifted his head and the force of the crossbow bolt that Morrak fired threw him onto his back. He was dead before his skull met the floorboards.

"Why did you do that?" Thorric hissed at Morrak. "He was about to tell us everything!"

Morrak scoffed. "No, he wasn't. Check his hands. The Northern King said not to hesitate, and that's the first thing you do. Y'know what? I'll show you why you don't hesitate with these bastards."

He knelt and carefully pried open the man's fingers,

revealing a small vial, still sealed with a cork and wax covering.

"Y'know what this is?" Morrak snarled. "It's an incendiary! Y'know what happens if this glass breaks or the top pops off? It's a liquid fireball that would burn this room, and all of us, to ashes, as soon as it hits air. *Don't. Hesitate.* A Trifecta brand means they would die rather than run, hide, or talk. They'll fight anyway they can to keep the snake's head intact. Understand?"

Morrak pocketed the small vial and reloaded his crossbow, muttering under his breath. I paused and knelt by the corpse, pulling aside his shirt and finding the mark, this time tattooed on over the man's heart. Morrak caught sight of it and met my eyes.

"Remember when I said the other man didn't choose his path? This one did. A tattoo marks the willingness of a man to sell his soul to the Trifecta. It's...incredibly rare that someone obtains a tattoo."

"How do you know all of this?" I asked.

"I've done a lot of research on these bastards. Every one of them deserves to die."

"You have a history with them."

He nodded. "I'd like to keep it that way, too. I hope you understand."

"I do." I understood the trauma, and I realized that Morrak had suffered loss at the hands of the Trifecta. I wasn't going to pry. I didn't want anyone prying into my situation, so I wasn't about to tear open Morrak's wounds.

"I hate to interrupt, but this might be something that Ragnar wanted us to investigate..." Althaea said, trailing off as she held up a small scroll to read.

Details of shipment 317-B; 22 individuals, 850 gold paid in full.
Overseer Grimwold disciplined for repeated escapees.

"You don't think," Thorric breathed, pointing at the word *escapees*. "Tell me it's somethin' else."

"There's nothing else it could be," Althaea said quietly. "We need to check the room, their pockets, we need to find the people and free them, fast!"

We entered the room and saw a sparsely furnished room, set up with a few cots, two trunks, and a lockbox hidden under the table. Dividing and scouring the room, we found nothing but a handful of gold and a few trinkets in the lockbox, and nothing of use in the trunks. The sun was shining through the boarded window and I realized that Kona was fixated on it, and began scratching at the wood. Before I could open my mouth to speak, Morrak knelt in front of the sunny spot on the floor, and pried the floor-board up, digging his knife into the crease. It wriggled up with only a little hesitation, and he tossed it aside, reaching in and pulling out a smaller lockbox. I pretended not to notice his hands shaking as he picked the lock, a bead of sweat running down his forehead. Sealed with the symbol of the Trifecta in wax as red as blood, a single letter was the sole occupant on the box. Morrak handed it to Thorric, and the dwarf unsealed it immediately, opening it and reading. Althaea read over his shoulder and covered her mouth with her hand, fingers trembling. I took the note and read it, and I knew why Ragnar wanted every one of them dead.

Expedite the human cargo.
Destroy the unprofitable.

Seal after reading.

"Every last one of them," Thorric growled, his weapon glowing with a holy vengeance. "They're all gonna die."

"Look!" Althaea said, reaching into the floorboards. Faintly glowing, a dull red stone lay in the dusty void.

She took it and squeezed, and in the common language, a gruff voice floated above the stone.

"Shipment arrived, barely alive. The King's patience runs thin. Send the next group in two nights. Discreetly. Rofellos expects his deliveries uninterrupted. Dispose of the evidence if compromised, by order of the Silver Fang."

Thorric clenched his jaw and Morrak spat on the floor, the disgust in his face unmistakable.

"The Silver Fang?" Althaea asked quietly, "that sounds so familiar, I just can't place it...not here."

"We clear this place, room by room," Thorric ordered.

We rose, and Thorric placed the scroll, the letter, and the sending stone in his bag. Room by room, we ended the lives of five men on the ground floor, all bearing the scarred brand of the Trifecta. We approached the staircase and I stopped in my tracks. Kona took a few steps back, whining as her eyes grew wide with fear.

"What...what is that smell?" I whispered.

A putrid and stomach churning filled the air; I knew the scent and wished it were anything else. Morrak shook his head and gripped his crossbow tighter. The scent clawed at my senses, my nose burned and my eyes watered as we reached the top of the stairs. Kona stayed behind on the main level, the scent too strong for her sharpened senses. The odor was palpable in the air as we stepped into the open landing, and as we carefully crept around, I discovered the probable source, unable to approach the door at the end of the hall without choking. Thorric led the way and held his breath as his fingers curled around the doorknob. He opened it a crack, peered through, and fell backward as the door creaked open. Althaea dropped to her knees, hiding her face as she wept. Morrak stood motionless, pale and breathless.

We had found what the Trifecta deemed *unprofitable*.

CHAPTER 25

THE OFFER
OF FREEDOM

The bodies had been thrown without care, the corpses of the women and children piled high in the room. Thorric closed the door and whispered shakily under his breath, a pleading prayer to his god, before returning to us and resting a hand on Althaea.

"Clear the other rooms," he ordered, his visage haunted by what we had seen.

The room next door contained empty iron cages that lined the walls. The next room contained the same. The room opposite the hall had a locked door, and Thorric threw his shoulder into it, throwing it open. Whimpering and cowering in front of the cage stood an older boy in Trifecta armor. I counted five women and seven young children locked in the cage, beaten, starving, and filthy. As Morrak raised his crossbow to the Trifecta member, a woman in the cage darted forward, shouting at him to stop. I shoved Morrak's arm and his bolt buried in the wall, and he whirled.

"He's one of them! He dies!" he snarled.

"No!" the woman cried. "He's not one of them, I swear it on my own life!"

"He wears their colors, he bears their mark!" Morrak shouted, grabbing the boy by the collar and wrenching his shirt aside.

Only a smattering of bruises colored his chest, faded yellows and greens overlapped by deep reds and purple. There was no mark of the Trifecta, branded or tattooed.

"Please, I-I'm not one of them," the boy said quietly. "I thought it was the safest thing to do. I haven't taken the mark, I-I was supposed to, but I couldn't do it. They stuck me up here to watch over the old man and I...I didn't know what they were doing."

"Yes, you did," Morrak spat, giving the boy a shove into the bars of the cages. "You did, don't lie."

"What was I supposed to do about it?" the boy shouted back, a sob erupting as his voice cracked, "I already lied and told them that the women and children were sick, sick and contagious so they'd leave them alone! I couldn't let them end up like the others!"

"Why did you do that?" I asked, stepping between him and Morrak.

He slid down the bars and fell with a thud on the floor, hiding his face as he cried. I took a step back and saw a scared boy. I glanced at the woman who had come to his defense and her face was streaked with tears.

"He's trying to do the right thing," she whispered. "He's innocent of this violence. Help him. If you have any heart, any sense of good and evil, you've felt it. You *know*. If you're a mother, you know this is true."

The pain seared deeper than a knife. I had never carried a child, something that had gnawed at me for many years. Though I had no biological children of my own, I had become a surrogate mother to Ragnar's children. Bjorn had been old enough to understand what had happened to his mother, Amelia as well, but Ivar had been an infant when his mother passed. When Ragnar introduced me to him, he had just turned ten. Full of wisdom beyond his years, Bjorn was fully committed to the protection of Tachá and her people, vicious Amelia was focused on becoming the best warrior Tachá had; past, present, and future, and Ivar was left with his books and mind. Ivar had quickly become my favorite, his similarities to his father residing and ending in the icy blue of his eyes. Ivar was taller than me by the time he was fifteen, lean and lanky, and quickly became a student of magic and stealth. While his siblings preferred to fight face-to-face, Ivar could pick off his enemies from afar, shrouded in shadows with his bow. Ivar had become adept with arcane arts, and while Ragnar didn't understand the complexities of magic, I did, encouraging Ivar to continue to hone his natural gifts, and it had brought us closer together. I loved Ivar as if he were my own child, and though he had never called me *Móðir*, he treated me as his mother, and that was all I could ask for.

"What's your name?" I asked the boy in front of me.

"Allyn. Allyn Bauer of Blackreach," he said, inclining his head.

"How old are you, and how did you end up here?"

"I'm fifteen. My parents said that I had to go with 'em, because otherwise they would take my sisters. Mama was scared, she was cryin' and beggin' not to take 'em," he mumbled, trying to hide his quivering chin. "Da' said to take me instead. Said I'm a hard worker, to leave the women, and take-take me instead. Mama got to hug me 'fore I left with the soldiers, and she told me...she told me to remember who I was and what kind of man she was raisin' me to be."

"And who are you? Who did your mother raise you to be?"

"Not a murderer. She raised me to protect my sisters from anything that would hurt 'em. This, comin' here, this was my way to protect 'em all."

I glanced at Thorric, he nodded. "He's truthful."

Morrak poked Allyn in the chest. "Why didn't you take the mark?"

"'Cause I was so scared of the fire," he said. "Nobody wanted to hear me screamin' as they burned me, so they punished me, instead."

"How?"

"Made me stay in the room...the one at the end of the hall, for a whole day and a night. Then I had to sit with the old man for the rest of my time," he mumbled, squeezing his eyes shut at the memory of the room.

Morrak dropped his head and sighed. "You don't know how lucky you are, kid."

"I don't feel very lucky," he said, his eyes welled with tears. "I just wanna go home. I want my Mama."

My heart broke for the boy as he cried in front of us, his arms wrapped around himself as he sniffled. I could see Ivar, years younger, in the boy's emotion and vulnerability, and every part of me wanted to embrace the boy. Beside me, Althaea wiped a tear from her cheek.

"Then it's settled," she said. "We're taking you home to your mother. We'll take these women and children back to town where they're safe and free."

"Hold on, who's the old man? Where is he?" Thorric interrupted.

"Here, in here with us," one of the women said, pointing to a cot.

Sleeping soundly and covered with a couple moth-eaten blankets, an old man lay on a cot, his back to us.

"Who in the hell is that?" Morrak asked, lowering his voice as the old man snored softly.

"He's half-deaf, love, he ain't wakin' up," a woman said. "His name is Jonathan, this is his house. His family has lived in this area for generations. He says his wife passed away some years ago, and he was all alone. Until the men showed up to keep him company."

"Is he...complicit to the Trifecta?" Thorric asked. "Is he marked?"

One of the women approached and leaned against the bars. "He has what my old Nan had. His memory, it's not there anymore. It comes and goes, but mostly it goes. He knows his name, but he doesn't even realize that this is his house anymore. He's been sleeping more and more, I pity him. He was just a lonely old man who let the wrong sort into his home."

"Then we'll take him with us," Thorric said, a soft smile matching Althaea's. "Let's get that cage door open and get you all out."

"One of the guards downstairs has a keyring," Allyn said. "The one who has the tattoo."

"I remember where we left him," Morrak said with a sharp nod, darting out of the room.

"Is anyone hurt? Can you all manage to walk a few miles if we can't find a cart?" Althaea asked as the women nodded.

"What about the others?" one of the women in the back said as she approached. "What'll happen to them? We can't leave them there like that."

"I'll take care of them," Thorric said softly. "I know the words and the prayers. They'll be accompanied to their halls of honor."

Morrak returned with the keys and the cage door was opened. The women gently woke the old man and he chuckled heartily, delighted to go for *"a nice walk in the meadow."* Freed of the iron bars, they looked down the hall at the tightly shut door, weeping silently.

"Leave the house, head due south. Stay hidden as much as you can, but head straight for Gray Tide. We'll not be far behind," Thorric said, turning to the boy. "Allyn, you are responsible for seeing that these women... and Jonathan, get back to town safely. Defend them, protect them, and if anyone forces it, fight for them. D'you understand? And take off that armor. Get rid of anything that ties you to the Trifecta."

"I will," he said. "I won't let you down. I'll keep them all safe."

Allyn led Jonathan and the women carefully down the stairs, and I kept an eye out the window as they left the house, the sun shining on their faces.

"Are we ready for this?" Thorric asked, motioning down the hall. "Each soul needs and deserves to be blessed. I'm the only one that's able to do so, but I'll need help making sure everyone is accounted for."

"We're with you, every step of the way," Althaea said, resting her hand on Thorric's shoulder.

FIVE HOURS PASSED before the last body, laid out and posed with respect, was blessed. Small coins covered every eye of the dead, and we covered each face with patches of white cloth from the linen cupboards we had searched. Thorric was exhausted, more so than the rest of us, having to pour his heart into every prayer. Fifty-two souls departed for their resting place, thirty-three women and nineteen children. The stench of death permeated our very bones, and as we descended the stairs, Morrak paused. Kona waited near the doorway, the front door left open from the departure, and she whined.

"Let's get back to the bird and take a rest, please," Thorric said, his face pale from exertion.

"Ragnar told us to burn the place down," Althaea said quietly.

Thorric paused, and turned back to the house. He inhaled deeply and summoned a golden flame in his hands.

"May the light of this flame purify the evil that once resided here. Let goodness rise from the ashes," he whispered, his brow furrowed deeply as he formed the ball of holy fire.

The glowing orb launched from his hands and sailed through the front door, landing in the middle of the front entry room. Flames spread as if fueled by willpower and Thorric turned away. We took the same wide arc in silence back to Axel, perched atop our bags with his head tucked into his feathers, snoring surprisingly loudly for a bird. Morrak kicked the bag and Axel woke in a flurry of feathers and obscenities.

"How'd it go?" he asked, looking past us as the flames surrounded the house. "Ah, I see. Mission accomplished?"

"Yes. Now, be quiet, we're going to rest up a little before we head back to Gray Tide," Thorric said, his tone not to be questioned.

I picked up my bag to use as a makeshift pillow and

found it significantly heavier than I had recalled. I opened the bag to see what was causing the differential and covered my mouth to keep my scream quiet. As if it had been placed with care, nestled in my bag, the hilt of a dagger protruded. The serpent's head, carved meticulously into the pommel, was an exact match to the one from my dream, and I fell backward, nearly toppling into Morrak.

"What the hell, Val?" he mumbled, "I was almost asleep-what the hell is *that*?"

He pointed at the barely visible pommel and sat up.

"I-I, wait, you can see it? It's real this time?" I stammered, unwilling to touch it, recalling the way it had wrapped around my wrist in my nightmare. "It's real... this is real..."

Morrak approached quietly as the others rested, staring into my eyes as if I were a fear-crazed animal about to attack. He put on a pair of gloves, the thick leather surprisingly soft and pliable, and pulled the dagger free. Holding it up, the blade caught the sunset's light, and similarly in my nightmare, the hilt glittered like multicolored scales. The blade curved like a fang, coming to a point that I knew was sharper than anything a mortal could hone. He brought the blade close to his face, his eyes poring over it, and he blinked hard, staring at the blade.

"See that? Those tiny little green veins running along the edges of the blade? Do you know what that is?" he asked quietly.

"It's magic," Althaea said, her eyes open as she watched us from her bedroll. "Do you know what kind of magic?"

Morrak shook his head but sighed after a moment. "I

have a feeling it's a very dark magic, but someone who knows a lot more than us could tell us for sure. I might know a guy, but he's in Enguard."

I cocked my head. "I was told to seek someone out in Enguard who might be able to help me, too. I wonder if it's the same man."

He gave a shrug and paused as he held the dagger out to me. I leaned away from it and he cried out as the dagger transformed into a black asp, its body thin and lithe as it slithered from Morrak's hand. It curved through the grass, finding its way back to my bag, where it crawled inside, maneuvering around until its head emerged from my clothing. It gave a chilling hiss and formed into the solid pommel of the dagger.

"That...that's not normal, Val!" Morrak shouted, waking Thorric. "What the hell *was* that?"

"That...it's a long story," I stammered, heat creeping up as panic threatened to close in. "I can explain, okay?"

"Val, I think you need to start explaining," Thorric said. "I want a satisfactory explanation by the time we reach Gray Tide."

I hung my head as I shouldered my bag, the weight now returned to its normal load. There was no more evading the truth, but at least I could control the truth and how much I revealed. Axel landed on my shoulder and I groaned, bracing myself for a sarcastic remark or inappropriate comment. Instead, he asked me, quietly and in Nordmaarian, if I was going to tell them the whole story, or just the parts they needed to know, and I sighed, hiding my face in my hands as we began the journey south to Gray Tide.

"For the past few months, longer than that," I began,

"I have had recurring nightmares. The subject of those nightmares have been the death of my husband, by my own hand, with *that* dagger."

"Are you sure they were just nightmares?"

"I always hoped they weren't, but the Seer of my homeland said she didn't know."

"Your Seer...didn't see anything?" Althaea asked, taken aback as I shook my head.

"Not a thing, so she suggested heading south. On my way, I happened upon an old, trusted friend. She suggested the same but gave me a name and a specific location. I'm supposed to seek out Mr. Winchester in Enguard."

"So how'd you end up in Gray Tide?"

"I assumed that he would have come for the wedding, I suppose the banshee distracted me a little," I mumbled.

"But the dagger," Thorric said, "where did you get it?"

"I didn't get it anywhere," I replied. "This is the first time I've ever seen it in reality. It's always just been in my nightmares. I don't know how it actually appeared."

Thorric fell silent as he thought for a long moment. He cleared his throat and pulled the sending stone out of his pocket.

"Okay. We'll deal with that later, then. For now, we should update Ragnar on what we found," he said. "There's no use pondering something we know nothing about."

"Tell him about Rofellos' involvement and the humans we rescued," Morrak said.

Thorric lifted the stone and spoke, slowly, clearly, into the stone.

"Thorric and party here. Evidence of Rofellos with

Trifecta in hand. Freed the women and children, burned the house. No surviving Trifecta. Headed back to Gray Tide, awaiting further orders."

The stone glowed as the message was sent and only a few moments passed before the response was received.

"Report to my agent in Enguard. Report to Floki. Val, Floki will order you to return home. Obey his orders and your king's."

Every eye met my face, set in stone as I refused to reveal anything. The walk was uneventful, Kona trotted ahead, hunting the small rodents that lived in the grassy plain, and every so often she would bring one back for me.

"She's feeding you?" Morrak asked. "Isn't it supposed to be the other way around?"

I smiled. "We take care of each other. Though ground squirrel isn't high on my list of favorite foods."

Kona snapped up the rodent in her jaws, crunching bones as Morrak grimaced. Kona seemed to smile brightly, and she loped around us as she filled her belly. As she trailed something, her nose to the ground, she stopped suddenly. Lifting her nose to the air, she let out a long, low whine that morphed into a growl. Squinting into the distance, straight ahead of us plumes of black smoke rose in the air.

"Is that..." Althaea whispered behind her hands, pointing to the smoke.

"Gray Tide," Thorric said quietly. "Move. Quickly."

We ran while Axel flew ahead, vanishing in the distance. As we drew close, the wind shifted and brought the acrid stench of smoke toward us.

"What do you think happened?" Morrak panted as he

ran, the outskirts of the town visible from the plain. "What's the worst thing that could have caught on fire?"

"The stables, the inn, maybe even the town hall that Rofellos and Ragnar met in?" I panted back. "Hopefully no one was hurt."

"I don't see flames, maybe the townsfolk took care of it," Thorric called.

Althaea's bag began moving as she ran, a muffling coming from inside it. We paused, and as she opened the bag, Axel climbed out, coughing and panting.

"Practically the whole lower part of the town is torched. Nothing left near the docks, it's awful," he said between coughing fits.

"Thank you, Axel," I said. "Are you okay?"

"No! I'm *not* okay!" he shouted. "I had to dive headfirst onto a rock to die! I ain't doin' that again!"

Althaea looked horrified and I waved a hand. "I'll explain later, we need to find Allyn and the survivors of the Trifecta house, we sent them to Gray Tide!"

A burst of energy filled us, the motivation of search and rescue pushing us onward. Allyn was a survivor, maybe not a fighter, but I knew he would protect the women and children no matter what. Reaching Gray Tide, we paused to catch our breath, and as I raised my eyes to the city's arch, proudly displaying the name Gray Tide in weathered print, my heart stopped.

I fell to my knees and a guttural scream tore through my throat. Horror and grief sank into my chest as I struggled to breathe. Morrak staggered backward and hit the ground hard, his eyes unwavering from the sight. Althaea's sobs echoed and rose with the smoke and Thorric stood motionless, disbelief washed across his pale face as he poured prayers under his breath, his hands trembling as he clutched the holy sigil around his neck.

Hanging from the arch, the beaten, broken bodies of Allyn, Phil-lip, and little Luka swung gently in the dusk breeze.

EPILOGUE

~

The streets were abandoned. Not a soul was seen as we approached. Althaea held Phil-lip's body in her lap and sobbed as Thorric cut the rope, freeing the gnome's body. Morrak carefully lowered Allyn while he fought to keep from crying, failing as his tears fell, dampening the boy's ashen face. In my arms I held Luka, smoothing his unruly mop of hair, now matted with blood.

"Why did this happen?" Althaea said raggedly through her tears. "I don't understand...*why!*"

Axel stayed quiet as he made soft, unusual coos. I realized it was his way of crying and I swallowed the grief in my throat.

"Someone knows what happened. Someone saw something," I said, an edge of righteous anger lacing my heartbreak as I held Luka closer.

Thorric stood frozen, his eyes locked on the remnants

of rope still suspended from the city archway. Unmoving, he simply stared as he wept. From the wooded area behind us, an elderly woman approached, a priestess of Apollo, her ears softly pointed similarly to mine. She hesitated and took a few more steps toward us, her snow-white robes torn and greyed with smoke.

"Are...are you kin to them?" she asked softly. "Do you know why this happened?"

I bit the inside of my cheek hard enough to taste blood and looked down at Luka's face, his eyelids half-closed as his bloodshot eyes looked nowhere.

"I wish we could talk to them, just one more time," Althaea wept.

"You can, you know," the priestess said. "If your bond with them is strong enough, if they are willing, you may converse with them."

"Do it," Thorric muttered. "They can't die in vain. We need to know everything they can tell us. Do it now."

The woman bowed to him and led us toward the forest, where another priest of Apollo waited, a small chest at his feet. We carried the fallen to the edge of the wood and the priestess took a large censer from the chest.

"Lay them down, please."

Morrak laid Allyn down gently, taking care with the boy's hands, his fingers mangled and some missing. As I looked at what remained of the terrified young man I had promised to free, blame began to crush me. His face, once holding a youthful gleam, now held dark shades of purple, the blood staining a sticky, dark red. I couldn't tell where the torture had begun, and I couldn't tell where it had ended his life. From his broken fingers to his missing ears, Allyn had suffered tremendously.

Beside Allyn, Althaea laid down Phil-lip. The bright,

beaming smile that I had quickly come to associate with the gnome was gone, his mouth swollen and nose broken from fists. Althaea wiped his face with a handkerchief, her tears dampening his cheeks as she cried. Phillip's legs stuck at unnatural angles, and as Althaea tried to correct the positioning, the shattered bones crunched under her touch as they resisted. She turned her head and vomited, sobbing as she apologized to our dear friend.

I let Luka rest beside Phillip, and I took one of Luka's hands. I saw that they had tried to start with his finger-nails, but the boy had already had them anxiously bitten down to the quick, so his attackers had broken his hands, instead. I could see the outline of a boot heel over the top of his bruised hand. Gently, I kissed his little hands before resting them in his lap. The priestess walked in a circle around us and a soft, golden ring of light surrounded us from the smoke that wafted. She stood outside the ring and sniffled, asking us to rise to our feet.

"What are their names, please?" she asked as we replied in turn. "Allyn, we ask that the veil not shroud your soul quite yet. Bless us with your presence, help us understand what happened to you in your last moments."

A smoky figure appeared and stood beside Morrak, taking the shape of Allyn, unharmed. Morrak could barely meet Allyn's eyes and set his jaw as he fought tears.

"Who did this to you?" Morrak asked through clenched teeth.

"You already know who," the echo of Allyn said. "They wanted information, names, and descriptions. They're searching for King Ragnar's Queen. They plan to kill him and they're gonna use her to do it."

"This wasn't supposed to happen," Morrak said, his

voice breaking. "I'm sorry. I thought you'd be okay. I didn't know they were here."

"It's not your fault," Allyn said. "The Trifecta are everywhere, always. I was able to keep the women and children safe, they're hidden in the woods. We saw the smoke and I went ahead to make sure it was safe. It wasn't."

Morrak ground his palms into his eyes and wept. Allyn's spirit rested a hand on his shoulder and Morrak raised his head.

"I was strong," he said softly. "I didn't tell them anything. I figured out who they were looking for but I still didn't say anything. Even after they took my ears, and my fingers, I didn't tell them anything."

"Are...are you going to be okay?" I asked Allyn.

"Yeah, my family is waiting for me, actually. Right after I died, they found me. Thank you for helping me, all of you, I won't forget you." Allyn gave one last grin and faded from sight. The glowing ring dulled for a moment before regaining its brightness. The priestess let us grieve for a moment before she spoke again.

"Phil-lip, we ask that the veil not shroud your soul quite yet. Bless us with your presence, help us understand what happened to you in your last moments."

Althaea knelt, struggling to look at the hazy figure. As the gnome appeared, his round face beamed with the wide smile that he always wore.

"My dearest friends!" he said joyfully, shifting to embrace Althaea. "I'm so glad you came back, I wished to see you once more before I went to my resting place."

Althaea lowered her eyes in shame as Phil-lip watched her, his eyes full of love. "Phil-lip, I'm sorry this happened to you. You didn't deserve any of this pain."

"No, I didn't, but I'd go through it all again, because it was for *you*. It was for you *all* that I endured it. My death means that you'll stay safe and sound. I could hope for nothing less for my friends."

"Can you tell us what happened?" I asked, my hand reaching out to grasp his fingers, extended out to me.

"Of course," he said. "I saw them coming and I knew why. They shouted about a dwarf-woman and a gnome and I knew that they wanted Thora, probably because of what she saw in the mine. She wasn't gonna go, but I made her. I gave her one half of the teleportation gem to Enguard, and she made me promise that I was coming, too. I tried to keep the promise, but they were too fast. I couldn't have closed the portal in time, they were already at the door. I...I broke the stone so they couldn't follow her, and so she couldn't come back, either. I've never lied to my friends before, will you tell her I'm sorry, please? I hope she forgives me."

"I'm sure she will," Althaea said sweetly, taking his other hand. "Phil-lip, why did this happen to you?"

"Well, they were angry that the stone was broken, but then they got very angry when I wouldn't answer them about the little boy," he said quietly. "They wanted to know where the boy was, the one with the special eyes. I truly didn't know anything about him, but then I heard them talking about you all. I knew that the boy was a friend of yours...so that made him a friend of mine, too. I always protect my friends."

"Thank you, Phil-lip," I whispered. "I'm so sorry that you're gone."

He smiled, a genuine, sweet smile that held love. "I have no greater honor than to die for my friends. I love you all," he murmured, fading away in the same way Allyn did.

The priestess let her tears flow unhindered as the golden ring dulled. As it came to glow brightly again, her hands trembled. She opened her mouth to speak, but Luka was already next to me, his spirit looking at his body.

"Hi, Val," he said, his voice tiny and timid as he looked at me.

"Hi, Luka," I said in a whisper, unable to control my tears from flowing. "Are you okay? I'm so sorry this happened to you. I'm so sorry."

"It's okay," he said, reaching his hand to touch mine. It was as if my hand had been touched by a cool fog, the pressure barely discernible.

How could I explain that it *wasn't* okay? How could I make him understand that it was my fault he was dead? Luka looked at me, his face wrinkled in confusion.

"It's not your fault, Val," he said. "You didn't do this."

"I-I promised that you would go to live in T-Tachá with me," I said, my resolve shattering into pieces as I sobbed. "You were supposed to be safe. I promised you a family!"

"I know, but I'm not mad at you," he said, the innocence of his voice breaking my heart. "Besides, it didn't go on for a long time."

"What do you mean?"

"When they hurt me, I didn't hold on for too long. I didn't say anything, though. I was brave."

"You're very brave, Luka. The bravest boy I know," I said softly, touching his cheek as he smiled.

Kona approached on my other side and Luka giggled

as he rested his hand on the top of Kona's head. She sniffed at the spirit form and cocked her head, confused at the spectral appearance, and Luka wrapped his arms around her neck.

"Luka, thank you for being such a brave boy," I whispered through my tears. "I'll never forget you."

"I'll never forget you, either," he said, shifting from Kona to me as he hugged me around my neck, the cooling sensation bringing an unexpected shiver. "Bye, Val."

"Bye, Luka, be safe, okay?" I said as he stood up, disappearing as he gave me one last smile, waving with an unbroken hand.

I hung my head and sobbed over his broken body in front of me, praying to whichever god would hear me to keep the boy safe. The golden ring faded and didn't glow again. The priestess exhaled softly and the incense censer was covered.

"They're gone," she said softly. "They have found peace."

Together in hushed tones, we dug the resting places for each one of them, and from the shelter of the woods, the women and children that Allyn had led emerged. They had crafted simple markers from the forest's greenery and presented them to us. We thanked them and arranged the markers quietly, honoring each soul. My heart ached and my mind raced, and I looked to Thorric. Althaea and Morrak followed my lead and we waited as Thorric spoke, his tone low and full of a fierce vengeance.

"We know now that the Trifecta has no limits to their evils. We will bleed the Trifecta dry and ensure that no innocent blood is shed again. We are consumed now by a holy and righteous vengeance. There is no force in this realm or any other that shall stay our hands."

The breeze carried our vow across the city, through the charred buildings and deserted streets, our resolve unwavering in the smoky haze.

ACKNOWLEDGMENTS

~

This novel could not have been created,
let alone finished, without you, James.
Þakka þér, ást mín, eiginmaðr minn.
Ek unna þér.

Connor & Michael, you boys are amazing and have been
so patient through this entire novel, thank you, go grab a
snack.

David & Diane, level up, you earned it.

ABOUT THE AUTHOR

~

Jessica Sturtevant is the author of three fantasy novels where adventure, magic, and heartfelt storytelling intertwine. A lifelong lover of immersive worlds, she draws inspiration from her time at the Dungeons & Dragons table, particularly the imaginative campaigns crafted by her game-master husband, which she transforms into richly layered, character-driven tales of heroism, sacrifice, and heart. When she's not writing, Jess can be found painting custom tabletop miniatures, from fearsome monsters to the heroes who face them, and running her Etsy shop, Brushes & Blades, alongside her husband.

Follow her Amazon Author page here to stay up to date on all upcoming books!

~

Don't forget to support this indie author and leave a review here!